figurehead

figurehead

Patrick Allington

Published by Black Inc.,
an imprint of Schwartz Media Pty Ltd
Level 5, 289 Flinders Lane
Melbourne Victoria 3000 Australia
email: enquiries@blackincbooks.com
http://www.blackincbooks.com

The National Library of Australia Cataloguing-in-Publication entry:

Alington, Patrick.

Figurehead / Patrick Allington.

ISBN: 9781863954365 (pbk.)

A823.4

Book design: Thomas Deverall
Printed in Australia by Griffin Press

To Zoë
And to Douglas Allington, Jan Carpenter,
Lisa Allington & Matt Allington

Trapped in the side-wheel of a ferryboat, saving himself from drowning only by walking, then desperately running, inside the accelerating wheel like a squirrel in a cage, his only real concern was, obviously, to keep his hat on.

—James Agee on Buster Keaton

Prologue

1991

Yesterday I woke up expecting to be repulsed but instead I witnessed a scene that so filled my heart with hope that I felt I might pass out. For yesterday Mr Nhem Kiry – mouthpiece to the Khmer Rouge's mass-murdering leader, Pol Pot – tried to return to Cambodia's capital, Phnom Penh, for the first time in more than a decade.

You might remember – you probably won't, that's part of his genius – that Nhem Kiry was a member of the Khmer Rouge leadership group that threw a vast sheet over Cambodia in 1975. The conjurers practised their tricks for nearly four years, but when their magic failed they set about elimi-nating the audience. In 1979 the Vietnamese saviours arrived to banish Pol Pot and his cronies, Nhem Kiry included.

Yesterday Nhem Kiry did not sneak into Phnom Penh like the criminal he is. No. He arrived at the airport as a guest of honour. The United Nations laid out the red carpet for him as the Khmer Rouge's representative in the burgeoning peace deal.

Peace? With the Khmer Rouge? Why not give Pol Pot the Nobel Prize and be done with it?

But the good people of Phnom Penh, ordinary folk who live in slums and ramshackled apartments, showed the UN a thing or two. They flocked to Nhem Kiry's new mansion. They taunted him and then they invaded his house. They split his head open and found, to their surprise and delight, that he bled just like them.

The United Nations called this moment a 'setback in the march towards peace and rehabilitation.' I call it a courageous and truly democratic act. And I'm proud to say I was there. I sweated in the crowd, I surged forward with them, I screamed 'Bloody murderer,' I picked up a stone and I threw it at a window. I pushed others aside so I could squeeze inside. I stormed the stairs and I called out 'Harrah.'

—Edward Whittlemore, 'As I See It,' syndicated column

Nhem Kiry's face was a marvel. Despite decades of struggle and revolution – frustration, pain, fear and mud, victory disguised as defeat, defeat disguised as victory – his soft cheeks, mellow camera smile, gentle eyes and pale full lips remained great assets in his politician's armoury. He knew it, too, and had for years cared assiduously for his skin. If these days he overdid the moisturiser and the wrinkle cream, he liked to believe that he was compensating for the years of jungle living, where no man's complexion is unaffected. He did not care to acknowledge that he enjoyed the routine, the wiping and smudging, and especially the sudden coldness of the regenerating agents filling his pores. All the preening made him glow, and helped him present to the world the sweet eleven-year-old boy who lived within the tired 62-year-old veteran. Or so he believed.

After years of experimentation, Kiry had established that his skin responded best to Marie Weston's No. 5 Replenishing Lotion. It wasn't greasy. Even better, it was not tested on animals and it was fully organic. He could, in an emergency, eat it. But at fifty US dollars a tub, the extravagance bothered Kiry. Of course, he could have shovelled the precious goo from its sleek packaging into some battered old pouch. But that had never been his way. He valued his reputation for austerity, so every second week he exposed himself to the doubtful benefits of a cheap vitamin-E moisturiser.

Kiry was not vain. Rather, he knew that his work, his life, was about diplomacy and negotiation but also about image. At news conferences and ceremonies, especially when he shared the rostrum with foreign leaders, and during photo opportunities, he had to present himself as a member of the global club of political figures whose differences could be endured, massaged, maybe ultimately overcome, by the fact that they all dressed the same.

Still, spending big on Italian suits left him agitated in the change rooms of exclusive Bangkok boutiques and nauseous afterwards. He usually compensated by selecting a size too broad for his wiry frame, perhaps hoping to imply that he relied on hand-me-downs from ex-politicians.

At state dinners these days he not only had to look pristine, he had to be demure. He maintained a strict personal protocol. In particular, he never waved his cutlery around while he talked –

there was usually someone in his vicinity who feared that his fork might end up embedded in their sternum. He avoided sudden movement, animated chat, or eating with his mouth open. You can't leave anything to chance, he knew, when you're selling a million and a half dead people.

Halfway between Pochentong airport and Phnom Penh, ready to join the interim government, ready to do everything within his power to help the UN keep the peace, Kiry pushed his wraparound Ray-Bans up his nose, fixed his smile in place, wound down the window of the Toyota all-terrain vehicle and placed himself on display. Beside him on the back seat his nervous bodyguards, led by the quietly agitated Ol, pleaded with him to sit back.

'It's too windy.'

'You'll get all dirty.'

'You'll mess your hair up.'

'There might be snipers.'

Ol, whose war medals were his enormous shoulders, dead eyes and malaria, made himself ten years old again. 'Please, please, can I sit by the window? I've never been to Phnom Penh.'

Kiry raised a hand. They fell silent and snooty, except for Ol, who redirected his exhortations to his front-seat colleagues. First, he pleaded with Akor Sok, Kiry's chief aide, to intervene. Sok shrugged, though he agreed that in a perfect world the window should stay closed. He then wound down his own window.

Ol then asked Nirom, the chain-smoking driver, to slow down. Their other vehicle, full of bodyguards and luggage, was stuck behind a swarm of motorcycles and a truck full of pigs. Nirom, who had trouble keeping his cigarette in his mouth while he talked, did not reply or slow down.

A young woman swept past on a motorcycle, her long black hair flying behind her. She braked suddenly and drew beside the vehicle, causing a truck to swerve and the thirty or so passengers in its open tray to hug each other. The woman stared at Kiry. He removed his sunglasses and nodded at the chubby boy who was nestled between the woman's thighs and the bike's handlebars. The woman sniffed, loaded her mouth and spat. She hit Kiry on the bridge of his nose. Allowing for the wind and the speed at which they were travelling, Kiry had to admit she had a marvellous aim.

Kiry continued smiling at the child. Only when Ol, with a growl, leaned across and closed the window did Kiry shake his head and wipe himself with his handkerchief. Sok's face turned red and Nirom chomped his cigarette in two, but the boy's smile consoled Kiry. As a rule, children liked him. He didn't talk down to them. He didn't harangue them and then rub their ears. Not like Americans, who, he believed, had trouble telling their offspring from their dogs.

He tapped his breast and a piece of paper rustled. This was no important document, but a letter from an everyday American, Brendan H. Margaretti of Barron, Pennsylvania. *Dear sir,* it read. *My young son Jimmy saw a photo of you in our local newspaper. He was delighted because he thought you were the real life Mowgli (the Jungle Book is his favourite video). Anyway, I thought you might like to know that your picture is now stuck to his wall, next to a drawing of Mr Snuffleupagus, an imaginary creature much loved in this country. But I have to tell you, I know a thing or two about what you've done in your life. I am going to keep your photograph, even after my boy grows tired of you, because when he is older I want him to recognise the face of evil.*

Kiry had cut the letter in half and thrown the nasty piece away. He did not need CIA Nixonites dissecting his character. And only in a world overrun by UN committees could such correspondence ever have found him. But he kept the stirring portion of the letter in the top pocket of his suit, amongst his ballpoint pens. Often when he met a diplomat or a politician or a UN representative – and during the peace talks he felt as though he had met hundreds of them – he took it out and read it, always adding, with a shy but mischievous grin, and a raising of one eyebrow, 'Of course, we Asians all look the same.' At the end of one especially unproductive meeting he waved the letter about and suggested that the UNHCR fund his book proposal, *Children's Letters to War Criminals.* It was a rare undisciplined act, but he was amused by the poorly concealed revulsion of all those in the room.

Kiry's entourage was chaperoned by a police truck. Kiry had demanded a quiet entrance but once they reached the outskirts of Phnom Penh the police driver took possession of the very centre of the bumpy road. Horns squealing and lights flashing, oncoming traffic scattering, they became a parade.

The traffic was a tangle now. The genesis of a crowd easily followed them on foot. Kiry continued to fill the window, defiantly and proudly, though the blue-black glass now hid him. He spied quizzical looks, a glimpse of anger, a placard or two. If that's the worst of it, he thought, I'll be happy.

They were stuck for ten minutes on Street 182 near the Russian Market. A policeman with a lopsided grin dealt with the traffic by waving vehicles from all directions into the centre, where delicate, intricate calisthenics became necessary. The staccato honking of horns rang out, less road rage than a special language of negotiated settlement. As they inched forward, Kiry played tour guide to wide-eyed Ol.

'That way is Independence Monument – Sihanouk put it up twenty years too early, of course, but it's a nice enough piece of stone. Down there and to the right is the Royal Palace. I once lived back that way, with my mother.'

He paused to watch a one-armed man skirt around vehicles and run to them. The man slammed his fist on the hood and kicked a headlight. As he sprinted back to the footpath and disappeared into the crowd, the policeman applauded.

Eventually they reached the villa, a pleasant whitewashed two-storey rectangle. The waiting crowd numbered ten thousand. They held up signs – in Khmer, in English, in French – made from thin bedsheets or flattened cardboard boxes: 'Khmer Rouge Killers,' 'Nhem Kiry Criminal,' 'Not Forgiven.' They chanted, 'Murderers, murderers, murderers.' They shook their fists. Some of them fell on their knees and howled. They jostled each other and pushed against the shabbily erected wooden barricade.

The crowd closed in; the police fell back. Kiry's gaze floated amongst the sea of young men, then focused on an old woman with a bad hip and orange teeth. She limped forward, clambered onto the bonnet and stared down Nirom, who took solace in a fresh cigarette. She wrapped her arms and legs around the bullbar. The purpose of her particular protest was unclear even to her many admirers, who cheered her anyway.

Kiry put his hand on Nirom's shoulder and said, 'Whatever you do, don't run her down.'

Eventually, someone from the crowd – a hospital orderly who as a boy had fought for the Khmer Rouge against Vietnam, and as a youth for Vietnam against the Khmer Rouge – took hold of the old woman's shoulders. It took him a moment to untangle her: she had quickly ceased being an active protester and had become a passive prisoner of her own intricate knots.

Finally, the vehicles passed through a narrow gap in the barricade. Nirom butted his cigarette on the dashboard and manoeuvred so that Kiry could step straight from his seat to the villa's front door. As they alighted, Kiry tried to sneak a glance at the crowd. As staged events went, he thought, these actors had passion. Ol pushed him inside. Sok followed close behind, leaving Nirom and the bodyguards to gather the baggage and evade flying stones.

Kiry was tired. He wanted to lie down before the evening reception at the palace, perhaps even snooze. Then he wanted to sit quietly with a gin and tonic and check his speech, or plan what he might say to the media. He wanted to phone Kolab, his wife, and tell her that he was really here. He wanted to read the newspapers or even a few pages of that Kissinger biography. He desperately wanted to wash his silver hair.

He greeted Son Sen, the Khmer Rouge's defence minister, who had quietly entered Phnom Penh a few days earlier. They shared a few words, a private moment, surrounded by lesser beings who contrived not to listen. Kiry nodded at the various aides and the villa staff, who stood in a line trying to look cheerful. He shook hands with a couple of French photojournalists, who had been waiting since dawn to record this moment. He inspected the villa, pronouncing it pleasant, comfortable and, but for the protesters, perfectly acceptable. He briefly posed for a photograph with Son Sen, the two colleagues cajoling tense smiles out of each other.

As he began to climb the stairs, tailed by Sok and his bodyguards, a car battery came through a window, shattering the glass into thousands of diamonds. He turned and watched the battery bounce end on end until a table leg stopped its progress.

'I think that's ours,' Nirom said.

Kiry sighed. 'I'm going to rest. Somebody sort this out.'

Outside, the crowd surged forward. The barricade buckled. The crowd came at it again. The barricade did not merely collapse, it exploded, and some in the crowd armed themselves with its shattered remains. They ran to the villa, peering through the windows and beating on the walls.

Inside, Kiry unlaced his shoes. They were too tight. The leather was so new and hard that he was sure that his toenails would blacken and drop off. He stretched out on a bed. Sok brought him a damp cloth to cover his face.

Outside, the prime minister, Hun Sen, arrived in a bulletproof limousine. He made his way to the first-floor balcony of the villa across the street. 'Calm down. Go home,' he yelled into a megaphone. 'There is no use in killing them now. Go home. Go home. Go home and remember not to vote for them.'

'He got here quick,' Sok said. 'What was he doing, waiting around the corner?'

'Oh well.'

'He's responsible for this. He planned it.'

'Probably.'

'Why are you so calm?'

'All this is to be expected.' Kiry sat up. 'Do you have a comb?'

As Kiry poured water from a jug into a glass, adding a slice of lime, some in the crowd smashed the door of the villa and spilled inside. Others climbed the outside stairs and banged on the door and window of Kiry's room. Across the street, police congregated. Their uncertain leader, unwilling to fight the people, sought guidance from a walkie-talkie. From above, Hun Sen pleaded, 'Please be calm. Please control yourselves.'

Some of the rioters attacked the pyramid of suitcases sitting near the door. They ripped them open and flung clothes and documents and passports around. Some of them slashed the furniture, threw it against walls, carried it outside. One man swung on a chandelier. When it broke from the ceiling, landing on him and leaving tiny cuts on his body, he lay on the Indian rug roaring. He then carried the metal skeleton outside, holding it above his head like a trophy, bleeding triumphantly.

Some of the rioters ran up the stairs, looking for Kiry. When they burst into his room he was waiting on a sofa, arms folded in his lap, legs crossed at the ankles, his face arranged at its most serene.

'Hello,' he ventured, before his bodyguards formed a shield in front of him. The French photographers, trying to locate a panoramic view, instead found themselves book-ending Kiry's line of defence, staring down an angry mob.

The protesters packed the small room so tightly that their attack on Kiry seemed to occur in slow motion. First, they dealt with the bodyguards. Someone shoved Ol against a wall. He hit his head on the sharp edge of a windowsill and slid to the ground with a groan. The other bodyguards fell down or flailed about amongst the throng.

The attackers momentarily froze with indecision, stunned by the ease of their raid and intimidated by the reputation of the man who gazed at them demurely. Then one man, a road worker, stepped forward. Kiry straightened, still believing the whole event was for show. He was so surprised when the road worker's crowbar connected with his eyebrow that he felt no pain. He slumped in the armchair, confused, and in the moment of stunned peace that followed he sought to reassess his situation and rearrange his face. He stopped considering the implications for the peace process, or the wording of his letter of complaint, or the propaganda possibilities. He took note instead of the blood dripping off the end of his nose, and the loathing in the man's face as he took aim to strike again. His façade cracked and, trying to stand, he collapsed. He grabbed the ankle of one of the photographers, looked up at her and said, 'Don't let them kill me.' She nodded and patted his shoulder, but not before she snapped the photograph that later adorned page three of *Le Monde*: Nhem Kiry as if dug from dirty ice, eyes glassy, skin pallid, deep lines of fear running across his face.

The road worker swung again but missed. Kiry bounced on his buttocks and scrambled on all fours into a wardrobe. Sok dived in after him, making it a tight squeeze, and pulled the door closed.

'Kill him,' someone cried, and then the chant commenced, down the stairs and into the street. 'Kill him, kill him, kill him.'

They ripped the wardrobe doors from their hinges and dragged Kiry into the middle of the room. One man pulled a reading lamp from a power point and cut its electricity cord free. He threw it over the ceiling fan and fashioned a crude noose.

Kiry's bodyguards fought back. Ol pushed Kiry into the bathroom, where the photographer vacated a chair for him. Government soldiers, in riot gear and now armed with instructions that Nhem Kiry must not die, rushed the stairs. They forced those engaged in the lynching down the staircase and into the street, where the crowd lauded them and Hun Sen counselled, 'There is a better way.'

Blood flowed from the cut on Kiry's head. 'It looks worse than it is,' he assured Sok. Bruises already rose from his elbow, his buttocks, his side. His shirt was ripped and bloody. His wristwatch was cracked. Ol, concussed and confused, berated Nirom for driving into a tree. The other bodyguards nursed minor wounds. One of the photographers reported a dislocated finger.

The crowd fuelled a bonfire with the villa's furniture, the paintings from the walls, the long table from the kitchen, the dried flower arrangements, the shredded luggage. They burnt Kiry's passport. They burnt his toiletries – Marie Weston's No. 5 Replenishing Lotion bubbled and spat as its container melted. They burnt his ripped jacket and, within, Brendan H. Margaretti's letter. They burnt his briefcase, including his speech: *I cannot express how very happy I am to be here at the beginning of a new peaceful era for our country. I hope to be here for many years to come. I pledge to work with all parties who truly have the interests of the Cambodian people in their hearts.*

One by one, Kiry and his entourage climbed down the outside stairs and into an armoured personnel carrier. As Kiry descended, Ol stood staring up with his arms outstretched to catch him should he fall … and gallantly fainted.

*   *   *

Ted Whittlemore was not in Phnom Penh on the day Nhem Kiry flew in and flew out. He did not, as he wrote, throw a rock at a window; he did not storm any stairs. He was in neighbouring Vietnam, in Ho Chi Minh City, where he'd based himself for the last few years.

Ted woke early that day, early enough that he could have – had he been capable of it – hitched a lift to Phnom Penh on a dawn flight and been at the Royal Hotel in time for the first sitting of breakfast. He could have walked the streets to gauge the mood of the city, something he always liked to do when he arrived in a place. He could have loitered outside Nhem Kiry's villa and watched the crowd form. He could have taken his time selecting the very best rock to throw: not too light, not too heavy, something to make a decent impact but not kill anybody.

Instead, he spent most of the day sprawled on an old settee on the balcony of his apartment. When he slept he moaned; when he was awake he grumbled and swore and clenched his fists. Occasionally, he struggled to his feet and shuffled into the apartment to fill up his water jug ('Don't get dehydrated,' his doctor had told him) or to urinate sweet yellow nectar. The apartment was quite spacious, for one person at least, but it gave the illusion of being tiny because all four of its rooms were crammed with old furniture from the Núi Café, the bustling establishment above which Ted lived. That day, tables, chairs, sofas and ice chests seemed like mines laid out in his path.

A few days earlier Ted had collapsed in the Núi Café. This came after weeks of unease that he had self-diagnosed as mental rather than physical, with symptoms so vague he tried to ignore them. But in the café Ted had suddenly fallen so ill that he slid off his chair and passed out on the floor in a pool of warm jasmine tea. He sprang back to life a moment later, appalled at this public show of mortality, but in the ensuing days the dizziness came – and passed – in waves, and he endured, in a pattern so random he felt sure it must mean something, a sharp stabbing pain to a bewildering variety of body parts.

Ted was disgusted by his body's sudden and pathetic weakness. He was dismayed that he was missing Nhem Kiry's homecoming. It might have been a mere footnote in history, but it was big news in Ted's world. Late in the afternoon he made the mistake of tuning into the BBC World Service and heard that he had missed a riot. He lost all sense. I'll get the next plane to Phnom Penh and view the scene, he told himself, and then I'll fly to Bangkok and I'll demand that Nhem Kiry show me his wounds.

Ted packed a bag and got halfway down the stairs when dizziness overwhelmed him. He grasped the railing as the world circled faster and faster. Finally a passer-by – one of the boys who repaired Hondas and sold dope from a hole in the wall a few blocks over – noticed him swooning and helped him back to bed.

Late in the afternoon Ted's friend Hieu, who ran the café, brought him a bowl of beef noodle soup. Ted found eating hard work but afterwards he felt much better – well enough, in fact, to pour himself a glass of armagnac (he knew it was fake, but they'd done such a good job, with whatever chemicals and colours they'd thrown into the alcohol, that he didn't mind). He settled in at the typewriter and began work on his weekly column.

Yesterday I woke up expecting to be repulsed but instead I witnessed a scene ...

Ted stopped writing and pondered this blatant lie. As if in punishment, a wave of light-headedness forced him to close his eyes. Nausea rose up from his gut then fell back. His tongue felt huge in his mouth. He had an image of bile spilling all through his body, flooding his organs. The thought of it made him retch into the empty soup bowl. He began shivering so hard that he wondered, as he fought to control himself, if this was epilepsy.

After a moment he opened his eyes and stared at the words on the near-blank page: *Yesterday I woke up expecting to be repulsed but instead I witnessed a scene ...* Although his hands were shaking so hard they were blurred, he tapped out the rest of the sentence ... *that so filled my heart with hope that I felt I might pass out.*

Finally, the shivering passed. Ted wandered his apartment, splashed water on his face, wiped deodorant under his arms for the fourth or fifth time that day and brushed his teeth. He pulled the piece of paper from the typewriter and grabbed a pen. With one hand gripping the railing, he made his way very slowly down the steps.

The Núi Café was busy and full of noise. Ted's favourite table was occupied by four men playing cards. He limped past them and Hieu ushered him to a seat near the kitchen.

'Tea, Ted?'

'Coffee.'

'Coffee bad. Doctor said coffee bad.'

'Coffee,' Ted said.

Snot began to pour from Ted's nose. He wiped it clean, ignoring the smattering of blood that appeared on his handkerchief. Hieu wanted to chat, wanted to know how he was feeling, but Ted waved him away and settled back to compose his eyewitness account of the attack on Nhem Kiry. He wrote it in a single burst. The coffee was still hot when he read it back to himself.

He was pleased. Very pleased. For a moment, he felt healthy. This shocked him, for suddenly he grasped how awful he had been feeling. And at that moment, right there and then, he decided that the column about Nhem Kiry would be his very last. No matter how horrific an idea it was, his doctor was right: he had to retreat or die.

He asked Hieu for a glass of red wine. 'Make it a bottle.' When Hieu refused – 'Doctor's orders!' – Ted burst into tears. All conversation in the Núi Café ceased – even the card game went into hiatus – as Ted howled then whimpered then fell asleep.

I should have been there, that time in '91. Of all the bloody shit-holes I've dragged myself to in my life for the sake of a story, for the sake of being an eyewitness, I missed Nhem Kiry getting the shit beaten out of him. But I had to respond somehow because they – the useless bloody spineless UN – were treating Kiry like royalty. I don't mind telling an out-and-out lie if there's no other way, so I wrote the column. Said I was there. Really, when you think about it, what difference does it make? Everybody tells stories their own way. Everybody sees what they want to see. What they need to see. I hear people say, 'I know my history.' But what is history? Some nameless faceless disembodied voice thrusting his own partisan beliefs at the world. History isn't rain. History is a water cannon, loaded, aimed and fired.

So I lied, but like any good forger I made sure I slipped in a kernel of truth: 'I felt I might pass out,' I wrote. Ha. That – passing out – was about all I was bloody well good for.

I'm not a violent man. I'm pretty sure I've never killed a human being. I've never fired a gun, except to find out how it feels and except for a few times when I found myself in a spot of bother on the frontline – but, honestly, whenever I tried to aim it was like I was drowning, limbs flailing about and bullets flying everywhere except where they needed to go.

I'm not a violent man, but I would give anything to have had the chance to land a blow or two on Kiry's scrawny little body that day in '91. Just to sink my fist into his stomach a couple of times and to elbow him in the ribs. Break his nose, maybe. Kick him while he's down. I wouldn't have enjoyed it, but it would have been cathartic. Cleansing. Like that pink stuff they make me drink when I haven't shitted for too many days in a row.

It would have been a good way to end. I would have gone full circle. The first time I ever saw Nhem Kiry, in '61, I watched Lon Nol's police beat him up. I'd heard about this boyish left-winger who wrote brave and blunt newspaper columns and who talked openly about the evils of corruption. One of my spies tipped me off so, as if by chance, I was across the road when five men (one of whom looked a lot like my spy) dragged Kiry into the street, stripped him naked and pummelled him. As Kiry lay counting his ribs, his left eyelids fused, the men taunted him and laughed at his penis. They photographed him and distributed copies around Phnom Penh. I bought one for a few packets of cigarettes and a bottle of plonk, but when I sent it in with the story my editor said, 'I don't publish pornography, no matter how tasteless.'

Back then – in '61 – I felt pity for Kiry. But more: in the photograph of a naked, bleeding man I thought I caught a glimpse of hope and maybe even of greatness. I thought I saw a man who was a radical but who could still make friends with the entire world. And now?

Part 1

1967

Late one afternoon Nhem Kiry, Member of Parliament, left his tiny office. He retrieved his pushbike and rode out into the heavy Phnom Penh heat, but not before he tucked his white cotton shirt into his trousers so it wouldn't flap in the wind. There would be creases in the shirt later but no matter; he was finished at the office for the day.

Kiry rode slowly along Monivong Boulevard, upright in the saddle, his face so impassive that if his legs hadn't been pumping he might have been mistaken for a statue. He veered around a cyclo and said to himself, 'I am a happy person. I *am* a happy person.' He cracked a smile but his mouth locked into place as if he was letting out a silent scream.

Kiry was on his way to see his friend Bun Sody, who was forever telling him that he was too stern. Kiry did not agree: if he was more often sombre than full of joy and light then that was because life was a serious business.

Besides, Kiry thought that Sody took things too far. Kiry had seen him tell some caustic joke and then collapse on the floor, shaking uncontrollably, his limbs crashing into furniture; he once saw him giggle with such gusto that he vomited all over himself. Kiry did not think there was anything *that* funny about life in Cambodia.

While Sody played the clown, Kiry ventured into the countryside to listen to the poorest of the peasants tell how the authorities systematically and legally stole their rice. He remembered all the details of these stories – not names but places and paddy yields – and he built up in his mind a panoramic vision of miserable inequity.

Whenever he said goodbye to these peasants, Kiry flashed a smile so full of empathy and genuine warmth that they knew for certain that he really and truly was on their side. It would have shocked Sody, had he seen it; and then, Kiry suspected, reduced him to a hopeless mess of giggles.

Kiry rode on. Even as sweat began to run down his armpits, a sensation he disliked intensely, he showed no outward discomfort. He rode a bicycle to remind all of Cambodia that he had refused a free Citroën and a chauffeur. His parliamentary colleagues had finally come to understand that he was incorruptible, but not before they'd offered him everything from warehouses full of cognac to women of all shapes and sizes and nationalities to teenage boys to suitcases full of US dollars to a cottage in the south of France. He'd rejected it all, yawned politely in their faces, and from that day on they'd tiptoed around him as if he were a landmine half out of the dirt. Kiry carried on as best he could, drawing strength from what Gandhi once said: 'First they ignore you. Then they laugh at you. Then they fight you. Then you win.'

Kiry turned left, as did two motorcyclists following an indiscreet thirty metres behind. Everywhere Kiry went these days, the secret police followed. Kiry knew that they reported to General Lon Nol but he suspected that Prince Sihanouk was in on it: for a man who went about with his eyes squeezed shut, Sihanouk seemed capable of seeing vast distances.

Lon Nol had started rumours that Kiry was in communication with the communists in the jungle – which was true enough, for there was a certain man who delivered news and instructions in the dead of night. But now Lon Nol was publicly accusing him of orchestrating the peasant unrest out west. The very idea was ludicrous, Kiry thought. His constituents were in the south. Nobody in Kandal province was rioting or killing police, although Kiry would not have blamed them if they had been. All over the country, he believed, the peasants were waking from a deep sleep, rubbing their eyes, looking at the rich and powerful in Phnom Penh and thinking, Why do I work myself to death so they can live in palaces and sleep on mattresses stuffed full of money? Kiry had not incited any peasants to violence, although it is true that his man in the night had warned him what was going to happen out west. Still, he understood the rioters; he honoured them; and now his mouth turned dry whenever he thought of Lon Nol's men beating or shooting them.

Kiry pretended not to notice that the secret police were following him. Nothing could make them leave him alone and, anyway, feigning ignorance gave him a certain freedom. They claimed he was responsible for orchestrating the riots and yet they tagged him as simple and naïve and cowardly.

Kiry turned left and then immediately left again down a narrow lane. He stopped by a pile of rubbish. Another man, dressed in exactly the same clothes as Kiry, mounted a replica of Kiry's bicycle and pushed to a start. The two men did not make eye contact or speak. Then, as the other man began to peddle, Kiry hissed, 'Tuck in your shirt.'

Kiry crouched down behind the rubbish, sending a black rat scuttling away. Once the motorcyclists had trundled past, he remounted and sped in the opposite direction.

Ten minutes later he entered a house. He removed his shoes and wiped his underarms and chest with his *krama*. He entered a windowless room just as Ted Whittlemore yanked the tops off two bottles of beer.

'Here you go, mate,' Ted said, handing a beer to Bun Sody, who grinned and lifted his shirt to mop his face.

Kiry wondered if Sody was ill. He seemed as delighted as ever with life but his eyes, two huge expanses of white, were abnormally bright against his reddish face. And Kiry noticed that his belly jutted out and his neck listed to one side, although his shoulders and his thighs looked as powerful as ever. Maybe he was stressed. Maybe he'd had too many late nights, fraternising and spreading the word that change was coming.

'Well, well,' Ted said. 'Mr Nhem Kiry. What an honour. A drink?'

'Whittlemore: I thought I made it quite clear that I wanted nothing more to do with you,' Kiry said.

'Aw, come on mate, don't be grumpy. I'm on your side, you know.'

'He shouldn't be here,' Kiry said to Sody. 'Have you read that rubbish he's been publishing in the US? He's Sihanouk's poodle, nothing more.'

'I invited him,' Sody said. 'He says he has news.'

'That's right,' Ted said. 'Big news. Important news. But first have a drink with us. I'm not sure what I've done wrong exactly, but let me make it up to you. Pretty please?'

'Either he leaves or I do.'

'Look, I'm sorry I wrote that your mates in the jungle are amateurs, but I have to call it how I see it. You people have got to be nicer to your friends. Like the North Vietnamese. And Sihanouk. And me. So: a beer?'

'No.' Kiry was scanning the room, as if he was trying to decide which of the two doors the secret police would shortly burst through.

'Just one? Come on, all good commies drink beer. Just look at me.'

'You can't support us *and* support Sihanouk.'

'Why ever not? Come on, have a beer, they're perfectly cold, if that's what you're concerned about.'

'I'm not concerned about anything.'

'Well, from what I hear, that's not wise, not wise at all, mate. But surely you'll have *something*? Whisky? Tea? Is there any Chinese tea here?' Ted yelled to no one in particular. 'I know: armagnac. Your favourite, right?'

Kiry sat down at the table, hands clasped, and stared at a spot on the ceiling where the paint was beginning to fray. 'Tea, then, if I must,' he said.

'That's the way. Tell you what, I'll put the armagnac in the teapot. That way, you can have what you really want but me and Sody will be none the wiser. Sounds like your sort of game, doesn't it?'

'This whole thing is a game to you,' Kiry said. 'You're forever bouncing back and forth between us—'

'Remind me, who is "us"?'

'Between us and Sihanouk. Who'll be your favourite next? Lon Nol? Lyndon B. Johnson? You'll break bread with anyone for a good quote.'

'We need an empty teapot and a cup and saucer in here. Bone china if you've got it,' Ted called out, apparently to the wall. 'Cheers, then. Here's looking at you. Here's looking *up* to you,' he corrected himself. 'Here's to the man who can save Cambodia from itself. With a little bit of help, if he's smart enough to accept it.'

'Why is he here?' Kiry asked Sody again.

'To take you to dinner,' Ted said. 'To bury the hatchet. Surely you can eat in a restaurant occasionally without doing damage to your precious reputation.'

'I don't like restaurants. Anyway, I eat with my mother.'

'Every night? No wonder people talk.'

An elderly man entered the room, shuffled up to Ted and handed him a teapot and a cup and saucer. 'Thank you, Uncle,' Ted murmured. He poured armagnac from a bottle into the teapot and then from the teapot into the cup. He handed it to Kiry, who grimaced but took a sip.

'Milk and sugar?' Sody inquired.

'Come on, everybody likes restaurants. Bring your poor old mum along. When's the last time she had a night out on the town? I bet she'd just love that new French place across the river.'

'Oh yes. La Guillotine,' Sody said.

'That's the place,' Ted said. 'The frogs' legs are out of this world. And the wine. Afterwards we could all go to the cinema. That'll show the upper class that you're well-rounded, not such a sourpuss, not such a peasant stick-in-the-mud.'

'No.'

'Sihanouk's new masterpiece is playing, the one about the doomed love affair between the air hostess and the fat old politician. It's beautiful. And so realistic. Your mum will cry and cry.'

'And that hostess, oh my,' Sody said. 'I'd go flying with her any day, ha ha ha. Oh happy landings, if you take my meaning.'

'But if my information is accurate – and I'm certain that it is – then tonight might be our last chance.'

'What's going on?' Kiry said. 'What is it that you think you know?'

'I'm told that Lon Nol is blaming you for the peasant riots.'

'Of course he is,' Kiry said, irritated. 'His goons have been harassing me since it happened.'

'I'm told that Sihanouk believes him. My information is that they're going to arrest you, probably this week. Sody too.'

'Guilty by association?' Sody moaned. 'The story of my life.'

'Who's your source?' Kiry said.

'No. No names.'

'Then why should I believe you? Your informants are figments of your imagination. And your loyalties shift like the wind.'

'Not at all. My loyalties lie with you *and* with Sihanouk.'

Kiry snorted.

'Come on. Imagine you and Sihanouk together: what a team,' Ted said. 'You'll be like Simpson and Lawry. Lennon and McCartney. You'll—'

'I thought I was going to be Lennon,' Sody said. 'I want to be Lennon.'

'You'll be like Jack and Bobby Kennedy,' Ted said.

'Only alive,' Kiry said. 'And competent.'

'You and Sihanouk in partnership, believe me, it's the best way, it's the—'

'The best for you maybe. The Royal Radical, that's what they call you.'

'But listen—'

'I've done nothing but listen since I got here.'

'*Listen.* I saw a truckload of heads today. Lon Nol's got his goons out Battambang way slaughtering anybody who's in the wrong place at the wrong time. In response to the rioting. He doesn't care who dies just so long as it's loud and bloody and there's lots of witnesses. And he wants proof that his boys are doing a good job. So they're bringing him home heads to count.'

'I heard that rumour but I didn't believe it,' Sody said. 'I still don't believe it. You must be mistaken, Ted. Perhaps your scouts are making up stories to scare us?'

'I saw the truck myself. There were a hundred heads. Maybe more. Lon Nol's coming for you. Tomorrow, the day after, the day after that, a week, a month, I don't know. But he's coming.'

Kiry sighed. Although he found Ted's pretence of omnipotence tiresome, he could not ignore this warning. He knew that Ted walked the corridors of Sihanouk's palace like he owned the place and that he had contacts in every bar and down every blind alley in town.

'What do you think?' Sody said to Kiry.

'It's time. We go, like we always knew we would.'

That night, Nhem Kiry lay down on his mattress fully dressed. He closed his eyes but did not sleep. In the corner of the room his mother snored and occasionally whimpered. Kiry sat up and watched her skeletal outline. She'd grown old so quickly she could barely move about the house. She claimed that when she walked she could hear her hip slowly grinding to dust. Kiry suspected she was imagining the noise but he did not doubt that her pain was real.

Kiry wanted to say goodbye, but he knew that if he revealed his plans she would start wailing and the whole neighbourhood – and the secret police – would come running. So he turned, faced the wall and tried to pretend she wasn't there.

Before dawn, Kiry slipped outside. He lay on his stomach in the dirt and crawled slowly past houses, through a rancid, muddy ditch, across a couple of roads, until he came to a man who stood waiting with a pushbike. Kiry mounted the bike and the man whispered directions in his ear. Kiry nodded and set off. He took a circuitous route, avoiding main roads and staying close to buildings. He saw no one, although a dog chased him for a couple of blocks, barking and snapping at the back wheel.

He rode for five minutes until he came to a man sitting on a motorbike. The man revved the engine as soon as Kiry climbed on behind. They rode through streets and alleys Kiry did not know. When they passed a man scratching his bare chest and considering the pre-dawn darkness, Kiry buried his face in the driver's back.

Soon they stopped at an abandoned warehouse near the river. Bun Sody stepped forward and whispered a greeting. Before them stood their transport out of the city: a mound of rubbish on a cart. Kiry and Sody wrapped *kramas* over their mouths and noses, then crawled along a tunnel dug into rotting fruit and vegetable peelings to a hollowed-out cave. A trusted man flicked at a buffalo's ear and they trundled forward.

Kiry lay perfectly still, although every time the cart's wooden wheels went over a bump a pineapple head scraped back and forth across the bridge of his nose. He could hear Sody's breathing, more shallow than his own. It's easier for him, Kiry thought. He has soft curves and flab to protect him.

How apt it is that we are taking this trip together, Kiry thought. As young men – boys, really – Kiry and Sody had taken a boat to Marseille, sharing a cabin barely bigger than the hollowed-out space they now endured and almost as rank. And they had shared an apartment for the first few months in Paris, until Kiry felt more confident about his foreign surroundings and moved elsewhere because he wanted to read and think in solitude.

Kiry could have reached out and touched Sody's hand. Sody would have liked that. But Kiry did not want Sody to know that he was uneasy. So he contented himself with wiggling his fingers and toes and with moving his jaw up and down, even though it created a curious sensation in his inner ear, as if a worm was crawling out of his head.

Kiry had never forgotten how forlorn Sody looked when Kiry told him he was moving out of their Paris apartment. He had taken pleasure in the revelation that Sody needed him. And he had admired Sody for saying 'Fair enough' even as his eyes filled with tears.

I was pissed off that neither Nhem Kiry nor Bun Sody – not even Sody, who was always waiting for the next party – joined me for dinner the night before they fled Phnom Penh. What a fine last supper we could have had, the saviour and the saved. What a celebrity I would have been the next day: Ted Whittlemore, journalist and free-thinker and the last person to see the two martyrs alive.

By mid-morning the whole city was talking about it. Almost everybody I spoke to was certain that Lon Nol's thugs, with Prince Sihanouk's 'don't tell me and I won't know' approval, had executed Kiry and Sody. 'They were gagged and bound and burnt alive in an irrigation ditch,' one of my sources told me, a mid-range public servant who I had previously believed supplied impeccable information. For appearance's sake I slipped him a couple of notes but I never used him again. Then I went to see Sihanouk.

'How was your dinner at La Guillotine?' Sihanouk wanted to know.

'Ah, Your Majesty. I see you're as well informed as ever. The food was excellent. But unfortunately, because I was eating alone, the owner kept sending me female companionship.'

'Unfortunately? Edward, you surprise me. You should change your diet if you are a little limp in that area. Are you getting enough red meat? Or frogs' legs? They always remind Sihanouk of a woman's thighs. I lick the salt off them and then one thing leads to another and—'

'Your Majesty, what do you make of the disappearance of Nhem Kiry and Bun Sody?'

'Ah, them! Who knows? Who cares? Sihanouk is not responsible for the whereabouts of every cowardly man in the country. But if you want my opinion: if you travel to the north I think you will find them alive and well and enjoying the rural air. Why, what do you think has happened?'

What an excruciating moment. I saved two men's lives, that's the plain truth of the matter, but what good is a delicious secret you cannot share? What is the point of making history if you cannot brag about your great deed?

'I haven't a clue,' I reluctantly told Sihanouk.

I knew the truth but in my column I repeated the whispers on the street: 'Leading left-wing politicians, Mr Nhem Kiry and Mr Bun Sody, disappeared overnight. While it is possible that they have fled to the communist maquis in the far north of the country, it is more likely that the authorities have arrested and summarily executed them.'

When Sihanouk read my column he summoned me and then refused to speak. I stood before him, arms by my side, paying silent penance for my sins, waiting and waiting for him to dismiss me.

But Sihanouk had too many real enemies to stay angry with his friends. I went to Vietnam for a month and by the time I returned he had entirely forgiven me. Soon we were once again eating and drinking and making music together. Soon he was whispering in my ear again about every aide or family member he suspected of treachery.

No one understood Sihanouk like I did. He felt schemed against every moment of every day by every single person in Cambodia, alive and dead, and by every foreign diplomat and politician who took his hand and praised him. But he had an amazing ability to move on, to forgive and forget. People thought this proved that he was stupid or weak. But I knew better.

1970

A plane stood stone cold on the far edge of a Soviet military air-
field, empty of fuel and food. While they waited, Prince Norodom
Sihanouk and Ted Whittlemore played badminton on the tarmac.
Seven of Sihanouk's aides and a Russian pilot stood in a line and
made a net. On Sihanouk's insistence – 'Everybody knows that a
net has no holes' – they held hands.

Monique, Sihanouk's wife, was so stupendously bored she
agreed to umpire. But she soon displeased Sihanouk.

'You must concentrate, my gorgeous burst of sunlight. Really,
your poor grasp of the rules does you no credit.' In response
Monique produced a copy of *Vogue* from within the folds of her vast
mink coat. Sihanouk then took it upon himself to umpire as well as
play.

'Another point to me! Sihanouk takes control.'

'What? *What?*' Ted said.

'Ha ha, too bad, Mr Aussie. Your commoner's blood is no match
for the Great Svelte Asian Neutralist. That's 12-5 in favour of Sihanouk. Just three more points and the game is mine.'

'But you caught the shuttle. That's my point.'

'You are ignorant. You are white trash. You know nothing. Nothing. 13-5.'

'12-5. But I protest. It should be 11-6.'

'13-5. Sihanouk's serve.'

'No, really, with the greatest respect, I insist on hearing the
umpire's ruling.'

'Very well. What do you say, Monique, my beautiful wife? Isn't
she beautiful, Ted? She's as sexy as a movie star, don't you agree?
She crouches down and moves like a tigress, she—'

'Let Ted have the point,' Monique said.

'Oh my sweet mango, what a thing to say. Sihanouk cannot give away that which is not his to give. Surely you remember: if the rally goes more than six shots, both players must lift their left leg and play only on their right leg. If a rally goes more than twelve shots, they must switch legs. This rally went thirteen shots. Ted, plainly, is standing on the wrong leg. Nobody can change that. Nobody can give him his point. His point does not exist to be given.'

There were murmurings along the net. A Russian official had just handed one of the aides a note, which relayed the news that in Cambodia General Lon Nol and Sihanouk's cousin, Sirik Matak, had engineered a coup d'état. Sihanouk was no longer prime minister. The parliament and the palace were no longer his.

A whispered argument broke out along the net. Some of the aides wanted to break the news to Sihanouk immediately. Some wanted to wait until the plane was airborne and flying across the tundra towards Beijing. Only the Russian pilot seemed happy. Smiling and nodding and holding hands, he was captivated by the idea of being friends with people to whom he could not say a word. When Ted called out to him in Russian – 'Having fun, comrade?' and then 'Cat got your tongue?' – he grunted, aggrieved.

Just as Sihanouk was about to serve a car sped towards them and screeched to a halt. Sihanouk served a fault.

'That doesn't count,' he cried. 'The awful noise, that black, pungent exhaust, the ugliness of the car's lines have put Sihanouk completely off his game.'

'Fault,' Ted said. 'My serve. 5-12.'

'13-5. Cheating does not become you, Ted. Give me the shuttlecock. That car put Sihanouk off his game. Play two, play two, by royal decree play two.'

'Excuse me, Your Royal Highness.' Behind Sihanouk, black-suited, grey-skinned and grave, stood the Soviet premier, Petr Mironov.

'Premier, what a delightful surprise. Where did you spring from?'

'From my car.'

'You honour me with your presence. Might I dispatch my unworthy adversary before we confer? I'm just two points from a quite famous against-the-odds victory.'

'Please forgive me, Your Royal Highness, but this cannot wait.'

'Oh very well.' Sihanouk placed his racquet on the tarmac and wiped his face with a towel handed to him by an aide. He waggled a finger at Ted. 'Sihanouk strongly suggests you review your tactics. They are predictable. And reform your morals. Sihanouk is saddened by your win-at-all-costs approach.'

Mironov led Sihanouk away from the group before he spoke.

'Your Royal Highness, you have my deepest commiserations. Might I inquire, what have you decided to do?'

'I can do nothing. I am informed that the plane is delayed so I will wait. Sihanouk thanks you from the bottom of his heart for the hospitality you have shown him by loaning him your personal plane and he is happy to wait.'

'But ... Nobody has told you? Oh dear, oh dear: Mr Prime Minister, Your Royal Highness, it is my melancholy duty to report to you that I have news from Phnom Penh: the National Assembly has voted to strip you of all your powers.'

Sihanouk took one step back. He blinked once, nodded, and blinked twice more. His ears turned red. He slumped, shielded his eyes with his hands and then slowly, with a supreme effort, lifted his head and snapped his shoulders back into place.

'Ooh la la,' Sihanouk said eventually. 'It has happened? They really have done it?'

'They have,' Mironov said.

'But ... Done it, really and truly, not just talked and threatened and then cowered in the corner when the time for action has come?'

'They have completed the task.'

'But ... I cannot believe it. Cambodia belongs to Sihanouk! The people are my sons and daughters, my little children ... What of General Lon Nol? Imprisoned? Dead?'

'My information is that General Lon Nol led the coup.'

'I ... I smell an American plot. Sihanouk smells cheeseburgers. Sihanouk smells hot apple pie. Excuse me, Mr Premier, but I must consult my wife.'

Sihanouk trembled in the strengthening wind as he told Monique the news. They held each other and wept. Ted watched as Sihanouk's hands moved slowly down until they cupped Monique's buttocks. He squeezed and squeezed as his shoulders heaved.

'Perhaps it is time we went to France,' Monique said eventually.

'What? I will not run. Sihanouk is no quitter.'

'But we could retire to Mougins. After all you have done for your people, they show their appreciation by knifing you in the back. So let them flounder. Let them fail. And then watch them come pleading to you to return and take charge.'

'No. No. Sihanouk will fight … Ted, Sihanouk will fight. 13-5, Sihanouk's serve, come on, Ted, pick up your racquet.'

'Your Majesty, my deepest commiserations at this shattering though not unexpected turn of events,' Ted called across the net.

'Not unexpected? *Not unexpected?* Dear oh dear, Ted, do you have to be right about everything?'

'I apologise, Your Majesty.'

'No matter. Let's not think about it. Sihanouk's serve: are you ready?'

'Are *you* ready?' Monique muttered, retrieving her *Vogue* from the ground. 'Does anybody know when we are leaving? Or *where* we are going?'

'Beijing, as planned. Where else?' Sihanouk said. 'Chou En-lai will know what to do. He will snap his fingers and fix everything. Beijing, I say, but not until we finish our game. And not until that plane is full of food: Sihanouk wants a feast. Come on, Ted, concentrate so Sihanouk can beat you fair and square. The winner plays Premier Mironov.'

Sihanouk served. The shuttlecock went high and long with the wind, then dropped suddenly. Ted back-pedalled and hit his return hard and flat, just missing the head of the Soviet pilot. Sihanouk dived full-length onto the tarmac but hit the shuttlecock into the stomach of one of his aides.

'Are you hurt, Your Majesty?' Ted said.

'You think this coup is a good thing. Don't deny it. I can feel it in the sudden finesse with which you hit the shuttlecock and the way your feet dance.'

'Your Majesty, I protest.'

'You think I will embrace your friends the communists now. You think Sihanouk will make a fine Khmer Rouge king, swathed in red and doing what he's told? 14-5: come on, let's play.'

'It's 12-6, Your Majesty. I *do* think you would be wise to ally yourself with the resistance movement, if you will permit me to say it. I believe that you and the Khmer Rouge could be formidable partners for the common good. But I beg you, please believe me when I say that this coup is unacceptable. Unforgivable. Unconscionable. Unbelievable. I—'

'You once told me that politics is getting the right result by any means.'

'I don't support the coup, Your Majesty. Please do not say such a thing. But—'

'Aha! But what?'

'But there is such a thing as an arranged marriage. Maybe now you and the Khmer Rouge might learn to love each other.'

Sihanouk served. Ted closed his eyes and swung madly. He missed the shuttlecock entirely.

'Game!' Sihanouk cried out triumphantly, hopping about waving his arms.

'Oh, thank God,' Monique said. 'Can we please go now?'

'Sihanouk wins again. Sihanouk wins again,' Sihanouk called.

Sihanouk hopped all the way to the plane, his entourage trailing along behind, some of them weeping, some of them dumbstruck. Ted boarded last. He knew that Sihanouk was right about him. He felt a surging, tingling optimism and all sorts of plots began fermenting in his head. It was a feeling he knew well, and he had long ago stopped bothering to be ashamed by his capacity to revel in bad news.

Ted entered the plane at the rear. He ran down the aisle until he found Sihanouk, who sat whimpering, his head buried in Monique's lap.

'I'll write a book about it,' Ted said. 'The whole sordid thing.'

Sihanouk looked up. His eyes cleared. 'We'll write it together. Yes, yes. Sihanouk and Whittlemore: two for the price of one. Move out of the way, my gorgeous fruit salad. Give your seat to Ted. We have work to do. Have you got pen and paper, Ted? Come on, come on, I am ready to write our book ... Now, first things first: what shall we call it?'

I honestly believe that sovereignty rests with the people: remember that in 1955 I abdicated as king so that I could rule as head of state. There have been many wildly inaccurate accounts of the coup d'état that deposed me, the rightful leader of the Kingdom of Cambodia. What we can say for certain, despite the prevarications of the tame Western media, is that the United States of America intervened deliberately in the internal affairs of a tiny, defenceless Asian nation. I have no doubt that CIA operatives planned and helped carry out the coup, replacing strong and independent Sihanouk with the compliant traitors Lon Nol and Sirik Matak. I responded by accepting the hospitality of my fraternal hosts, China, and by forming, not out of mere necessity but with pride and hope, an alliance with the left-wing patriots, who already have liberated vast numbers of grateful rural Cambodians from the imperialist Lon Nol-ists.

For forming this alliance the West castigates me but I make this promise: after we save the country from the Yankee imperialists our internal policy will be socialist and progressive but never communist. Private enterprise will work in partnership with state monopolies. There are Marxists and non-Marxists amongst my new allies and supporters but all of us agree on the principles of social justice, equality and fraternity. All of us agree that the corrupt Lon Nol-ists, who love American dollars but care nothing about the fate of ordinary Cambodians, must be excluded from public life until they reform.

I have chosen to tell my story to a marvellous Western writer who understands Cambodia. In contrast to so many of his peers, who refuse to comprehend that non-alignment is a matter of the greatest national necessity and pride because our needs do not coincide with America's needs, Edward Whittlemore shows the greatest concern for the hopes and dreams of ordinary Cambodians. He has been a loyal and passionate advocate of my position. He is my dear friend.

—from the preface to *The CIA Ambush of Cambodia* by Prince Norodom Sihanouk as told to Edward Whittlemore

1971

In the elevator of the United Nations, rising to the twenty-eighth floor, a grey-suited American leaned close, his peppermint breath all about, and said in a firm voice, 'Mr Edward Whittlemore?'

'That depends.'

'On what?'

'On what you want me for.'

'Yes, please excuse me. My name is Larry Phillips. I am a senior aide to Dr Henry Kissinger, the US national security advisor.'

'Thank you, I know who he is.'

'Excellent. Dr Kissinger would be delighted if you would join him for lunch tomorrow. He understands that you have no pressing engagements.'

'Does he indeed?'

'He means no offence. He knows that you are a busy man. *Very* busy. But he would be delighted if you could fit him into your schedule. Will you meet him?'

'Here?'

'No, I should have made that clear. He would like to see you in Washington DC. Will you go?'

'I don't believe I can.'

'No?'

'It's nothing personal, of course—'

'Of course.'

'But given that Mr Kissinger is so well informed about my movements he must also know that my visa stipulates that I stay within thirty miles of the UN building.'

'Ah, yes. That.'

'All because of the disturbance at that university last time I was in the US.'

'The New Haven riot?'

34

'"Riot" is a very strong word. But, anyway, that had nothing to do with me. I was inside a basketball stadium giving a speech.'

'The decision regarding your visa was not mine. Nor Dr Kissinger's.'

'No, of course: I suspect your Senator Jackson is behind it.'

'Senator Jackson does not speak for the Nixon administration.'

'What do you suppose he and Nixon discussed last week at the Washington Redskins game?'

'I can assure you, President Nixon never mixes politics and sport. As I understand it, he spent the whole game designing plays and eating hotdogs.'

'Well, it's very disappointing, this thirty-mile thing. I was so looking forward to visiting Las Vegas this time. I understand that the showgirls are a sight to behold. And the neon lights. On top of that, now to miss the chance to meet the national security advisor.'

The lift doors opened. The speechwriter to the president of Zambia and an aide to the UN ambassador to Sri Lanka entered the lift. Ted greeted them effusively while his new friend retreated and hung his head. For an American, Ted thought, he shows admirable restraint.

Five floors later, when the two of them were alone again, Larry Phillips continued talking as if he had never been interrupted.

'*Dr* Kissinger feels certain that if you were to catch the 7.15 train to Washington, no adverse consequences regarding your visa would eventuate.'

'7.15 ... What, in the morning?'

'Will you go?'

'Would he consider sending a car for me? And a driver?'

'Dr Kissinger feels it would be an excellent opportunity for you to see some of our great wide land. And to gain some insight into the travelling habits of everyday mom and pop Americans.'

Ted peered closely at Larry Phillips' face but the American betrayed no hint of humour. Ted caught the 7.15 train. He demanded a window seat and then slept the whole way, his head resting on the shoulder of a retired farmer from Ohio who peered past him, enthralled by the landscape.

I suspected Kissinger was not a man at all but some sort of top-secret committee. When I went to Washington I imagined a posse of Henrys would encircle and interrogate me, all high and mighty and intimidating with their wacky hairdos, their ill-fitting suits, their low centres of gravity.

'What's the capital of Botswana?' these Kissingers would yell at me. 'Do you prefer your bread rolls cold or at room temperature?' 'Do you think that Le Duc Tho is the best person to negotiate for the North Vietnamese?' 'Rank Stalin as a leader out of one to ten. Come on, hurry up. Now Hitler. Now Idi Amin. Now Nixon.' 'Do you honestly believe that there is any way other than the American way?' 'Why do you swear and curse so much? Did you have a traumatic childhood?' 'What sort of Australian are you to be so anti-American?'

But up close Kissinger resembled a normal human being. Only so much smarter. His eyes were creased not by tension or sarcasm but by a playfulness I was befuddled to find alluring. When he smiled, which he did often, he exposed slightly crooked teeth. This utterly disarmed me: why, given the power he wielded, didn't he get them straightened? And whitened?

But then – not a moment too soon – I realised that Kissinger was seducing me and I settled back to give as good as I got.

'I hate formalities. I'm going to call you Henry,' Ted said.

'Welcome to the White House. And thank you for coming.'

'I'll eat with anybody if it's free.'

'Ha! You should be a diplomat. I thought we might chat for a while before lunch,' Kissinger waved Ted to an armchair. 'Do you agree?'

'All right.'

'You must allow me to apologise for the quality of the coffee. It's true what they say.'

'*They?*'

'That American coffee is the worst in the civilised world.'

'Surely you're in a position to do something about that.'

'*Me?* What can I do about entrenched historical mediocrity?'

'The Vietnamese make fine coffee.'

'Indeed.'

'Actually, they do many things well.'

'Yes, I agree. It's a pity that they – let me clarify: it's a pity that some of them – say one thing when they mean another. It makes it

hard to praise them for all those things they do well. Such as coffee.'
Kissinger paused, then said, 'You understand that this is a private
conversation, not an interview?'

'I assumed as much. Well, I won't tell anybody that I was here.'

'Well, I certainly ask that you don't write about today. But feel
free to recount our conversation to any relevant third party.'

'Did you have any particular third party in mind? I'm not sure
I'm privy to whatever inference you're making. Remember, I'm no
diplomat.'

'No?' Kissinger laughed. 'Well, allow me to put it like this:
should you happen to find yourself amongst your North Vietnamese friends, you can tell anybody you deem it worth telling that I
am open to the possibility of talks.'

'The possibility of *further* talks, you mean?'

'Quite so.' Kissinger sipped his coffee and grimaced.

'Then I must tell you that I have a great deal less influence than
you imagine. I'm a simple reporter who happens to go to the North
Vietnamese briefings instead of yours.'

'Oh come now, you're too modest. Simple? I read your column
all the time. You have access at the highest levels.'

'That's true. I'm here, aren't I?'

'Do you know the problem with the Vietnamese? I've been giving this a lot of thought.'

'The North Vietnamese, you mean?'

'Quite so. The problem with the *North* Vietnamese,' Kissinger
said, sweeping his arm in such a way that he implicated Ted, 'is that
they are impatient. They are extreme. They want everything all at
once. They want the south handed to them as if it was theirs by
right.'

'Many people – most people – agree that it *is* theirs by right.'

'But the Viet Minh won't concede a thing. And the way they talk:
"You must do it this way" and "We expect this of you." That is not
the appropriate language to use with a great democracy such as the
United States of America. Why don't they understand that? Why not
say "We prefer" or "Would you possibly consider" or "We humbly
submit" or—'

'How about "With your permission"?'

Kissinger's eyes narrowed and then he leaned back and laughed.

'That's the sort of thing. That's it, exactly. But, really, all we want is a fair settlement. We will not capitulate, no matter how many hippies march and refuse to cut their hair, because we want a real peace for *all* the people of Indochina, including those who have put their trust in us.'

'What about Cambodia?'

'What about it?'

'Prince Sihanouk sits in exile waiting for the chance to fix things in his country. Would you be prepared to meet him also?'

'Such a stock-standard question, Ted, you disappoint me. Very well, let's get our little press conference over and done with so we can enjoy our lunch. Yes, of course I would meet Sihanouk. Under certain circumstances.'

'There's always "certain circumstances." You know your problem, don't you?'

'America's problem, you mean?'

'Exactly. You've picked a loser in Lon Nol. And now you're stuck with him.'

'But we didn't pick Lon Nol. We were as shocked as anybody by the coup that deposed Prince Sihanouk. We have maintained open lines of communication with General Lon Nol and his forces because circumstances have forced our hand.'

'Oh come on, don't give me the official line. They must be the dirtiest bunch of cronies you've ever jumped into bed with.'

Kissinger failed to suppress a grin. 'Obviously I am unable to respond to such a provocative statement. But if – if – I was to reply, I might ponder aloud the wisdom of you denouncing Lon Nol while extolling the virtues of the Khmer Rouge.'

'The Khmer Rouge aren't perfect but they're good people doing what they have to do for their country.'

'Oh Ted, you mustn't say such things out loud.'

'Did you know that Lon Nol determines policy by poking about in the stomachs of chickens?' Ted said.

'As long as he eats the chickens afterwards it's no concern of mine. Waste not want not, I always say.'

'He cuts their heads off, calls them ducks and sells them to his own army at five times the price.'

'So many ducks, so few bullets … But really, Ted, your Vietnamese friends left us with no choice but to support Lon Nol. They expanded the war into Cambodian territory, after all: the Viet Cong sanctuaries, the arms shipments arriving through the port at Sihanoukville. We merely responded.'

'How very convenient.'

'Not at all. Many of our soldiers, our young men, died as a direct result of Sihanouk's encouragement of the Vietnamese. One cannot be neutral merely by proclaiming "I AM NEUTRAL." One must actually behave in a neutral fashion. Besides, the United States is now obliged – let me clarify, we oblige ourselves – to do what we can to help the innocent people of Cambodia. They depend on us now more than ever. They have asked for our help. We must render it. It is a matter of honour.'

'You get to help out and wage war simultaneously. What could be better?'

'We could probably work with Sihanouk in the unlikely event that it proves necessary. But we cannot countenance a dialogue while he insists on this alliance with the Khmer Rouge. The United States of America expects a gesture from Sihanouk. Something that indicates he's trustworthy.'

'The Cambodian people trust him. Isn't that enough?'

'Sihanouk is no better than your Vietnamese friends. He refuses to negotiate with Lon Nol—'

'Surely you understand that Lon Nol is not his favourite person. He did betray Sihanouk, after all. And sentence him to death.'

'But Sihanouk places so many unacceptable conditions on talks that he ensures that talks cannot possibly eventuate. It is a tired tactic. Just like your Vietnamese friends who—'

'Who you happily negotiate with.'

'Sihanouk's terms and conditions are ridiculous and then he blames me for my intransigence. The nerve. Does he really want a negotiated settlement? Or is he hiding behind his Maoist friends in the jungle? Is he sure he can control the Khmer Rouge? Those people are thugs.'

'What do you care whether or not they're thugs? They're not your thugs, that's what you really mean. You trampled all over Cambodia's neutrality and—'

'Oh, come now, Ted, so simplistic. You're such a journalist.

Don't let's have a conversation that can be reduced to half a column.'

'Fair enough, but let me finish. You trampled all over Cambodia's neutrality. You bombed neutral territory. And then you had the CIA help Lon Nol get rid of Sihanouk—'

'I hope you like fish.'

'And now you have the temerity to slander the Khmer Rouge, who are patriots and honourable nationalists and—'

'We're having fish for lunch. I hope you like cod.'

'Boneless?'

'Boneless. Spineless. Poached in white wine, I believe. Now, I don't want to argue, Ted, we can do that any old time and we certainly don't need to be in the same room. Let's chat.'

'I don't speak for anybody, you know, other than me. I hope you didn't bring me here thinking I have some authority in Vietnam just because you read it in some CIA gossip column.'

'Do you know what I want? Do you know what I hoped for when I asked you here?'

'Illumination?'

'Yes, of course, ha ha. But the other thing I wanted – I'm still hoping for it, call me a dreamer – is that you might listen to my viewpoint rather than dismiss me according to your preconceptions. Do you know your problem? Please, it's nothing personal, but you have the same disease as all the journalists who are so sympathetic to the anti-war movement. You're all so caught up in the big picture – forcing the geopolitics to line up with the way you imagine the world works – that it never occurs to you that I mean what I say. And that President Nixon might mean what he says.'

'How can he mean it if he doesn't understand it?'

'Now, now, Ted. Don't go falling for your own propaganda. All I'm suggesting is that you consider the possibility that we are pursuing a morally upright and honourable solution in Vietnam. And that what we say in public is exactly what we mean. President Nixon and I are the strongest two anti-war Americans you will ever find. More coffee?'

'You're kidding, right? My tongue is already damaged irreparably.'

'Taste buds have remarkable powers of recuperation. Trust me, I know from experience. But would you prefer a glass of beer?'

'What, now? It's 11.30. Are you trying to get me drunk?'

'I think we both know there's barely any alcohol in a Budweiser.'

'All right then. I'll have one.'

'Good.'

'And you'll join me?'

'Good heavens, no. I couldn't possibly.'

One of the phones on Kissinger's desk rang.

'Yes? ... What about? ... All right, put him on.' He put his hand over the receiver, whispered '*New York Times*' to Ted and rolled his eyes. 'Henry Kissinger speaking ... Hello, Brad ... No problem, I can only spare you a moment but it's great to speak to you again ... Yes, I'm aware of the turn that particular demonstration has taken ... Well, I can't condone their methods. Lying down in the street seems a singularly ludicrous exercise. People need to be able to get to work. They need to be able to get their children to school. On the – please, Brad, let me finish. On the other hand, I am sympathetic to the demonstrators' frustrations. I share those frustrations. That's why we're redoubling our efforts to find a peaceful solution in Vietnam that is acceptable to all parties. But we can't just walk away. We have responsibilities to the American public. And to the Vietnamese people ... You're welcome, Brad, see you around. Am I right in thinking you wrote yesterday's editorial? ... A most intriguing perspective. Utterly wrong, of course, but fascinating.'

He hung up and turned back to Ted. 'Poor fellow doesn't know his history. Now, where were we?'

'Disagreeing.'

'Oh yes. My point is quite simple. What are the North Vietnamese doing most successfully at present?'

'Destroying you on the battlefield.'

'No, Ted, no. Certainly they have their little victories and I'm sure they seem marvellous if you happen to be there to witness them. But no. Their greatest success is in influencing American domestic opinion. I know you won't tell me who's masterminding it, but—'

'It's not me, if that's what you're suggesting. I'm proud to say I've never been in charge of anything in my life. I'm not even in charge of myself.'

'Well, whoever is in control of Vietnam's public relations is brilliant but desperately misguided. They are the very people who need to understand that we really are genuinely trying to negotiate. Don't you see?'

'You want the Vietnamese to like you?'

'No, no, don't be a simpleton. They tie me up and then complain when all I can do is wiggle. They demand that I think in the absolutes of right and wrong, like a member of the public. But I cannot work like that unless I am willing to fail the American people, politically and morally. I do not have the luxury of idealism or of conforming to some theoretical notion of pure rectitude.'

'You'd bend in the wind so long as the *New York Times* didn't report it?'

'Bend? I'd snap myself in two if I thought it would help. But never in public.'

'And in the meantime Vietnamese and Cambodians die.'

'Americans, too… If only there was some way to negotiate the peace without having the actual war.'

1973

On a sunny afternoon in Siem Reap province, in the Khmer Rouge's Liberated Zone, Nhem Kiry, Bun Sody and Prince Norodom Sihanouk stood on the causeway that led to Angkor Wat. Facing them, Akor Sok crouched beside a stone lion and with dusty hands changed the roll of film in his camera.

Kiry was dressed in simple black cotton: loose trousers and short-sleeved shirt. A single ballpoint pen poked from his breast pocket. His hair was freshly cut, perfectly straight and combed back. That morning he had shaved meticulously with a razor and a tin cup half-full of cold water. After six years of living in the Liberated Zone, in rough camps and tiny hamlets, he looked clean and healthy, although a little thinner than the day he had escaped from Phnom Penh. He had the calm assurance of a leader who commanded the respect and support of all of those around him. And all week, preparing for the photo shoot, he had been practising a special smile: open, honest, relaxed, reassuring, authoritative.

Inwardly, Kiry was seething at Sihanouk's presence. He hated all this feigned affection. It made him feel dirty, as if he'd given in to lustful thoughts and dragged a prostitute into an alley. But, still, he knew that he had to keep Sihanouk happy – and Monique, too, although that was probably asking for a miracle.

Sody sensed that Kiry's focus was melting in the heat. He dug him in the ribs and whispered, 'I'm sure that I could be a movie star if I could get out of this place.' Despite himself, Kiry grinned. It was unpleasant but essential work, he reminded himself, and he was honoured to be playing a part.

A small crowd stood nearby. Princess Monique scowled and drank water from a glass bottle. Her personal attendant stood at her left elbow, holding an umbrella to create shade. Several smooth-faced soldiers stood around caressing their rifles and fighting the urge to fall asleep in the late-afternoon heat. Several Khmer Rouge luminaries – Hu Nim and the famous sisters, Khieu Ponnary and Khieu Thirith – stood waiting for their turn to have Akor Sok photograph them. A little further away several other Khmer Rouge leaders stood: Son Sen, Ieng Sary, Nuon Chea.

A cheerful, vacant figure called Saloth Sar hung from the crowd like a loose thread. His hands rested on his belly. His slightly chubby face was a carefully constructed mask of amused indifference. Sihanouk recognised Sar. He was the little brother of a woman who had lived and worked in the royal palace. She and Sihanouk had fornicated from time to time.

As they all stood marvelling at the architectural miracle of Angkor Wat, Sihanouk took the opportunity to launch into a speech. His rotund tummy pushed against his khaki shirt as he pontificated and waved his arms about: 'It is three years since the ultra-traitor Lon Nol stole my country from me. Three years, oh my, three long years. I love my friends in Beijing, but Sihanouk can only eat so many egg rolls in one lifetime before he himself turns into an egg roll. Meanwhile, Lon Nol eats suckling pig in the Royal Palace. Lon Nol and my evil cousin Sirik Matak claim that they run Cambodia when everybody knows that they follow Dr Henry Kissinger's instructions. Anyway, how can Lon Nol take himself seriously when Sihanouk stands at Angkor Wat unmolested? Lon Nol can do nothing. Lon Nol *is* nothing. Lon Nol does not even know that Sihanouk is in Cambodia. What a shock he will get when he sees these photographs.

'There is nowhere in the whole wide world as wonderful as Angkor Wat. Where else can Sihanouk remind himself of the virtues of his little children, the Cambodian people? Where else can we all remember what can be achieved when a great leader and a kingdom full of labourers come together? Angkor Wat is the emblem of our country and our struggle and our potential and our greatness, and what better person than Sihanouk to stand here? Thank you, thank you, thank you my dearest friends, thank you especially Brother Nhem Kiry, for inviting me to visit the Liberated Zone. You have granted Sihanouk his most ardent wish: to again be amongst his darling children. He is so emotional he can barely speak.'

'If only that was true,' Nuon Chea muttered.

'Everybody is so delighted,' Ieng Sary whispered, 'that His Majesty Prince Norodom Sihanouk is finally pregnant. He has wanted to be a mother for so long. He's so large that the doctors suspect twins.'

Son Sen and Nuon Chea sniggered.

'Please, friends,' Saloth Sar said quietly. 'Have some self-discipline.'

'Sirik Matak: him I can understand,' Sihanouk continued. 'My little cousin with the great big forearms, always so angry that he was born to the wrong parents, so jealous of Sihanouk's abilities, Sihanouk's manliness, Sihanouk's shapely wife, tee hee. Oh the way he used to look at my sweet Monique, ooh la la: I could never tell if Sirik Matak wanted to kiss her or kill her.'

'But Lon Nol? Lon Nol owes everything to Sihanouk. Lon Nol *belongs* to Sihanouk. How could he betray me? How could he go and—'

'Excuse me, Your Majesty,' Kiry said. 'Comrade Sok needs us to move over here to where the light is better.'

'Yes, yes … I admire your dedication so much, you know.'

'Thank you, Your Majesty.'

'To live exposed to the elements for so long. And amongst such … how can I say it? … mixed company.'

'I confess it is difficult sometimes, Your Majesty. Occasionally I must endure a minor digestive complaint. Sometimes I contract a mild fever.'

'I eat if I am feeling unwell,' Bun Sody said. 'It's a sure-fire cure.'

'But never fear, Your Majesty, Comrade Sody and I are feeling particularly sprightly,' Kiry said. 'Especially as it is widely supposed that we have been dead these last six years.'

'In any case, dead or alive, it is an honour to serve you, Your Majesty,' Sody said.

'Six years, ha ha ha, dead for six years, tee hee. And what's more, it was *I* who supposedly killed you. What a terrible job I did of disposing of the bodies, tee hee,' Sihanouk said.

'Your Majesty, do you recall that I began to tell you earlier about the many serious offences committed in the Liberated Zone by our Vietnamese brothers?' Kiry said.

'Yes, these stories upset me. I am eager to hear more but perhaps some other time. Why not write me a memo? I know Ieng Sary loves to carry pieces of paper to Beijing for me to read. It is so kind of you to find all those little jobs to keep him occupied.'

'The Vietnamese soldiers go into our villages,' Kiry said, 'and they steal whatever they want – even though the peasants are happy to share any surplus, as we have humbly and politely asked them to do. The Vietnamese take the peasants' rice and chickens, buffalo, fruit. They take so much that there is nothing left for our own soldiers. And they take carts, clothes, bicycles, anything they can find.'

'Brother Son Sen, Sister Khieu Thirith, have also told me about this. But—'

'But if the villagers complain, they rape the women and the girls. Sometimes they beat and kill the men whose only crime is to want to survive and play their part in liberation, for Vietnam as well as Cambodia. It's true, I tell you. And that's not all, they also—'

'But we must continue to work with our Vietnamese brothers if we can, mustn't we?' Sihanouk said. 'Are not the Americans our greatest enemy, and also the greatest enemy of our Vietnamese brothers?'

'Of course, Your Majesty, you are correct. That is why we endure the situation, complaining with tact and humility. But America will leave here one day soon – they no longer have the stomach for the war in Vietnam – whereas the contemptible Vietnamese will always cast a shadow over Kampuchea. They are imperialists first and good communists second.'

Sihanouk shuffled in the dirt. He had no interest in Kiry's complaints, whether or not they were true. Such petty squabbles were not his problem. Besides, he recalled the advice of the Vietnamese general who had delivered him into the Liberated Zone: 'Please, Your Majesty, do not speak too openly about all of the help we have been giving you recently. Our Khmer Rouge brothers would not approve.'

'Will we be finished here soon, do you think?' Sihanouk said. 'My darling wife looks very tired.'

'Of course, Your Majesty. We need several more photographs but, yes, we can leave soon. I am sure that you are eager to spend some time alone with Princess Monique. And to eat. Comrade Sok, please hurry up. His Majesty cannot wait all day.'

'Yes, comrade, I am ready,' Sok said, fiddling with a light meter. 'Please forgive me, Your Majesty, the conditions are not ideal. Now: please stand close together.'

Sok looked through the viewfinder of his camera. He imagined that the small circle, designed to centre the image, now enclosing the tip of Sihanouk's nose, was a rifle sight.

'Please stand closer to Comrade Kiry, Your Majesty.'

Sihanouk took a short step to his left. The two men's shoulders kissed.

'Please smile, Your Majesty.'

Sihanouk beamed and stood to attention, his shoulders pulled back hard, as if someone was poking the small of his back with a stick. The sun illuminated his face. As he smiled his moist lips glued together. His cheeks turned into crescent moons and shone.

'Are you ready?' Sok said. 'Excellent, excellent. Brother Kiry, please smile. A little more. Good. Brother Sody, could you perhaps smile a little less. Good. Perfect.'

Kiry grasped Sihanouk's hand.

'Liberation,' Sihanouk said.

'Solidarity,' Kiry said.

'Peace,' Sody said.

Above them, the mid-afternoon sky bled into the tree line.

1975

At dusk, Bun Sody crouched at a riverbank and splashed his face. Although victory was near, he was troubled. He thought it very possible that his old friend Saloth Sar – Pol Pot, as he was now calling himself – might be going a little crackers. Pol Pot had declared that as soon as the Khmer Rouge took control of Phnom Penh and the other cities and towns, the people should all be herded into the countryside. Every single one of them.

'We must ask him to reconsider this madness,' Bun Sody told Nhem Kiry, who paddled about in the river's deeper water, clutching a cake of soap. 'Surely there are other ways to wipe the slate clean.'

Kiry waded out of the water. He patted Sody on the shoulder and murmured something so quietly that Sody suspected he had made gentle, soothing noises, like a mother cooing at a baby, enticing him to sleep.

'What? *What?*' Sody said. 'I can't hear you.'

'I said, don't worry so much. It doesn't become you. I said, let's eat.'

That night Bun Sody slept badly. He passed in and out of consciousness, burdened by the thoughts of his countrymen tramping to all corners of the country for no sane reason. What was Pol Pot thinking? he wondered. Did he really believe the people were so tainted that they needed to be born again?

The next morning, Sody decided he must relay his unhappiness to Pol Pot, who was camped a day's walk north. The young man he chose to deliver his message was sensible and trustworthy. Years earlier, at a high school in Phnom Penh – when the prospect of a communist take-over had seemed like nothing more than a dream – Sody had taught him mathematics by day and Marxist theory by night.

'Tell Brother Pol Pot that in my opinion his strategy to empty the cities is not completely rational. Tell him, with the greatest respect, that it will cause great pain and create widespread problems – problems we will then have to fix, at great cost to both our reputation and the national budget. Tell him it's not too late to do things differently. Tell him I stand ready to come to him to explain an alternative strategy. Tell him I honour and respect him and cannot wait to embrace him in liberated Phnom Penh. Tell him I've had my fair share of harebrained ideas, so I know what I'm talking about. Tell him that I stand ready to serve the movement in whatever capacity he sees fit … but that if he chooses to appoint me as, say, foreign minister, then I would be joyful beyond words.'

Three days later, in the heat of the early afternoon, Sody lay in a hammock composing a sonnet on the subject of the female form and drifting towards sleep. The messenger, Sody's former student, found him lolling with his eyes closed and his dry, cracked lips silently moving.

'Wake up, comrade, Brother Pol Pot sends you news. But we must talk in private,' the messenger said.

The messenger led Sody along a winding path that cut through thick foliage. Sody had come this way earlier in the day, just far enough to find a spot where he could squat in privacy to shit. He had groaned at the effort. Not for the first time, his intestines were rebelling against living rough. Sody couldn't wait for all this to be over. Phnom Penh beckoned. Or somewhere even better: maybe Pol Pot really would appoint him foreign minister. Even minister for trade would do. If not, perhaps he could plead for an ambassadorship, get himself posted to Paris for a couple of years, recuperate with galleries and concerts and gourmet food and fine beaujolais and a city full of white women.

The messenger took Sody's elbow and led him off the path and into the jungle.

'Is this necessary?' Sody asked, but the other man did not reply.

After a short time, less than a minute, they reached a small clearing. Three soldiers, barely more than boys, stood waiting. Two of the soldiers trained their rifles on Sody; the third held out a shovel.

'What is this? I demand that you explain yourself,' Sody said, although he knew instantly what was happening. 'Do you have a message for me or not?'

The boy soldier threw the shovel at Sody's feet.

'Dig. That's your message. Dig your grave.'

A little while later the messenger returned to the camp. He approached Nhem Kiry, who was sitting amongst a group of soldiers and aides, eating a bowl of rice flecked with greens.

The messenger leant close and whispered in Kiry's ear. Kiry frowned slightly, then nodded. He stood up and walked to a spot by himself, where he crouched in the dirt and continued eating.

*   *   *

Nhem Kiry reached the centre of Phnom Penh a day and a half after the first Khmer Rouge troops. Fifty metres from where he stood, past an abandoned car and upturned cyclos, sat the convoy of jeeps that had borne him and his personal battalion into the city. A radio operator sat in one jeep, twiddling the dials of a box that occasionally stopped farting to relay a message. Four soldiers stood by, three boys and a girl, battle-hardened and clear-headed, guns trained north and south. The other soldiers, their weapons protruding like tentacles, surrounded Kiry and his awed chief aide, Akor Sok. This strange organism proceeded north along Monivong Boulevard.

Kiry paused in front of the twin-towered dirty white cathedral. Catholic architecture did not interest him – he had lived in Paris for three years without visiting Notre Dame – but he needed a reason, however flimsy, to pause. Not for the first time that day, Kiry's body felt too light: his fingertips tingled, his kneecaps wobbled and the tip of his tongue kept catching in the gap between his front teeth. He thought he might vomit or faint or float away.

He steadied himself by briefly touching Sok's elbow. Sok mistook the contact to be a command and obediently commenced a disdainful assessment of the four-metre statue of Jesus that stood above the cathedral's entrance.

'What's he doing there, imposing himself on our city? Look, he's all dirty. No one has washed him in years. What is that, dove shit? Look, the plaster's peeling off him. They don't care about him. Pathetic.'

Kiry drank from his water canister and tipped the last of it over his head. The flow ran dry at the base of his neck, where his top vertebrae bulged. Sok blinked, surprised by this uncharacteristic show of waste. He sensed that Kiry might be ailing and began to fuss.

'Are you unwell, comrade?' He handed Kiry a fresh canister of water. 'Are you dehydrated?'

'No.'

'Have you got stomach cramps again?'

'No.'

'Have you got a temperature? Please, no, is it malaria?'

'Stop it. I'm suffering from exhilaration.'

'I understand,' Sok said, flabbergasted.

Seeking respite from the sun, mostly seeking a quiet place to sit alone and gather his thoughts, Kiry pierced the circle of soldiers and moved towards the cathedral. He made stuttering progress up the widely spaced stairs. When he glanced at Jesus, who looked down his nose at him, he tripped. He broke his fall first with the palms of his hands and then with his ribcage. He lay half in sun, half in shadow, marvelling at the first thought that entered his head: finally, a legitimate war wound.

'Quick, comrade, get up,' Sok whispered. 'They'll think you're praying.'

Kiry laughed at that unlikely proposition. 'Praise be to God,' he said. 'I'm going inside.'

'We will stop here for now,' Sok called out.

Several soldiers stayed with Kiry. Others sat on the road, nursing the blisters on their feet. A couple lobbed stones at Jesus. One young man entered a bakery. He emerged pushing a woman, who half-turned to protest. He raised his rifle. She ran. As he lowered the gun he let off a shot. The bullet thudded into the woman's thigh. She collapsed, howling. The soldier blinked – his stunned face suggested the rifle had come to life of its own accord – and turned away.

Kiry stepped inside the cathedral. The air was heavy with the smells that encapsulated the building's history: the lake of lemon oil rubbed into the walnut pews; waxy effluent from thousands of candles; the mustiness of damp, black-spotted hymn books, which still sprouted like mushrooms on every pew; small pyramids of refuse left by refugees who were now filling the roads out of Phnom Penh.

'It stinks,' Sok said.

'It's the memory of the French.'

'That's what I said: it stinks.'

Discomforted by the silence, Sok quickly spoke again.

'So, we've done it, comrade. We've won.'

'So it seems.'

'You doubt it? Is there something more to come?'

'No. We are here.'

They sat for a time until Kiry grew tired of Sok's fidgeting.

'Did I tell you that I met Chou En-lai last month in Beijing?' he asked

'No, comrade, you never mentioned it,' Sok lied.

'He was propped up in his hospital bed. He tried to smile when I arrived but it only made him lose his breath. Do you know what he said to me?'

'No, comrade.'

'He told me to pursue a gentle revolution, a gradual revolution. Can you believe it?'

'No, comrade.'

'I was polite but I told him the truth. I promised him that our revolution would be pure as rain.'

'How did he respond?'

'He didn't say anything. He sighed and one of the machines he was connected to lit up. He was so unwell; delirious, probably. I suppose I could have been gentler with him. But the truth is always best.'

'I agree, comrade.'

Kiry peered through the gloom. 'Oh, look, a miracle: that baptismal font has arms and legs.'

Sok followed Kiry's gaze to where an old woman, despite abject thinness, failed to conceal herself.

'Quickly, men, over here. Grab her.' Sok's eyes widened with excitement as the soldiers obeyed his commands. 'The rest of you check the building. You, look there; you, check back there; you, through there.'

Kiry winced as Sok's bellowing bounced from wall to wall. He craved silence – an hour, even a few minutes – to close his eyes and clear his mind. Instead, soldiers stormed the centre aisle in pursuit of an old woman incapable of flight. Above the beat of their footsteps on the floorboards Sok continued yelling. Kiry bowed his head and played deaf and dumb.

One of the soldiers approached the old woman, who cowered and continued to delude herself that she was invisible. She breathed heavily now, her chest poking out through the gaps between her ribs. Finally, submissively, she commenced a coughing fit. The soldier slung his rifle over his shoulder, lifted the baptismal font and threw it against the altar. Brackish water sprayed the woman. She attached herself to Sok's legs, panting, clasping her hands together.

'You must leave the city,' Sok said. 'You must go to your home district. Stand up and walk.'

The woman hauled herself upright by grabbing a tuft of Sok's black shirt. 'Look at me. I am lame,' she said, swivelling in a tight circle anchored by her right leg. She finished where she had started and, unable to maintain her balance another moment, collapsed at Sok's feet.

'You are not special,' Sok said. 'Everybody must go.'

'I cannot. Please, I cannot. The other soldiers I met earlier, by the river, they told me I could stay if I kept out of the way.'

'The Americans are going to bomb the city. You can come back soon if you want to but now you must leave.'

Then the old woman saw Kiry.

'Oh, oh, oh,' she stuttered and lost control of her breathing.

Several soldiers converged on the old woman as she scrambled towards Kiry. Her sarong unravelled and threatened to stay attached to a wide splinter that reared out of the floor, providing Kiry with an unexpurgated view of the opalised ulcer that ran from her calf to her thigh.

'Honourable Uncle, is it really you? They said you were dead but I never believed them. I am so happy that you are here at last. Have you brought Prince Sihanouk with you? Please tell these people that I cannot walk. Please let me stay here. Please tell them. I know you understand me.'

'You must leave, Auntie. There is no other way.'

'But I am not strong enough to walk. What will I eat? I have no bowl, no rice.'

The woman reached out to touch Kiry. Sok kicked her in the ribs. She whimpered as a soldier grabbed her by her good ankle and dragged her down the steps and onto the road. She did not scream or complain further. She squatted then stood and with a lopsided, comical gait hobbled away.

Then one of the soldiers, looking for food, discovered a priest hiding in a closet.

'Careful, boy,' the priest said in Khmer to the soldier, who waved a gun in his face. 'I'm French.'

As the soldiers crowded around the priest, Kiry turned his back and commenced studying a stained-glass window of Jesus ascending to heaven. He had met this priest a few times. He was, Kiry remembered, a compassionate man who held presumptuous but surprisingly perceptive opinions on the question of progress for the Cambodian peasant. He had also, or so Bun Sody had insisted, fallen madly in love with his housekeeper, a plump girl whom he had first employed when she was fourteen. 'She cooks him onion soup,' Sody had claimed, 'and every morning she washes him head to toe with a sponge. She offers more but he refuses.'

'I don't want him to see me,' Kiry told Sok. 'Take him to the French embassy. Be polite. Don't let anyone hurt him. Do it now.'

'Yes, comrade.'

'And while you're there, find out who's hiding inside the embassy. I want a full list. I want to know if Lon Nol really went with the Americans. I want to know if they're sheltering Sirik Matak and Long Boret and—'

'Will you be all right here without me, comrade?'

'Just get me that list. And see if you can be of any use at the hospital. Then go and see that everything is under control elsewhere.'

'Elsewhere, comrade?'

'Anywhere. I don't care. Just go.'

Sok approached the priest, who was arguing with one of the soldiers.

'But I just came to collect a few things. My stoles are precious to me. One of them comes from Mexico. Peasant workers made it by hand, using the same cotton that—'

'No.'

'And my Bible. It's in the vestry, just back there. My grand-mother gave it to me the day I began school. I refuse to leave with-out it.'

Sok stood so close to the priest that they could smell each other's mouths. 'Okay, but you have one minute. That is all. Then we will go to the embassy.'

'Oh, I can walk there myself.'

'We will escort you. The street is very dangerous.'

'I'll be fine.'

'We *will* take you.'

'Yes. All right.'

'You should have run away with the Americans.'

'Yes.'

Finally it was quiet. Kiry sat on a pew, breathed deeply, held the rank air within his lungs, counted to ten and exhaled through pursed lips. None of the minor triumphs or quiet moments of self-satisfaction he had experienced in his life had prepared him for the elation that now threatened to immobilise him.

He remembered the excitement of his boat trip to France – he was twenty-two years old – and the sense of accomplishment he attained simply by arriving safely in Marseille. That was a pleasant memory, he supposed, although the truth was he had vomited the whole way and had irritated Bun Sody, who was his cabin compan-ion, by implying he knew so much more about the world than he did.

From his time in Paris he remembered a deep conversation in a café with a young French woman about Lenin and Trotsky and the eternal revolution. His restrained delivery of his passionate argu-ment so convinced her – he had long ago forgotten her name but she was tall and had long brown hair – that she followed him to his tiny apartment and stayed the night and most of the next day, an outcome he desired but would never have proposed. He was relieved when she left, having already come to believe that his moment of weakness had lost him thirty-six hours of reading time.

When she knocked on his door a few days later, he pretended he was out. When he saw her in the street, he ducked into a doorway. When she wrote him a letter, he burned it, unopened.

He recalled being joyfully mute when a panel of French academics heaped praise on his thesis. The work was rudimentary and speculative, he now knew. Still, he was proud that he'd produced a piece of research which somehow satisfied a panel of examiners who were at war with each other.

He remembered his elevation to parliament. How proud his irretrievably frail mother had been. Now he knew – in truth, he'd always known – that Sihanouk had chosen him because of his apparent meekness. Still, he was proud of his reputation for incorruptibility and hard work. It had won him a second term in parliament, a useless time notable mainly because he had somehow achieved it against Sihanouk's wishes. Still, the ordinary people had seen him in action and they considered him to be an honest patriot: what a useful tool that had been in the hard years that followed.

Kiry thought about his mother. She had died in 1973. One day, walking home from the market, she tripped and fell. She lay in the street moaning quietly until her neighbours came and carried her to the hospital. But the wards and the corridors were full of soldiers, so she went home. Overnight her leg blew up like a balloon, hard and black. One by one her organs rebelled, so that by the time she died a few days later the doctor could only guess at the cause. It was weeks before Kiry heard the news and months before he learnt the details.

Kiry thought about his brother Goy, older by one year. Goy had been a burly boy with manly shoulders, whereas Kiry was skinny and prone to falling over and skinning his knees. Inexplicably, Kiry always won their races to the well to collect water – even though he had the handicap of carrying the buckets. Kiry was twelve years old before he, too, learnt to lose on purpose. He wondered where Goy was now: probably limping to Kandal Province, assuming – fool that he was – that his well-connected brother would rescue him.

Inside an annex at the back of the cathedral, Kiry located a winding staircase. He began to climb and was pleased that his legs grew stronger and that he felt, at last, properly connected to the earth.

At the top of the tower he broke a couple of rotten wooden slats and leaned against the cold metal of a brass bell. As he admired the view his sandals crunched down on dried pigeon droppings. He was deaf – or indifferent – to the sounds the city made as it expelled its inhabitants: the din of two million shuffling people, the crying toddlers, the murmured survival plans that families debated and disputed, the occasional bursts of gunfire, the cries of the living as they saw corpses in gutters and floating like logs down the Sap River, the raucous backfires as victorious soldiers taught themselves to drive.

He could see a broken line of people leaving Calmette Hospital. Inside the hospital, Akor Sok herded the ill and the injured down a set of stairs and onto the street. 'Come on, keep moving, keep moving,' Sok ordered a woman with a bandage covering a useless eye, then a hobbling youth with shrapnel embedded in his thigh, then a man clutching his bloated bladder, then a woman holding a limp four-year-old girl, her operation aborted, her stomach wide open.

Kiry could see Wat Phnom, now abandoned. The smart monks had discarded their robes and transformed themselves into peasants, just as the sensible soldiers from Lon Nol's army had shed their khaki skins. The beggars had left too, suddenly no more disadvantaged than anyone else, indistinguishable from the privileged citizens who wore their oldest clothes into the street and strapped their jewels and their dollars to their bodies.

From this vantage point, Kiry let out a single whoop of delight. He felt as if he was flying and he didn't care whose shoulders he had leapt from. Anything was now possible. The view from the sky was so spectacular that nothing else mattered.

*   *   *

Make no mistake, Prince Norodom Sihanouk has heard every single ridiculous rumour about the new Khmer Rouge government in Cambodia. He's heard about the mass killings of so-called 'class enemies.' He's heard about chronic food and medicine shortages. He's heard that his own role as head of state will be purely ceremonial and he's even heard that his freedom and safety will be jeopardised if he returns to Cambodia.

As is so often the case, the truth is very different. Prince Sihanouk is currently in the North Korean capital, Pyongyang, where he spoke with this reporter. Shortly, with great optimism, with a song in his heart, he and his wife, Monique, will return to their beloved Phnom Penh.

Prince Sihanouk acknowledges that the Khmer Rouge have largely emptied the cities but he points out that most people returned to their home provinces, that families were not separated and that no one was forced to leave Phnom Penh if they preferred to stay. 'I am so proud that Cambodians are the first in the world to create a classless society,' he says. 'And the evacuation could not be avoided. Lon Nol had turned Phnom Penh into a Sodom and Gomorrah.'

This reporter has not yet visited the new Cambodia but understands, from Sihanouk and other sources, that the government has eliminated rich and poor, oppressor and oppressed, money and markets. Everybody in the countryside is working, either growing food and raising animals or creating and maintaining a reliable electrical supply or devising and constructing irrigation systems or making and repairing bicycles or weaving clothes or refining sugar or converting tanks into tractors. All this is simply the first step. The construction of a new, equal, and corruption-free urban society will soon follow.

Prince Sihanouk scoffs at suggestions that the Khmer Rouge have no use for him now that the war is won. 'The National Front over which I preside is the absolute essence of monolithic unity. Nhem Kiry and all the other leaders are genuine nationalists. They are working tirelessly to preserve the sovereignty of our country.' As far as Prince Sihanouk is concerned, Cambodia has regained the key principles that as head of state he always fought so courageously for: economic independence and political neutrality. 'And don't forget,' he says, 'that I am the only non-communist head of state ever to be chosen by communists in human history. I am an adopted Khmer Rouge.'

—Edward Whittlemore, 'As I See It,' syndicated column

Prince Norodom Sihanouk and Princess Monique stepped from their specially chartered plane into the harsh light of Pochentong airport. Rubbish whipped around in the wind and came to rest against the planes, trucks and jeeps that were scattered randomly about the tarmac. Sihanouk had always wanted to own a bomb that left property undamaged. He dreamed of clearing Manhattan and repopulating it with his family and friends; of emptying Paris and turning it into his getaway palace. But now, standing and looking about a place apparently cleansed of all life, he was profoundly unnerved.

Or maybe he was hungry. Sihanouk had eaten nothing on the plane but a shrivelled-up baguette. He had wanted to wash it down with champagne but Monique had told him to stick to water and to keep his wits about him. 'You are right,' he had said, shaking his head at the tragedy and watching mournfully as Monique sipped from a glass of chardonnay. Now he was light-headed and desperately in need of a decent meal. A deep queasiness invaded his empty stomach. He glanced at Monique. He knew what she was thinking – Why aren't we in Mougins? – and he willed her to say it aloud so that he had an excuse to rant at her about his responsibilities to his people, irrespective of his private wishes.

There was no red carpet for Sihanouk and Monique to parade down, just Nhem Kiry standing in front of a jeep. The driver kept the engine revving as Kiry stepped forward.

'Your Majesty, welcome home,' Kiry said flatly, his hands firmly clasped behind his back. 'And Princess Monique, what a great honour – what a treat – to see you again. Please, this way.'

They drove to the far side of a tarmac, where a battalion of soldiers dressed in black stood waiting. Kiry ushered Sihanouk and Monique to straight-backed chairs and clapped his hands. The soldiers began to march about. Sihanouk concentrated hard but he could discern no pattern. Still, they seemed to know what they were doing.

'Do you see the guns the soldiers are carrying, Your Majesty?' Kiry said.

'I see them.'

'American, every last one of them. Brand new. We captured them after the imperialists fled.'

'How wonderful,' Sihanouk said.

'And look. Look, Your Majesty ...'

The soldiers parted, revealing a group of M102 howitzers arranged like the petals of a flower. A convoy of tanks rumbled out from a hangar and circled the soldiers. Two helicopters descended and hovered. High above, a fighter plane roared past, banked, and then roared back again.

'The whole lot American,' Kiry said. 'We have many more helicopters, you know ... But unfortunately at the moment we only have two pilots.'

As soon as the parade finished, Kiry bundled Sihanouk and Monique back into the jeep. The drive into the city was fast. The only other vehicles they encountered lay abandoned on the fringes of the road. They saw almost no people, even when they entered Phnom Penh. Sihanouk stared out of the window. Every now and then he would shake his head, almost imperceptibly. This was like some cheap movie-set version of Phnom Penh. Where was the tickertape parade? Where were the brightly dressed schoolchildren singing songs and waving flags? Where were all his loyal subjects, his little children? Were they hiding, waiting to jump out of potholes and swing down out of trees and appear from behind buildings to welcome him home? Sihanouk glanced at Monique, but she had closed her eyes.

The gates of the palace lay open. A couple of guards stood to attention. Inside the grounds, several rows of soldiers, most of them children, engaged in manoeuvres. As the jeep stopped, Monique opened her eyes just in time to see a pig saunter past.

Kiry led them to a guesthouse, a pleasant free-standing building several hundred metres from Sihanouk and Monique's usual sleeping quarters. Monique had never been inside this building before. She was shocked by how small it was: a living room, with a table at one end and a couch at the other, two bedrooms (the second barely bigger than a cupboard), a bathroom and a study.

Sihanouk was more familiar with the guesthouse. Over the years he had rendezvoused here with certain 'special friends'. It was best not to mention that now, he decided. 'I never knew this place even existed. What a ... delightful bedspread,' he said morosely.

'Yes, I'm sure you'll be very comfortable here,' Kiry said.

'But what now?' Sihanouk said.

'If we need you we will send for you. And of course, you may ask to speak to me at any time. If I can manage it, I will visit. But for now, you must be hungry. I will arrange for food. And then, no doubt, you will want to rest.'

'But surely there will be a reception to mark Sihanouk's triumphant return to Phnom Penh,' Sihanouk said. 'Today is a great and historic day for Cambodia. I want to meet the members of the new government. Aren't they eager to see me so we can congratulate each other on our joint victory? Don't they want to hear Sihanouk's report on the outside world's views and opinions towards our regime?'

'Life is very busy in the new Kampuchea. We are making a new history and there is not a moment to spare. Perhaps at some time in the future there will be a chance to formally welcome you home. But not today, alas. And not tomorrow.'

'But I have written a speech.'

'You can give that to me,' Kiry said. 'I'll see that it is circulated, if appropriate. Now: I am busy for a few days. But after that I will return to brief you about your responsibilities. There is much important work for you to do. First, you must go the United Nations and put a stop to all the hateful rumours. Then you will go on a world tour to thank our friends and allies for their unwavering support.'

'And then?'

'And then you will return here, of course. To your home, where you belong.'

After Kiry left, Sihanouk lay on the bed with his hands covering his face and wept.

'What have I done?' he cried out.

Monique patted his thick thigh a couple of times. Then she slid her hand down the front of his trousers.

'What have I done?' Sihanouk cried out again. 'Why didn't you stop me?'

Monique bunched her hand into a fist but thought better than to strike. She pulled her hand free, wiped it on the bedspread, stood and walked to the window. She watched as the boy soldiers advanced on the pig, who stood with its backside facing them, eating grass, oblivious.

Part 2

1979

Happy days are here again! The murderous Khmer Rouge are gone, run out of town by the good sheriff Vietnam. Although information about the goings on in so-called Democratic Kampuchea has been scarce these last years, we have known that life was tough. But the truth is more horrific than any of us could have imagined. A million dead, maybe more. Mass starvation and illness. Widespread and wanton executions. Some of us – I, Edward Donald Whittlemore, stand before you as guilty as any man – did not predict the savagery of the Khmer Rouge. But nobody could have prophesised such mass depravity and anybody who claims otherwise is taking shameful advantage of a terrible situation. Things could have been, should have been, so much different in Democratic Kampuchea.

—Edward Whittlemore, 'As I See It,' syndicated column

Ted Whittlemore simmered in his own diminishing juices as the minivan passed through the Vietnamese military checkpoint at Moc Bai and entered Cambodia. The driver, Tung, rhythmically chewed a wad of gum. Whenever the flavour faded he would add another stick, switching flavours at random. Much later in the day, as they crossed Vietnam Bridge and entered Phnom Penh, he wound down a window and spat a wad the size of a golf ball into the Bassac River.

Ted stared out the window at a countryside that had seemingly expelled all life. How had this happened? he wondered. The pocked land was barren but for irrigation walls that reared out of the dusty fields and an occasional pile of rubble that had once been a rest station or a village. The only signs of life came from inside the minivan, where the occupants grumbled and panted and slithered across the vinyl seats.

An hour inside Cambodia the muffler on the minivan came loose and began recording the route in the dirt. Tung manoeuvred over a particularly large hole in the road, wriggled under the vehicle and set to work with a couple of tools and a roll of masking tape. The journalists all piled out except for the BBC fellow, who slept. Ted peered at him suspiciously. In Ted's experience, dozy reporters somehow saw everything.

Du, the Khmer-speaking guide from Vietnam's ministry of information, stood guard at Tung's feet, devouring cigarettes. Ted peeled the sodden shirt from his back and held it above his head, hoping to catch a breeze. Phillip Fraigneau, a freelancer, touched his toes a couple of times then dropped to his haunches. Masami Itoh from the *Tokyo Daily*, fearing landmines, stood on the road facing Vietnam and pissed between his feet. Hugo Reisch, senior writer for a glossy German weekly, rubbed cream into the stubble rash on his neck.

'Is that antifungal cream? Is it an antiseptic?' Phillip asked. 'Can I have some for between my toes?'

'It's toothpaste. It's all I've got.'

'Give me some.'

'Please.'

'All right, don't then.'

'Can't you people show some respect?' Ted said. 'Look around you.'

'Stuff you, Mr Vietnam, we're coming too. You don't get Cambodia to yourself and there's not a damned thing you can do about it,' Phillip said.

'Oh, leave him alone, he's just embarrassed,' Hugo said.

'He should be, too. Mr Complicity. Mr Trust-me-Pol-Pot-won't-be-so-bad-you'll-see-it'll-all-be-roses-and-universal-healthcare-and-full-bellies-and-perfect-equality.'

Ted turned away and spoke to Du in Vietnamese. 'How long is it since you were last in Cambodia?'

'Do you think I want to be here? *Do you?* My brother died in this shit-hole.'

The BBC man opened his eyes and wound down the window. 'What did he say, Teddles?'

'He said that although he would prefer to stay in Cam Ranh with his family, he is proud to be serving the cause of liberating the innocent Cambodian people from the murderous Pol Pot clique.'

'Yes, correct,' Du said in English.

'And stop calling me Teddles.'

Tung emerged, shaking himself free of road dust, and got behind the wheel. 'Bad,' he said in Vietnamese. 'Very, very bad.'

'What did he say?'

'He said, "We go now okay,"' Du said.

Two hours later, they encountered their first Cambodians. Tung braked hard, showering them with dirt. They were, it seemed, the remnants of a family: two women of indeterminate age, a man perhaps thirty years old who continually wheezed, and three hollowed-out children. The man and one of the women pulled a cart made of a house door attached to wooden wheels; two of the children pushed. On the cart sat a few clothes, a hoe, a small bag of rice, a cooking pot, the other woman and the smallest of the children. Exhausted and hungry, the Cambodians looked at the foreigners with polite and thorough indifference.

Phillip climbed onto the roof of the minivan, rummaged through his bag and came down with a large chocolate bar that had turned to oil in the heat. He gave it to the children. They rubbed their hands in the goo and licked their fingers.

The journalists closed in on the Cambodians, staring, blocking their path, worshipping them with cameras and notebooks and tape recorders. 'Give them space. Don't frighten them,' Ted said. But he too wanted to inspect them and when the BBC chap tried to push past him he stuck out an elbow. Ted snapped photograph after photograph of the survivors, partly to prove to himself that he really had seen the protruding skeletons and furtive eyes, the bruises and scabs, the rags for clothes; and partly because he'd always wanted to get one of his photos onto the front cover of the *Far Eastern Economic Review*.

The journalists supplied Du with questions to ask. Du and the older woman talked back and forth, his questions and translations taking longer than her replies.

'Ask them how they are feeling,' Masami said.

'Are they diseased? Contagious? Can we touch them? When did they last have a proper feed?' the BBC chap said.

'Where are they going? Where are they coming from?' Ted said.

'They are walking from Pursat Province,' Du said. 'They are—'

'How long have they been walking?'

'Many weeks. They stop and start. They are returning home. They hope they will be there very soon, two or three days more only.'

'Ask her about the children,' Hugo said.

'The two girls belong to her younger sister. She is hoping to re-unite them, but—'

'What if she doesn't?'

'I do not ask her this.'

'And the little boy?'

'They do not know who he is. They found him on the way.'

'Who are the other adults?'

'Her neighbours.'

'What do they hope to find in their village?' Ted asked.

Du asked his question, listened to the answer and shrugged.

'What? What did she say?'

'She says she has heard that her husband is killed but she does not know this for certain. Someone she met on the road told her one of her children was still alive six months ago but she does not know about her other children. She knows one of her brothers is killed. Her other brothers, her other sister, she does not know. Her parents, she does not know.'

'How does she think these people died?' Phillip said.

'She does not know.'

'Didn't you ask her?'

'She says Pol Pot killed them.'

'Ask her who she thinks Pol Pot is,' Hugo said. 'Here, show her this photo. Look, that is Pol Pot, see? Pol Pot: there, there. What do you think of him?'

The woman looked at the grainy image and muttered a few words.

'She says he looks Chinese,' Du said.

'Ask her if she's heard of Karl Marx,' the BBC man said.

'Did she witness any massacres?' Masami said.

'I do not ask her anything more,' Du said stubbornly. 'Now we are late.'

After they took Phnom Penh in '75, the Khmer Rouge refused to let me visit. At the time, I was beside myself with rage. After all I'd done for that bastard Nhem Kiry – who I assumed was running the show – he wouldn't even let me come and witness the victory. All I wanted was to walk the streets of lib-erated Phnom Penh, to take photographs and conduct a few interviews, maybe land a scoop or two. And to toast the new peace with Bun Sody.

Now I know how lucky I was. If I'd gone to Phnom Penh, actually set foot in the place, if I'd given Pol Pot the benefit of the doubt and praised Democratic Kampuchea as a colourful work-in-progress, my reputation would never have recovered.

I must have applied for a visa twenty-five or thirty times. I tried to sneak in with Sihanouk and Monique but I never got near the plane, thank Christ. I pleaded with every contact I had in China and Yugoslavia to put in a good word for me but nobody would – or could – help. It was as if the Khmer Rouge had wiped Cambodia off the map and removed themselves from the world. A heavy silence descended until the refugees started appear-ing on the border.

The minivan entered Phnom Penh close to dusk, its inhabitants dulled and dehydrated, sick of their own smells and small talk. Ted stared out of his window, as shocked as if he had stumbled upon the corpse of a friend. The Phnom Penh he remembered – his Phnom Penh – hummed and broke into frequent song: people laughed and argued and bartered; fish and poultry flapped to demonstrate their freshness and their firm flesh; pigs squealed and pork fat spat in intricate patterns from hot grills; cars and trucks gossiped incessantly; cyclo wheels squeaked and their drivers called out, 'Where you want to go?'; rice pots bubbled; one dog barked and a thousand harmonised; the wind cavorted through narrow streets, rattling windows and tin roofs; the sky was deep blue except for the fluffy white opium clouds that announced the beginning of the cocktail hour; wine bottles burped their corks free and glasses clinked along the riverside, where salacious yet sophisticated women strolled under parasols. Best of all there was Sihanouk, a human fireworks display. Back then Bun Sody was for-ever reminding Ted that the city had slums and backstreet assassi-nations. Ted knew Sody was speaking the truth but that just made him love Phnom Penh all the more.

This new Phnom Penh was a ghost city, the silence broken by occasional sounds and movements that jarred and echoed. As they drove towards the city centre there were occasional pockets of people but no crowds. The minivan passed by a row of shops that had once contained Ted's favourite French bakery. It was a shell, its windows glassless, its interior stripped. Two blocks further on, Tung braked to allow a truck laden with Vietnamese troops sitting on sacks of rice to pass between them and the skeleton of a rusting car. While they waited, Ted saw a young woman standing in a doorway. At her feet, flapping about on a dribble of water on a pan, were two small catfish. He opened a window.

'Hello, miss. How much?' he called out in his basic Khmer.

The woman stepped back into the shadow of the doorway, but first she rewarded Ted with a smile and a dip of her eyes. He savoured the contact.

'You're in with that one, my friend,' Phillip said. 'Buy the fish and she'll probably fuck you, no extra charge.'

Soon they reached the Royal Hotel, which the Vietnamese had renamed the Samaki.

'That's a Jap word, isn't it? They must have known you were coming,' Phillip said to Nikito.

'*Samaki*,' Ted said, 'is Vietnamese for solidarity.'

'If you say so.'

As they piled out of the minivan Tung threw a bucket of water across the bonnet. The motor sizzled, then fell silent.

'Ask them if I can have my usual room,' Ted said to Du. 'Room 28.'

'Bloody favouritism,' Phillip said.

'Sorry, Ted. Second floor closed for business,' Du said. He jumped onto the roof and began dropping luggage.

'Where's the best place to eat?' Phillip said. 'Hey, careful, I've got all sorts of equipment in there. *Careful*, I said. Will you vouch for the food? I simply don't have the time to get sick. Have you arranged my interviews with the leaders? Well? Is there hot water? Don't forget, I booked a room with an air-conditioner.'

Ted stepped out into the road to escape Phillip. The BBC chap appeared at his shoulder.

'Are you going for a walk? Can I come?'

'Well ... Yeah, sure, mate.'

'It's a god-awful mess, isn't it?'

Ted nodded.

'Do you think things will improve now? Are the Vietnamese any better than the Khmer Rouge? Really better, I mean, or do they just hide it better?' the BBC man said.

'You interviewing me?'

'Just making conversation. Being friendly.'

'Right ... Look, Vietnam has freed these people from something unimaginably wicked. Surely you can see that for yourself.'

'Yes, of course. Still, they've taken over a foreign country. An invasion is an invasion.'

'Nothing matters but defeating the Khmer Rouge. Nothing.'

'Hmm, maybe.'

'We must right this wrong.'

'We?'

'We – all of us, the whole world, led by Vietnam – must right this wrong. We must purge the Khmer Rouge once and for all.'

'Fighting words, Teddles. But tell me, how long do you think the Vietnamese will stay?'

'As long as they need to in order to set things right. But is that relevant right now?'

'Yes, actually, I rather think that it is. The clock's already ticking so far as the West is concerned.'

A couple of children shyly approached. Ted greeted them in Khmer but quickly exhausted his vocabulary. He tried French, then English, then Vietnamese. The children laughed but did not understand. Phillip arrived with chocolate – he seemed to have an endless supply of the sodden stuff. The children left with a bar each, which Ted suspected would make them ill.

'ROOsee, ROOsee, ROOsee,' the children chanted as they left.

The Englishman clicked his heels together and called out in a Russian accent, 'My name is Vladimir Ilich. You know me as Lenin. I've come to eat you all up.'

'ROOsee, ROOsee,' the children continued calling as they ran away.

'Come back. I want to take your photograph,' Phillip said,

chasing after them. 'Bloody kids, don't they know there's no such thing as getting something for nothing?'

The BBC chap and Ted walked on. Suddenly Ted stopped and stared.

'What's the matter with you?' the Englishman asked.

'I, I—'

'What is it? What are you looking at?'

'The cathedral.'

'What cathedral?'

'It's gone.'

Ted stood where the arched entrance of the cathedral had been and walked slowly down the centre aisle to his usual seat, near but not too near the back. Here he had often come to think – never to pray – and, when he was troubled, to try to catch up on sleep. But now he could only scuff the dirt. The cathedral was not damaged by artillery, not riddled with bullets and bloodstains, not rotting from neglect and high humidity, but simply erased. No rubble remained, not a single stone, no foundations, no pews or shattered stained glass, no trace of the statue of Jesus, just an empty block of land on which a few weeds eked out a basic existence.

'Goodness,' the BBC chap said. 'Just like Stalin.'

'Shhh.'

'Don't get all grumpy at me, Teddles.'

'Will you shut the fuck up?'

'You're the one who wrote what decent fellows the Khmer Rouge are.'

Ted shaped as if to punch the BBC chap but instead he grabbed his own shirt and yanked it open. Buttons flew into the air. He threw his shirt on the ground and began jumping on it, raising a cloud of dust. The BBC chap raised a handkerchief to cover his mouth and nose.

'Steady on there, Teddles. Why don't you try putting your head between your knees?'

In the grey light, Du came running.

'You must not wander about like this. I worry that you will get lost. For goodness' sake, Ted, put your shirt on ... Please, it will be dark soon. You must come and check in now.'

Ted looked at him. 'But where's it gone?'

'It went away,' Du shrugged, as if that explained everything. In Vietnamese, he added, 'Please, let's go. Before you get me in trouble.'

*   *   *

It seemed to Nhem Kiry that the whole world wanted to talk to him. As the new prime minister of Democratic Kampuchea, he barely had any country to rule over. But that only seemed to make him more popular. In the months since the Vietnamese had captured Phnom Penh and pushed the Khmer Rouge to the far west, he had criss-crossed the globe. First, he accompanied Pol Pot to the Cardamom Mountains, where they skirted around Vietnamese patrols and lived rough while they retrieved their pride and dreamed up a new strategy. Then, in April, when Vietnamese battalions pushed hard into Khmer Rouge territory, Kiry had walked into Thailand. From Bangkok he had flown to Beijing, Singapore, New York, back to Bangkok for a meeting with Pol Pot and Nuon Chea on the border, Beijing again, Florence and Belgrade. Today he was in Geneva and shortly he would begin a tour of four African states.

Although his limbs and especially his knees ached morning and night, he found the hard work, the urgency, invigorating. And he took solace from acting the grump. An hour earlier he had made Leang Sros, the Khmer Rouge's permanent envoy to UNICEF, completely clear his desk, even the drawers, just so Kiry could sit there for half a day and pretend it was his office. He leaned back in the chair and surveyed the desk, on which sat two telephones, a pristine blotter, an upturned metal stake onto which he had impaled several pages of briefing notes, and a silver-framed photograph of him, Kolab and their daughters that Akor Sok had produced as if by magic.

Kiry arranged his ballpoint pens, the lids slightly chewed, in a straight line on the left-hand side of the blotting paper, adjacent to a small flag of Democratic Kampuchea. He half-listened as Akor Sok briefed him on his imminent meeting with Dr Corinna Zophan, Director of Operations for the International Committee of the Red Cross.

'By all accounts she is unflappable. She speaks seven languages but not Khmer.'

'A good thing, too.'

'She speaks Spanish, German, English, French, Mandarin, Welsh—'

'Yes, yes.'

'By all accounts she is a very determined woman. She will not be easily swayed.'

'Yes, yes ... I like this chair.'

'I, um ... I like it too, Your Excellency.'

'Why? Have you sat in it?'

'No, Your Excellency, but it looks very comfortable from a distance.'

'I like that I can rock back on it. And swivel. Do you think we could take this chair with us to Africa? Do you think Comrade Sros will miss it?'

'I think they have chairs in Africa. You may insult your hosts if you bring your own.'

'I suppose so.'

'Dr Zophan recently gained considerable publicity for criticising the Pope.'

'Yes, yes. What is she a doctor of?'

'I, um, I do not have that information with me, Your Excellency. But I will check immediately.'

Kiry sighed. 'You must be fully prepared at all times. She has a doctorate in chemical engineering but it is fifteen years since she practised in her profession.'

'Yes, of course, I'm sorry, Your Excellency ... Please remember that in private Dr Zophan has criticised our revolution most severely. There is no telling what she might say to us behind closed doors.'

'She has no choice but to see me. So she will behave.'

There was a single knock at the door. Leang Sros entered and formally presented Dr Corinna Zophan. Kiry abandoned the sanctuary of his desk to shake hands. Her touch was firm but light, her skin cool and dry.

'You can leave us,' Kiry told Sros and Sok. 'Now.'

'As you wish, Your Excellency,' Sok said unwillingly.

Kiry directed Dr Zophan to a couch and sat opposite. A coffee table and two glasses of water kept them apart.

'I must thank you again for taking the time to visit me. The whole government of Democratic Kampuchea – and I personally – have the greatest respect for the work of the International Committee of the Red Cross. You honour me with your presence.'

'Thank you for inviting me, Mr Prime Minister. And my congratulations on your recent appointment.'

Kiry liked what he saw. This Dr Zophan was businesslike neat. Her starched white shirt was stiff as cardboard, her breasts a mystery. Her woollen skirt – brown, almost black – followed the curve of her thighs all the way to her knees. She wore dull stockings and sensible leather shoes that hid, Kiry felt certain, dainty feet.

'I understand that the Red Cross has received a letter from Mr Hun Sen in his capacity as foreign minister of the illegitimate Kampuchean government.' As Kiry spoke, and despite realising that he was behaving undiplomatically, he could not help but stare at the hem of her skirt. 'I understand that this letter requests Red Cross assistance.'

'That is correct. It's no secret.'

She had, Kiry noticed, clear hazel eyes. Her skin was pale, enhanced by smudges of pink on her cheeks. She had imperfect earlobes: one was noticeably fatter than the other, even when half-hidden by wisps of auburn and grey hair.

'As the principal representative of the government of Democratic Kampuchea, I am obliged to point out that your agreement to any such request would indicate that the Red Cross supports the illegal invasion and occupation of Kampuchea by the Democratic Republic of Vietnam.'

'Indeed?'

'Indeed. Such support would, with respect, breach the political neutrality of the Red Cross. What is more, the Red Cross would place itself at odds with the United Nations, which quite rightly refuses to recognise this new illegitimate regime.'

Kiry sensed that he should stop running his fingers through his hair. He laid them flat on his knees, spread them out like fans. A Bulgarian diplomat had once told him that he had the fingers of a pianist, but he supposed that wasn't appropriate information to share with Dr Zophan. Unless she herself commented upon the elegant beauty of his fingers.

'With respect, Mr Prime Minister, the letter from Mr Hun Sen is a plea for help. It takes into account a set of circumstances that are dire. The foreign minister predicts that many people will go hungry this season. As I am sure you know, I myself visited Phnom Penh in June, accompanied by Marcus Thompson of UNICEF. We were deeply disturbed by what we saw. The concern of the Red Cross is for innocent people – not for the politics of the matter. That is the essence of how we intend to apply our neutrality to these circumstances. Subject to negotiations with officials in Phnom Penh we will—'

'Surely you mean officials in Hanoi.'

'Once certain issues are resolved with the appropriate authorities, I must tell you that I intend sending a larger delegation to Phnom Penh, as a matter of urgency, to further review conditions and to begin the transfer of material aid as soon as possible.'

'Very well, though I must restate my objections. And I might remind you that any food shortage, any famine, that occurs inside the country is a direct result of Vietnamese imperialism.'

'Please understand me, sir, the humanitarian situation is my sole concern.'

'Of course. I simply wish to reiterate that my colleagues and I are not fighting an ideological struggle. We are defending our territory and we are defending the integrity of the Khmer race. This is our task and it is connected directly to the struggle of the Red Cross with regards to foodstuffs. Which brings me to another matter. We are doing what we can for the thousands of our countrymen who have fled from the Vietnamese invaders. You are aware of the refugee camps near Thailand?'

'Of course.'

'The situation in some of our camps is dire. In the interests of humanitarianism, as well as neutrality, my government requests Red Cross assistance in our territory.'

'Of course, we will consider your request. And as you know—'

'Good. We have hungry children too.'

'We have, as you might know, already spoken with Thailand and with various other interested parties. And as you are probably aware, we have taken initial measures in certain locations.'

'Yes. Good. Nevertheless, I reiterate that Democratic Kampuchea is the sole legitimate government so far as the international community is concerned. Therefore, we should receive all Red Cross aid available and we should be free to distribute it as we see fit.'

'Please permit me to ask you, Mr Prime Minister, why did your government never respond to our offers of help when you controlled all of Cambodia, when the situation, as I understand it, was also dire?'

'Yes, that represents an entirely different set of circumstances. And I hope you might recognise that the former Democratic Kampuchean government is much misunderstood.' Kiry paused and smiled. 'But I do not wish to upset you with all this political talk. I am very conscious of the difficult position you find yourself in.'

The door opened. An aide entered carrying a tray on which sat a coffee pot, two cups and saucers and a plate of sandwiches.

'Would you care for coffee?' Kiry asked.

'Yes, thank you, I will take a cup.'

'And, please, take a sandwich also.'

'No thank you.'

'No? Well, I will have one. Ah, cucumber and cream cheese: my favourite.'

After Kiry chewed and swallowed a tiny bite of sandwich, he said, 'I believe Pierre Dubrecilh works for you.'

'That is correct.'

'Good old Pierre. I met him when I was a student in Paris. We had some very good talks; he even convinced me to go to a bar with him a few times. He wrote a thesis about Algeria, as I recall. Are you sure, no sandwich?'

'Very well, I will take one. Thank you.'

'Would you prefer tomato?'

'Cucumber is most acceptable.'

'Please pass on my best wishes to Pierre. I remember him as a good man.'

'He is the finest of men.'

Kiry watched Dr Zophan's face closely. He found it wondrous that she revealed only the barest hint of the repugnance she surely felt. This was a woman he could respect. He imagined courting her: quiet dinners in French bistros; mercy dashes to impoverished Africa when famine took hold; and then, once they married, a house in Phnom Penh and another in Madrid. It would be so different, he felt sure, than the early days spent with the woman who became his wife. He had met Kolab in the Liberated Zone in 1971. Despite her bravery – she specialised in crawling so close to enemy snipers that she could lob hand grenades into their laps – Son Sen had pulled her from the frontline and set her to work teaching groups of children new ways to behave.

When Kolab and Kiry were alone, when she was certain that they could not be overheard, Kolab was opinionated and fiery. Kiry found this appealing in such a young woman. When he tried to instruct her in Marxist theory, she said, 'I already know all I need to know about that,' and he found himself growing fond of her. He did not fall in love with Kolab – then or later – but he respected her and the sex was decent: Kiry considered intercourse to be an essential bodily function, like emptying his bowels or clearing his ears of wax. Besides, he needed a wife to counter the rumours circulating about his listless manhood.

'If you will permit me to ask, Dr Zophan, if the Vietnamese want to own Kampuchea so badly, why don't they feed the people themselves?'

'The situation is most complex. You know this, I am certain. And I say to you again, the politics of the situation are not my primary concern.'

'Please believe me, I am simply expressing the fears of the Kampuchean people.'

'Indeed?'

'My compatriots are keen students of history. Our survival has depended on it for hundreds of years. We are used to resisting the Vietnamese imperialists, using whatever limited means at our disposal. Do you know that they stole the Mekong Delta from us? And Saigon too?'

'I hope you will understand that I cannot take account of such matters, historically significant though they may be in your view.'

'Of course. I do not blame you for Vietnam's behaviour. But, please, be very careful about sending food and medical supplies to Phnom Penh. The Vietnamese are like birds circling fruit trees.

They will fill their mouths and fly far away to where their own babies are waiting with mouths wide open.'

Dr Zophan stood and extended her hand. Her other arm hung loose along the curve of her hip. 'Thank you for seeing me.'

'The thanks are all mine. Please consider everything I have said.'

'But of course. And you too.'

Kiry gripped her hand a few seconds longer than he should have. He felt her disgust but he also sensed in her a flicker of attraction. She was conflicted, or so he hoped.

'Would you like to take some sandwiches with you for later?' Kiry said. 'I could have one of my aides wrap them up to keep them fresh.'

'No. No thank you.'

'A pity. I hate waste.'

After she had left, Kiry sat behind the desk, doodling and dreaming. What did she think of him now? No doubt she had shoved the thought of him aside, got on with her day as if nothing at all had passed between them. But when her work was done, when she'd finished reading some draft report on southern Africa or considered the latest research on inserting anti-malaria drugs into bananas, perhaps her thoughts would return to Kiry. Then he would rise like bile and fill her mouth until she gagged.

In his mind, she brushed her teeth then rinsed her mouth with baking soda dissolved in water. She stripped in a blur, uncharacter- istically leaving a pile of clothes on the floor, and immersed herself in a bathtub full of bubbles, her hair unfurled, loose strands of it steamed to her neck, her hand gently massaging her submerged belly. Then, finally, she gave in to her desires: she stood up in the bath and gave Kiry a full view of her naked body. She held out her hand for him to join her. He invented a headline: *Red Cross Head Elopes with Khmer Rouge Mouthpiece.*

He shook himself back into the real world, back to the shell of an office he would shortly abandon. He admonished himself for his weakness: he was forever telling Sok that lustful thoughts lead to evil acts, which made Sok a very evil man indeed.

*   *   *

That trip to Cuba in 1979 for the non-aligned-movement conference was dismal. Weighed down by facts I couldn't stomach – the Khmer Rouge catastrophe, China's shameless persecution of Vietnam and its ludicrous spat with the Soviets, Sihanouk's refusal to see me – I felt as if I was attending the funeral of my own life and times. I wanted to be friends with everybody but nobody else saw it that way. So I, too, had to take sides. Of course, I stuck with Vietnam but I was stunned – I'm still stunned – that I had to make the choice at all.

I arrived in Cuba feeling ill. The advance gusts of Hurricane John (or Robert) (or Edward) rocked the plane as we came in to land. I stayed nauseous the whole trip. None of these people, I realised, truly cared about the Cambodians (or the Afghans or the Palestinians or the Namibians). Half the delegates loved Russia and hated China, which made them anti-Khmer Rouge. The other half loved China and hated Russia, which made them pro-Khmer Rouge.

So that they could get on with their meetings and their parties, the delegates declared the Cambodian seat vacant. This they called 'even-handed' but it made me want to rage up and down waving a placard that read 'COWARDS, THE LOT OF YOU.'

I knew that the conference would upset me. I don't know why I bothered to go. Habit, I suppose. And because I wanted to see Nhem Kiry.

Several hours after he landed in Cuba, Ted Whittlemore pegged a tie to his shirt and wandered into a reception hosted by President Fidel Castro. He pushed his way through the throng with resigned determination. He could not see Castro, nor hear him over the tinkle of glasses and the hubbub of politicking, but he knew where he was by observing how the individuals who made up the throng positioned their bodies.

When Castro saw Ted approaching, he broke through a wall of minders and well-wishers.

'Ted. You made it then,' Castro said in Spanish. 'Sorry about the weather.' He lifted his arms in momentary excitement. Ted steeled himself for a brutal hug, but Castro merely clapped his hands and said, 'Good to see you, my friend.' Castro's translator, a tall woman with an Oxford accent, repeated the welcome.

'A present for you, Mr President,' Ted said, handing Castro a purple and orange Hawaiian shirt which he pulled from under his damp armpit.

Castro let off a low burst of words. 'Thank you, Ted, how delight-ful,' the translator said, her pursed lips indicating that she was not relaying Castro's first and spontaneous reaction. 'I'm sure I'll think of … some use for it.'

'You're looking fit, Mr President,' Ted said.

'But of course. Why not?'

'I heard a rumour about you when I was in London,' Ted whis-pered, leaning close.

'Oh yes? Was it the one about Castro arriving at the gates of heaven with three women: a blonde, a brunette and a redhead?'

'Better. Apparently, so the story goes, you've been dead for a decade or more. Your aides have stuffed you – "He's shinier than Lenin," my source says – and lodged a tape recorder in your chest cavity. They prop you up – "When's the last time you saw him when he wasn't leaning on a podium?" my source says – and move your mouth with fishing line attached to your jaw.'

'So I'm immortal? So nice of you to say so.' Castro clasped his hands together atop his stomach. 'I have a confession to make. I hope it will make you very happy.'

'Oh yes?'

'It's a Cambodian confession: right up your alley, I think. I'm afraid I have accidentally dropped Mr Nhem Kiry's conference accreditation papers in a bowl of punch. They are all wet and sticky.'

'Oh dear.'

'I know. I feel terrible. But I will certainly deliver them to him just as soon as they dry out.'

'Where are they now?'

'His accreditation papers? They are hanging from pegs on a rope in my garden.'

'It's quite windy outside. The newspaper mentioned something about a hurricane.'

'How unfortunate. But I have another confession to make.'

'Do you need a priest?'

'Probably but not now, Ted, I'm trying to confess: I'm afraid that this hotel is overbooked. I have, with great reluctance, been forced to house Mr Nhem Kiry and his entourage in another hotel. It is only a half hour or so away … depending, of course, on the state of the road.'

'Cuban roads are terrible.'

'I read something about that in the *New York Post*. But it's the best I could do. I feel dreadful, but as the leader of my country sometimes I am forced to make unpleasant decisions. Such is the lot of a president. Please believe me, the burden is heavy … What's the matter, Ted? You look like you've eaten a lemon.'

'If I may say so, Mr President, I believe it would be better to let Nhem Kiry speak, to let him be seen for what he is. To hide him away is to protect him and to make him a cause célèbre.'

'If you may say so? If? If? You've already said it.'

'Mr President, all I meant—'

'This is my home. I will not just go inviting any old riffraff into my home. If that bothers you, I don't care.'

'I want to interview him. Nhem Kiry. You don't mind, do you?'

'And what if I do? You are Edward Whittlemore, fearless and independent. What could *I* do to stop *you*? And why would I bother? If you want to waste your time, feel free, just don't ask for my endorsement. Mind you, you might need a good map to find him.'

Castro turned his back on Ted and handed the Hawaiian shirt to his translator. 'Get this thing out of my sight. I wouldn't blow my nose on it.'

For the next three days and nights Ted wandered around buffets and cocktail parties, engaging in small talk while eavesdropping on as many conversations as he could manage. He sat through a hundred or so interminable speeches, not one of which was interesting or controversial enough to report to the world.

He witnessed the signing of several memoranda of understanding – pieces of paper that resolved some minor issue or other using words that, so far as Ted could tell, the signatories had only agreed to after years of painful negotiation to remove all possible meaning. If the parties deemed the resolution especially important, they signed their documents on a table adorned with a linen cloth and a bowl of flowers, after which they swapped pens. If their relationship had been truly poisonous, they hugged and kissed for the cameras.

At one point, desperate for signs of life, Ted sat in a toilet cubicle for two hours and collected three stories that he began with, 'Sources close to the delegation confirmed today that …' He was a close source, too: Ted felt intimately connected to these powerful men after listening to the animal noises they made as they relieved themselves. But when he finally emerged from his cubicle and headed to the basin to make a show of washing his hands, all heads turned towards him and all conversation ceased.

On the afternoon of Ted's last day in Cuba, after Hurricane John had blown itself out, Ted convinced a reluctant local to drive him to Nhem Kiry's hotel. Sitting in the lobby, sipping a beer, waiting to find out if Kiry would see him, Ted read a copy of the speech that Kiry had planned to read before the delegates had banned him from addressing the conference: 'The current tragedy in Kampuchea fills us with sorrow but also with exasperation. We cannot comprehend that a certain country, posing as a non-aligned friend, has used brutal force to occupy Kampuchea. If the non-aligned movement rewards behaviour that is so at odds with the principles of non-alignment, then the naked aggression currently being waged against innocent Kampucheans will surely spread throughout South-East Asia and perhaps even the world.'

'Good afternoon, Edward. What a pleasant surprise after all these years.'

Ted half rose, compelled to take Nhem Kiry's extended hand and shake it. Although Kiry did not squeeze hard, Ted fought to contain a shudder.

'Very nice to see you, Mr, uh, Mr Prime Minister. Would you care to join me?'

'For a moment. Thank you for coming. I've been rather bereft of visitors here.' Kiry paused, then smiled. 'Apart, of course, from my many friends and allies from fraternal governments and from the world's media, who have called on me to express their solidarity and to reinforce our mutual commitment to the dear principles of non-alignment.'

'Yes, I was just reading your speech.'

'What do you think of it?'

'Well, I haven't finished it yet. And it is such a detailed document that I confess I might need to ponder its complexities before I offer comment.'

'Really, Edward, you surprise me. Will you not speak your mind?'

'Very well. I was surprised to read that you are predicting World War Three.'

'You're right. You *do* need to ponder the speech's complexities.'

'Mr Prime Minister, I have sent you several requests for an interview in the last week. Have you considered them?'

'I think that will be impossible today. I'm waiting for a car. I'm going to take in the sights, now that this wild weather has eased. I am keen to visit the former residence of the famous writer, Mr Ernest Hemingway. If it has not blown away.'

'Might I ask you, Mr Prime Minister, your opinion of Hemingway? Are you a fan?'

'As a writer or as a man?'

'Well ... Let's say as a writer.'

'Off the record?'

'Yes, all right.'

'I think that Hemingway believed that war existed so that he could write about himself.'

'Can I clarify, Mr Prime Minister, are you referring to his reportage or his fiction?'

'It was all fiction, Edward. You of all people should know that.'

'You must be disappointed at not being allowed to address the Non-Aligned Summit.'

'Off the record? No, I'm not at all disappointed. I have found the last few days to be most revealing. And I have been gratified by the majority show of support for me and my country's sad predicament.'

'I have heard that Castro invited Mr Hun Sen, the new foreign minister of the People's Republic of Kampuchea, to a private dinner at his home. I believe that they ate steak. What do you think of that?'

'I have nothing against carnivores. I myself have been known to eat steak myself. Although only very occasionally, of course.'

'What about Castro?'

'No, I have no desire to eat President Castro. You've been listening to too many nasty refugee rumours.'

'But what's your opinion of Castro?'

'Off the record, I think Castro was once a fascinating man. But his time has long passed. I never thought I would see a revolutionary hero use base political tactics to prevent a legitimate and honourable government from taking its place amongst the family of non-aligned nations. Still, I would not dream of telling him with whom he should eat. I would have thought you'd be more worried about this than me: from what I hear, Castro's not so fond of you these days.'

'And what do you think of Hun Sen?'

'The poor boy. I feel sorry for him. Young minds are so pliable. I think Master Hun Sen is an ideal foreign minister in a Kampuchea so overrun by Vietnamese imperialists.'

'Are you in contact with Prince Sihanouk?'

'Ah, the prince. What wonderful talks we had during the years of the Democratic Kampuchea regime. Now, alas, he pretends not to know me. But what about you, Edward? Are you in contact with your old ally?'

'He won't take my calls.'

'You seem to be struggling to hold on to your friends at the moment.'

'Mr Prime Minister, how do you respond to the widespread claims – to the mounting evidence, to the inescapable truth – that the Khmer Rouge committed horrible atrocities between 1975 and 1979?'

'I do not respond to misinformed rumours.' Kiry smiled. 'Not even off the record.'

'But I've been to Phnom Penh since the Vietnamese liberated Cambodia and—'

'Liberated? Truly, Edward, that's a curious way to describe a foreign invasion.'

'I've seen it with my own eyes.'

'You've seen misinformed rumours with your own eyes? Yes, I've heard that you have been spending too much time in Hanoi. Well, you should not believe everything you read about the government of Democratic Kampuchea nor about me personally.' Kiry pulled a neatly folded piece of paper from his breast pocket, glanced at Ted, winked, and read a quote from a recent best-selling book: '"In trying to understand the worst excesses of the Khmer Rouge let us look first to the psychology of Nhem Kiry, their leading intellectual. Nhem Kiry has been

diagnosed with chronic impotence, which can result from profound hostility to an individual's environment. Nhem Kiry was
a sickly child, a friendless, bewildered youth, and a meek, per-
secuted man. When power came his way in 1975 he was overcome with vengeance."'

'Would you care to respond?' Ted said.

'Fervour is the weapon of choice for the impotent,' Kiry murmured, apparently for his own benefit. 'Needless to say, my wife
was shocked to learn of my condition. She cannot now understand
how our two beautiful daughters came to exist. It must be Immaculate Conception, I tell her, because books published in America
never lie.' Kiry stood up. 'But please excuse me, Edward, I am late
for my appointment with Mr Hemingway.'

'Mr Prime Minister, what can you tell me about the whereabouts
of Mr Bun Sody?'

'Bun Sody is missing. That is all I know.'

'Missing? What does that mean?'

'Exactly what I say. As I understand it he has been missing for
quite some time. Several years, in fact.'

'You don't seem too worried about it.'

Kiry bent down so close to Ted that their noses nearly touched.

'Bun Sody was my very good friend. My colleague, my confi-
dant. He disappeared a few weeks before our great victory. It was a
time of great confusion and activity. When I think of it, I am sad.
Of course I grieve for him. How dare you – you, of all people –
suggest otherwise? But do you want to know the truth about him?
He could not bear the idea that people might suffer. He was always
going on about suffering because he wanted everybody to know
how much he cared. But he wanted a perfect revolution without
hard work. Without sacrifice. He claimed that the revolution
meant everything to him, yet he did not have the willpower to
commit to the revolution.

'Maybe he realised the truth about himself – that he was weak
– and the shame of it destroyed his will to live. Or maybe he got
caught up in a dispute of the heart. He liked women, after all,
all sorts of women. Maybe an enraged husband assaulted him.
It wouldn't have been the first time. Or maybe he stepped on a
landmine. Or maybe he walked across the path of a stray bullet. If

you want my opinion – but I'm only guessing – I suspect an accident befell him. Perhaps he went to wash in a river and floated out to the middle – don't you remember how he loved to pretend he was Mao swimming the Yangtze? – dived and got tangled up in a sunken tree branch. Or hit his head on a rock. Or maybe he stole away to Vietnam. He was always fond of the Hanoi boulevards. And the food. And the women. And the Politburo. Scan the streets the next time you are there, why don't you?'

Kiry stood, buttoned his suit jacket and stalked away. After a moment he turned.

'The world is full of misery. Millions of people are hungry and oppressed. Why are you so worried, I wonder, about the fate of one man?'

Ted recoiled. His mouth twitched and formed into a silent snarl. He tried to speak but he couldn't think of a thing to say.

'I can ask you that – I have the right – because Bun Sody was my friend. A true friend, not some informant I leeched off,' Kiry continued, but then his expression softened. 'By the way, I never thanked you for what you did for Sody and me that time. If we hadn't left Phnom Penh when you warned us to, we would have been dead within the week.'

Kiry smiled, turned and left. Ted peered at the people scattered about the foyer, desperately hoping that nobody had overheard Kiry thanking him. He sunk back in his chair and tried to silence the rattling laughter that filled his head.

On my way home from Cuba in '79, stuck in Changi airport waiting for a connecting flight, I invented an interview with Nhem Kiry. I was beside myself that he'd thanked me for saving his life. Not with rage exactly. Not guilt. I don't know what it was: grief maybe. It was as if I'd donated bone marrow to him and now I wanted it back.

EDWARD WHITTLEMORE: How do you respond to the mounting evidence, indeed to the inescapable truth, that the Khmer Rouge committed massacres and other acts of atrocity in Cambodia between 1975 and 1979?

NHEM KIRY: The claims are ridiculous and unfounded. I will admit that we made some mistakes. We are not perfect. Many Kampucheans, maybe as many as one million, lost their lives during the war. But talk of massacres is propaganda spread by the Vietnamese to hide their own crimes. And by traitors who fled Democratic Kampuchea out of self-interest.

EW: Mr Prime Minister, would you comment on the claim that Democratic Kampuchea was excessive in its execution of so-called war criminals from the previous Lon Nol regime?

NK: Why must I answer this question again and again? Those criminals committed heinous crimes against our former head of state, Prince Sihanouk, and against the Kampuchean people. When we were victorious it was of course regrettably necessary to execute a few war criminals from the previous regime. The people expected no less of us. But any other killings were the work of Vietnamese agents and infiltrators and their supporters. I became a revolutionary because I love the people of Kampuchea. Why would I want to kill them?

EW: My suggestion is that the purges, once begun, found their own momentum.

NK: How many times do I need to say it? People die in wars. Boo hoo.

EW: What about your policy of emptying Phnom Penh and the other cities and sending all the people into the countryside?

NK: Please remember that when we arrived, Phnom Penh was full of refugees. The war had driven more than two million people into the city. Many of those who left the city were simply peasants returning to their homes. They were ecstatic to go. And never forget that Phnom Penh was riddled with vice and corruption. We gave the place a spring clean.

EW: Mr Prime Minister, you must have been disappointed at not being permitted to address the non-aligned conference in Cuba?

NK: I was not surprised. Some countries are neutral in name alone: Vietnam and Cuba colluded to keep the Kampuchean seat empty, to exclude us from our rightful place as a fully committed member of the non-aligned movement. Cuba's active discrimination against Democratic Kampuchea, the sole legal and legitimate government of the Kampuchean people, is a blatant attempt to legalise Vietnamese aggression against the Kampuchean people, who suffer gravely. Of course, I was heartened by the attitudes of so many sympathetic friends and colleagues gathered together in Cuba.

EW: Who is now supporting the Khmer Rouge and helping the Khmer Rouge to improve its strategic position within Cambodia? Is China aiding you? The ASEAN nations? What about Western governments?

NK: We have so many friends in the international community. The world loves Democratic Kampuchea, but I am too humble to name names.

EW: And what of Prince Sihanouk?

NK: You must understand that the real heroes of the resistance are the Kampuchean people, ordinary patriots living and breathing the illegal occupation. But all patriotic forces should come together. If Prince Sihanouk ever deigns to take an interest in Kampuchea, I would be delighted to work with him.

EW: If you win the war against Vietnam, can we expect a repeat of your past policies?

NK: Oh no, not at all. Our country had its chance for socialism but that time has passed. When we free Kampuchea from the imperialists, we will support capitalist enterprises, we will encourage local entrepreneurs and we will welcome foreign aid and foreign investment. Please understand that it is impossible to scramble an egg twice.

I was so pleased with the interview that I bribed a Qantas official to type it up for me. I whacked it straight into an envelope and posted it to my old friend, Malcolm Macquarie, long-time publisher of Radical Papers. *I wasn't Malcolm's favourite bloke by then, but I hoped he'd rise to the occasion and see my scoop for what it was.*

I was subletting an apartment in Phnom Penh. It took weeks and weeks for Malcolm's reply to find me. On the back of a postcard of the Statue of Liberty he scribbled 'Thanks but no thanks.' I got myself a little portrait of Ho Chi Minh, glued it to a piece of cardboard, wrote 'Asshole' on the back and sent it off.

Several weeks later Malcolm replied: 'My dear Ted, You must know that I have stopped publishing your work because you have abandoned all objectivity. When I want official comment from the government of Vietnam I will print their press releases and quote their spokesmen. If this observation offends you, please feel free to demonstrate your displeasure by submitting your rubbish elsewhere. As for this 'interview' with Nhem Kiry, what do you take me for? It is so blatant a fabrication that I hope it is a joke gone wrong rather than a serious attempt to sneak fraudulent material into the public domain. A word of advice: if you're going to write fiction, at least put some time and effort into it. I'm sorry, Ted, and I say this with our memorable association and our long friendship in mind, but the fact is I have been far too tolerant for far too long. All of us here remember your outstanding and brave dispatches from Cambodia and Vietnam. But this behaviour is reprehensible. Sordid, even. Apart from anything else, you do great damage to the cause you are so over-eager to serve. Regretfully, Malcolm.'

I read and reread Malcolm's letter. Couldn't help myself. There is nothing worse in life than getting caught red-handed doing the wrong thing. Still, I couldn't let him have the last word.

'Dear Mal,' *I replied.* 'Sordid certainly is the word. I can remember a day, not so long ago, when the editorial position of *Radical Papers* was to support the Khmer Rouge. I know this to be true because, to my eternal shame, I authored several of those articles. I cannot comprehend how any decent editor or publisher – any decent human being – would not now do everything in his power to recant that previous position, again and again and again. It is callous of you to deny me my right to reflect on the true nature of the Khmer Rouge, given that I once praised them in your pages. And I cannot believe that you are so indifferent to your reputation, which you surely realise requires immediate rehabilitation. You seem to believe that the war in Vietnam and Cambodia finished when Henry Kissinger says it finished. I never thought I would say this about you, Mal, but you have turned out to be an American first and a radical second. Just like all the others. Your little magazine would have faded into obscurity if it wasn't for me, you ungrateful bastard. If *Radical Papers* was essential Vietnam War reading, I made it so. Sordid doesn't come close to describing you. With my best wishes, despite everything, to you and to Jenny and the children, Ted.'

In the days that followed I wrote Malcolm another letter, a meandering, painfully honest mea culpa *that ran to twenty or so pages. I spilled my guts. I gave voice to my confusion about the Khmer Rouge and Stalin and Mao and Christ knows what else. I even owned up to a little bit of misconduct (the details of which don't matter now).*

But I never posted the letter. I ripped the pages to shreds and threw them in the Sap River.

Good thing, too.

1981

Three hours from Phnom Penh, returning from the ancient capital of Udong in an old, cramped Mercedes van, Ted Whittlemore was in high spirits. He sat in the back seat behind his old Vietnamese friend, Freddie, the most artistic driver on bad roads Ted had ever met.

Beside Ted sat Rachel Walker, a thirtyish Australian filmmaker who was directing a documentary about post-Pol Pot Cambodia. She had employed Ted to provide an alternative viewpoint – or, as Rachel had put it, 'Give me some controversy or you're no good to me.' Ted suspected Rachel had only hired him to make sure that the Vietnamese let her into Cambodia. He suspected she would later edit out everything he said and did but he didn't mind: she was fun and young and her money was real.

To Rachel's left sat Adam, the sound recordist. He slept slumped against Rachel, rubbing his perspiration all over her white cotton shirt. Ted thought that Adam's snores sounded suspiciously uniform. He leaned across Rachel and whispered in Adam's ear, 'In my opinion, if you're going to grope a girl you should have the decency to look her in the eyes while you do it.' Adam snored on.

In the front passenger seat sat Tom the cameraman. Overnight, his lower intestine had twisted into an engorged knot. Worried about landmines, he had squatted on the road to shit five times in the previous hour. The first time he did it the rest of them burst into applause and Rachel took a series of action shots with her brand new Leica camera.

Earlier that day they had filmed amongst the stupas and the ruins of Udong. 'We all know the history of America's crimes in Cambodia. They engineered the coup against Prince Sihanouk. They dropped more bombs than fell on all of Europe in World War Two,' Ted had told the camera, his hair slicked over his bald spot, a brand new *krama* draped over one shoulder. 'But in many ways their current behaviour is even more reprehensible. Nobody doubts the crimes of the Khmer Rouge, yet the Americans and their allies, dressed in UN camouflage, refuse to accept the legitimacy of the new and honourable Cambodian government, just because the Vietnamese helped set it up. The Khmer Rouge, meanwhile, regroup, re-arm and wash themselves clean, while the US averts its gaze. And, as we have come to expect, Australia falls into line behind America.'

'But the Australian foreign minister has recently taken diplomatic steps against the Khmer Rouge. That's a good start, isn't it?' Rachel asked.

'Hardly. He flirts with doing the honourable thing, he rubs himself up against it, but at the end of the day he's a virgin through and through. He makes bloody sure he does nothing concrete to upset the Americans.'

In the van, as they drove back to Phnom Penh, Ted said to Rachel, 'You really should go to Vietnam. I guarantee you'd be very welcome. I'd be willing to accompany you. For an additional fee, of course.'

'We haven't got the budget for Vietnam. Besides, you're the one who keeps insisting that the Cambodians are running Cambodia. So what's the point?'

'You could talk to Nguyen Co Thach. He's a wonderful man. I could arrange it. He will tell you the truth, the whole truth and nothing but the truth. You could ask him anything at all. No restrictions. No censorship. No games.'

Rachel gazed at Ted, amused. '*You* talk to him if *you* want to.'

Freddie tapped the steering wheel and started singing: '*It takes three years of graft and fret. It takes ... I ain't got no ciguhrettes ...*'

Tom lifted his head out of his hands. 'If you don't shut up I swear I'll open your door and kick you out.'

'*I'm a ma-hann of wunder, I'm the, ugh, ugh, king of the road ...*'

The first shots were high and wide. Ted heard dull thuds as the bullets struck dirt. He gripped Rachel's thigh. She swatted his hand away and said, 'You won't find much of a story down there.'

'Step on it, Freddie,' Ted said.

Freddie turned his head and as he met Ted's eyes he realised they were under attack. The air whistled and a C-40 rocket hit the road twenty yards ahead of them. Freddie accelerated and nearly drove off the road and down an embankment, where they would have sat like a tree waiting to be lopped.

Tom's bowels erupted. 'Shit! Shit shit shit.' He swivelled in his seat. 'Camera: come on, I need my camera. Now, NOW.'

Ted grabbed Adam's shirt and yanked him upright so he could retrieve Tom's camera from between his legs. Tom twisted in his seat, held his camera in front of his heart like a shield and commenced filming a clump of trees on the far side of a dry paddy field.

'Let's get out of here. Quick as you can, mate,' Ted told Freddie. He patted Adam on the back with one hand and squeezed Rachel's thigh with the other.

'Jeez, I wish I'd thought of that,' Freddie said. He veered around a ditch; the van bounced and Freddie's window shattered.

'Faster, you little fuckwit, faster!' Adam screamed.

Another rocket landed behind them, closer, on the fringe between the road and the field. Ted instinctively ducked, although he knew it was pointless: if a rocket hit the car they were all dead. When he looked up Tom was filming Freddie, who was bleeding profusely.

'I'm all right,' Freddie said. 'It's nothing. I hit my chin on the steering wheel.'

More gunfire followed. A third rocket landed further away; this time the car did not shake. When Ted looked out the back window he saw a truck rumbling across the paddy field towards the dust cloud that Freddie had whipped up, figures standing on its open tray.

'Faster, Freddie,' he said. 'They're coming.'

'What's the matter with you, are you fucking mental or something? FASTER!' Adam screamed.

'For Chrissakes, Adam, will you shut up?' Rachel said.

Freddie's whole torso was red now.

'Jesus, they've shot you, haven't they?' Tom said.

'I'm all right. It's just my shoulder. No problem, no problem.'

They reached a decent patch of road. Freddie accelerated. The Khmer Rouge quickly fell back and then disappeared.

'Tom, give me a shot of Ted. Can you get him? Good. Adam, are you right to go?' Rachel said. 'Ready?' she asked Ted.

'Ready for what?'

'Describe it.'

'I, well, describe what?'

'Tell me what's gone on out there. Tell me what's happening inside your head. Tell me how you formulate your thoughts, how your decision-making works. Come on, Ted, paint me a word picture.'

'*A word picture?*' Adam yelled. 'Jesus fucking Christ, woman, are you nuts? They're trying to kill us.'

'Come on, Ted.'

'I ... I mean, I'm thinking is Freddie all right to drive, how bad is the injury, I'm worried that he's—'

'I'm all right. It looks worse than it is. There's a checkpoint soon.'

'He's slowing down,' Adam yelled. 'Why's he slowing down? Why the fuck are you slowing down?'

Freddie twisted his head. 'I'm driving. And they're gone,' he snarled.

'We're still rolling, Ted,' Rachel said.

'All right.' Ted wiped the pouring sweat from his face, dried his hair, restored calm to his face, then sat up straight and said, 'Being in the heat of a battle is miraculous. Nothing else in life comes close. It's bedlam: imagine a swarm of ants and flies and maggots and foxes and coyotes and lions all ripping into a corpse.

'Yet time slows in a battle. For me – remember that I'm no soldier – the usual survival techniques don't apply because the whole point is to witness the action. As the bullets fly, as the air turns black, as the river of blood begins to flow, a voice inside – in my brain or in my soul, I don't know which – tells me to run forward or to drop onto my stomach or to shelter beside a tree. It tells me which soldier to crouch beside. It keeps me safe – indestructible, I've come to believe – amongst the carnage.' Ted paused. 'How was that? Pretty bloody evocative, I'd say.'

'It'll do for now,' Rachel said.

Ten minutes later they reached a Vietnamese checkpoint. A medic dressed Freddie's wound and declared it bloody but not serious while Tom peeled off his trousers and endured a couple of Marlboro-toting teenagers throwing buckets of muddy water over his shit-stained buttocks and thighs.

The Vietnamese captain waved his soldiers into a truck. They trundled off, the truck listing to one side like a boat going down, to see if they could find any Khmer Rouge to shoot at. Rachel stared wistfully after them. 'Is there any chance they'd let us tag along?' she said.

Later, after they'd dropped Freddie at the military hospital, after they'd showered in cold water, after Adam had shaved and doused himself in deodorant and done twenty push-ups because he'd read in a men's magazine that the blood would rush to his arms and make his muscles look bigger, after Ted had downed eight bottles of beer in quick succession, they filmed one last shot. Ted rocked gently back and forth as he spoke to the camera.

'Inferior war correspondents often say, "Whittlemore's a maniac" or "Whittlemore's got a death wish." But, actually, the opposite is true: I plan to work forever. If I ever get shot between the eyes I expect that the bullet will bounce off my skull or obliterate nothing more than that part of my brain that directs restraint, which I don't need anyway. If I ever step on a landmine, I'm sure that the explosion will catapult me unscathed into a trench from where I will witness, on behalf of the world, another moment of American military excess.'

'But it was the Khmer Rouge, not the Americans, who shot at us today,' Rachel said.

'Exactly. Exactamondo. Such a smart little girl. At Udong you filmed me complaining about America and, next thing you know, the Khmer Rouge come after me. It really does make you wonder if there's a hotline between Pol Pot and the US State Department. I've already spoken to one of my contacts about the attack on us, you know.'

'Who?'

'Well, obviously I can't disclose names – hush hush, secret service, cloak and dagger don't you know – but it was a Vietnamese military attaché with close ties to a Cambodian public servant with close ties to a Khmer Rouge military officer. There's no doubt that their mission was to kill me. "Bring me the head of our Number

One Enemy: Mr Edward Whittlemore," Pol Pot told them. And that makes me proud to be an Australian.'

Tom's head came from behind the camera. 'Stop speaking,' he mouthed.

'What? I can't hear you.'

Tom put his finger to his lips.

'Oh ... Really?'

'I'm sorry, Rachel, but there seems to be something wrong with my battery,' Tom said. 'I missed the whole thing.'

'Do you know, I don't think I can remember a word I said,' Ted said.

'Thank God,' Rachel said.

*   *   *

Prince Norodom Sihanouk, former head of state of Cambodia and now head of the Funcinpec resistance group, will this week receive the so-called leader of the Khmer Rouge, Mr Nhem Kiry, in the palace permanently loaned to Sihanouk by the prince's friend, the seriously wacky North Korean leader Kim Il-sung. The apparent purpose of the meeting is to discuss ways to form a common front against Vietnam's occupation of Cambodia – an occupation, never forget, that rid the Cambodian people of the Khmer Rouge. A third resistance leader, the KPNLF's Son Sann, will not be joining Sihanouk and Kiry for this round of talks. Perhaps he is too embarrassed to go: after all, he is supposed to be a democrat. More likely, his potential allies forgot to ask him.

Typically, Sihanouk has already downplayed this week's meeting. 'These negotiations will not achieve much. After we arrive at a stalemate I will suggest that we resume talks another time, if my busy schedule allows it.' But this is all some ghastly game: nobody should make friends with the Khmer Rouge. Nobody should even speak to them, especially Sihanouk, who has travelled that path before with horrendous consequences.

—Edward Whittlemore, 'As I See It,' syndicated column

The stench of furniture polish made Nhem Kiry's nose run. He dropped his propelling pencil. As he bent down to retrieve it he sniffed deeply and wiped his nose with the sleeve of his suit jacket. Upright again, he was drawn to the reflection in the redwood table, where his forehead merged with Sihanouk's ear. Sihanouk patted the table proudly – it ran almost the length of the rectangular room – and said, 'This was cut from a single tree. Can you believe that?' Hot air blew from vents in the floor. A portrait of Sihanouk and Monique – young, seductive and heavily varnished – hung in a gold frame above the fireplace.

'What a gorgeous room this is, Your Majesty,' Kiry said, refusing to allow the opulence to unnerve him. He stood and could not help but admire the view from the panoramic window: a frozen lake in front of low, well-rounded, snow-covered hills; a single sentry, still as a statue, his weapon glinting in the sunlight. Kiry stared closer at the sentry and decided it *was* a statue.

Sihanouk's butler deposited coffee and a plate of croissants and fruit. They were alone now, free to recite their lines, but Sihanouk procrastinated. He overfilled his coffee cup, then used a teaspoon to return the excess to the silver pot. He stirred through one and a half teaspoons of sugar – 'Sweets for the sweet, tee hee' – and added a dollop of thick yellow cream.

'We've got five cows. They've got their own shed – water, hay, straw, warm water. I wish I had their life, ha ha.'

Sihanouk peeled an orange. He giggled with mock apology when he squeezed too hard and sprayed juice all over Kiry's clasped hands. Kiry wiped himself with a napkin and suppressed his impatience.

'I have concerns,' Sihanouk finally said. 'Sihanouk has grave concerns.'

'I know. I read about them in the newspaper.'

'Sihanouk has concerns about a union between the resistance groups. I am not optimistic that our negotiations will succeed, and—'

'With the greatest respect, Your Majesty, then why initiate this meeting? Why bother to invite me here?'

'And, as you see, we could not even convince Son Sann to join us to talk – merely to talk and eat breakfast – so what hope is there?'

'When the time comes, Son Sann will do what his backers tell him to do. We do not need him here now.'

A chunk of croissant lodged in Sihanouk's throat. He commenced a coughing fit.

'I know the Heimlich manoeuvre,' Kiry offered.

Sihanouk shook his head, swigged coffee – 'Ugh, cold already' – and miraculously recovered. 'You know why I invited you here.'

'With the greatest respect, Your Majesty, I cannot imagine why anyone would call a meeting that they do not want to attend. We're alone. You can speak freely.'

'Alone? Of course we're not alone. Deng Xiaoping is in this room. The Thai military is in this room. Alexander Haig is here, Ronald Reagan is here. Alone? *Alone?* Pol Pot is in this room. And Nuon Chea and Ieng Sary and—'

'Goodness. Should we call for more coffee?'

'I will tell you my concerns.'

'I read them in the newspaper.'

'I will tell you Sihanouk's concerns.'

'Tell me, Your Majesty. Tell me all of them.'

'I want my flag back.'

'Your flag?'

'Sihanouk's flag. Cambodia's true flag.'

'Democratic Kampuchea's flag is a fine flag. Many patriotic men and women have fought and died for that flag.'

'Twenty-seven members of my extended family—'

'You want twenty-seven of them in the leadership? With respect, Your Majesty, that is impossible.'

'Sihanouk will speak: twenty-seven members of my extended family went missing under your Democratic Kampuchea flag.'

'People go their own way sometimes, Your Majesty.'

'Some are dead. I know this. But some I do not know their fate. Here is a list. I want to know what happened to every one of them.'

'Let's clear this up now: do you have a Paris phonebook on the premises?'

'I want to know who is alive and who is dead, how they died, why they died. I want their remains. Not just any bundle of bones. I will test them. My doctors can do that sort of thing—'

'I don't doubt it, Your Majesty.'

'If any of them are still in your refugee camps, then—'

'You mean the independent settlements administered by various neutral international aid agencies?'

'If any of them are in your camps you will locate them and release them to me.'

Kiry scanned the list. 'Paris. Paris. Don't know. San Francisco. Don't know. Oh, those two have defected to the Vietnamese imperialists.'

'Impossible.'

'He works for me. So does she. He lives in Melbourne, Australia. I believe he owns a McDonald's franchise. Ah: my sincere commiserations, Your Majesty, but your niece, Thyda, died a heroic death defending Democratic Kampuchea.'

Sihanouk's butterfly eyelashes fluttered.

'Sihanouk has other concerns: I will not lead a coalition called Democratic Kampuchea.'

'You do not wish to lead the coalition? What lesser role would you prefer? Who are you prepared to serve under? How will we tip-toe behind you if you are not in front?'

'I will lead. No one else. But I will not agree to the name being Democratic Kampuchea. And I must be free to speak my mind, to say whatever I want whenever I choose.'

'I know. I read it in the newspaper.'

'I must have freedom of expression.'

'If you would like to improve your oral expression, Your Majesty, I am happy to help. Perhaps a private tutor? Don't despair, Your Majesty: anybody can be made coherent with a little time and effort. Well, *almost* anybody.'

'I will not join this coalition if I must tape my mouth up in the name of solidarity. Unshackle Sihanouk, I say. Allow him to give interviews and offer his personal opinions. It is Sihanouk's right to speak on behalf of his people.'

'Your people ask only that you denounce the Vietnamese imperialists.'

'No: I have so much to say. So much. I will write a book. You can't stop me.'

'You will defeat Vietnam with words, then?'

'Sihanouk will engage the world in constructive debate, to counter Vietnam and to counter the wanton propaganda of certain other interested parties.'

'You will remain free, I am certain, to employ anyone you choose to write your books. I happen to know that your friend Whittlemore could use the money.'

'I want arms for my soldiers.'

'Goodness: words *and* arms?'

'The Chinese will arm and train my troops. They will treat them equally.'

'But we will be one group. Therefore, we will already be equal.'

'Sihanouk's soldiers will be armed and trained. Sihanouk's army will be a separate and distinct body. China must help Sihanouk.'

'I cannot speak for China.'

'Not out loud, at least.'

'Perhaps we should ask them to join us here. Or if you believe that the Chinese wield so much influence, perhaps they could simply tell us later what we must agree to. That would leave us free to go straight to lunch.'

Sihanouk pushed his chair back and paced the room, interrupting Kiry's view of the frozen hills. He had gained weight, Kiry noticed, but his powerful legs comfortably carried his ample belly. 'I must say, Your Majesty, you are the picture of health. In fact, you are the spitting image of your portrait.'

'After we achieve victory, after we have defeated the Vietnamese, after the Cambodian state and the Cambodian monarchy are restored, all our armies – mine, yours, the KPNLF – will disarm.'

'It will not take the KPNLF long to disarm. I believe that Son Sann has an antique French rifle and a box of wet ammunition in his storehouse. And a kilo or two of rice.'

'After the Vietnamese capitulate, after our glorious victory, we will all disarm.'

'Surely the new Kampuchean state will need an army?'

'We will invite the United Nations to guarantee security in the new Cambodia and we—'

'Ah. Replace foreigners with foreigners: ingenious, Your Majesty.'

'And then we will hold peaceful, democratic elections.'

'I remember your democratic elections, Your Majesty. How very popular you were.'

'The people are my children. They adore me so they vote for

me. It brings tears of joy to my eyes to think of it. Besides, have you forgotten that you won a seat in Sihanouk's parliament? Twice.'

'A lovely gift, that empty box. How will I ever be able to repay you?'

'So we seem to be at an impasse,' Sihanouk said.

'I know. I read it in the newspaper.'

'I have told you my concerns.'

'You have, Your Majesty. There is nothing left but for me to wish you health and happiness in your retirement. I hear you are renovating your cottage in Mougins. And then there is this place. It's magnificent, Your Majesty. I could well understand if you never wanted to leave here.'

'Oh no. No no no. Sihanouk will never abandon his children. Never.'

'With my deepest respect, Your Majesty, you can have your concerns, your provisos, or you can be reunited with your millions of children. You cannot have both.'

'And what then? Will you cellar Sihanouk and Monique again, leave us to grow old and dusty? Will we all be communists again?'

'The Khmer Rouge no longer think this way.'

'Oh no?'

'The world can change in an instant. We change with it.'

Sihanouk clapped his hands, licked his lips and opened his mouth wide, allowing his laugh its fullest range. 'And they call me a joker.'

1982

Nhem Kiry grasped the commemorative fountain pen. The fever caused his brain to expand. Hot fluid burst out of his eyes and a steady flow of pus and blood and brain matter ran down his nose and into his mouth. Or so it felt.

He opened his eyes and tried to focus on the document in front of him: *On this day the 13th of ... in Kuala Lumpur, Malaysia ... formation of the Coalition Government of Democratic Kampuchea ... Funcinpec, represented by Prince Norodom Sihanouk ... the Honourable Son Sann ...*

He couldn't make sense of the document, even though he'd written the first draft himself, taking a hard line with Sihanouk and poor tired old Son Sann. He hated to sign a document he couldn't properly read – it could say anything, it could be a forgery, it could be a trap – but the crowd had assembled at his own bidding. He had no choice.

He closed one eye to focus, signed his name and shook hands with somebody – Sihanouk? – then somebody else. Or was it the same man twice? He wasn't sure and didn't much care. He stood now, although he had no memory of having left his chair and he couldn't feel his legs. He wondered if he had stepped on a landmine. It was bound to happen sometime. Or had Sihanouk and Son Sann finally given into temptation and thrown buckets of boiling oil all over him? Or had somebody amputated his legs as some sort of bizarre anti-war protest? Was he going to have to sit like Buddha for the rest of his life? Was he halfway through a slow-motion assassination? Was this how it had ended for Bun Sody?

He suspected but could not prove that he was in another room now. He sat behind a table and put his hand on the white linen cloth, leaving behind a sodden imprint. He resisted an urge to pull the cloth off the table and wipe his face and neck with it.

'Drink some water,' a shape beside him said. It sounded like Kolab. She had no business being here.

'You haven't brought the children, have you?' he asked crossly. 'Put your clothes on, woman: this is neither the time nor the place.'

'Come on, Mr Vice President, just a little sip.'

He blinked at the shape but that didn't help. He squeezed his eyes shut and wiped away the fog with a flick of his arm, as if he was swatting mosquitoes. Blurry but unmistakable, grinning like a monkey, Prince Sihanouk materialised. He pointed at the jug. But Kiry found the task of getting the water into his mouth insurmountable. He burped, gasped and dry-retched.

'Oh dear, Mr Vice President, you need to brush your teeth. You need a peppermint,' Sihanouk said.

Kiry felt like weeping. He wanted to curl up under the table and let himself fall into a coma.

Somebody in front of him whispered something in an urgent tone.

'Shhh,' he said. 'It hurts to listen.'

'Your Excellency, can you hear me?'

'Who's there?' he said.

'It's me. It's Akor Sok. Are you all right, Your Excellency?'

'Of course. Stop asking me.'

'Here, drink some water.'

'Where have you been?'

'I've been here with you all this time.'

'Liar.'

'Can you answer some questions?'

'Your tie is crooked. For goodness' sake, have some self-respect.'

'Just one or two questions?'

'What do you want to know?'

'Not questions from me, Mr Vice President. Questions from these journalists. Some of them have come a long way to see you.'

Another wave of heat broke over him. He shuddered. 'Yes, yes, I will speak. Go away, get out of my way, give me some space.'

'President Prince Sihanouk,' a reporter said, 'how do you feel about being in an alliance with the Khmer Rouge?'

'I prefer to fly alone, but without wings even Sihanouk will crash to earth. All of us must join forces to remove Vietnam. The world agrees. We must repulse the Vietnamese army before they turn every single Cambodian into a refugee. Sihanouk will do what he must do. But I wonder if my new vice president for foreign affairs, the oh-so *Honourable* Nhem Kiry, wants to add something. Do you have a few words of wisdom for the people, Mr Vice President?'

'We will abide by all of the rules of the coalition,' Kiry said. He gripped the tablecloth. 'We will do everything in our power … to make the coalition work.' He paused and stabbed his finger in the direction of a pot plant. 'And don't let anybody tell you any different, do you hear? When—'

'If I may speak,' Son Sann interrupted. 'The KPNLF is compelled to join this coalition to save Cambodia from becoming part of Vietnam. But we are democrats. The KPNLF does not support the Khmer Rouge, has never supported the Khmer Rouge and will never support the Khmer Rouge.'

'With friends like that …' Sihanouk said, applauding.

'I'm going to vomit,' Kiry whispered. 'Kolab, where are you? Fetch me a bucket. Not that one that reeks of bleach.'

'Hold on, Your Excellency, you're doing wonderfully well. You can lie down very soon. I promise,' Sok said.

'Wait one moment, hold the presses, I believe our colleague, our new Mr Vice President, has something to add,' Sihanouk said, rolling his eyes. 'Oooh la la, he looks as if he needs to add it as a matter of great urgency. Those people in the front seats, I advise you to take evasive action.'

'Thank you. I am perfectly all right,' Kiry said.

'I think it's fair to say that Mr Vice President has been hot and cold on the question of the formation of the coalition. Is that correct, Mr Vice President? Have you been hot and cold but are you now boiling? Boiling with pleasure, with anticipation, with fraternal love? Yes, surely that's it: red-hot love,' Sihanouk said.

'Democratic Kampuchea … is resolute in its determination to form … this alliance of forces in opposition to the expansionist Vi … etnamese …' Kiry said. He began to shiver violently and his teeth clattered together. 'We believe with sober excitement that we can reclaim Kampuchea before it disappears forever into the abyss of Vietnamese imperialism … Now … you will excuse … me.'

Kiry pushed his chair back and stood up. Sok came forward,

took his elbow and led him through a side door. Kiry dropped to his haunches and retched, then toppled forward and lay in the vomit.

'Well, I think everybody here knows how Mr Vice President feels,' Sihanouk said, clapping his hands and winking. 'Nonetheless, Sihanouk pledges on behalf of his friends and partners that we will do everything we can to make this alliance work.'

1983

On the first morning of the Second World Conference to Combat Racism and Racial Discrimination, held in Geneva, Cornell E. Jackson – tall, broad-shouldered and chisel-jawed, like the champion quarterback he had always expected to become – bounded up the stairs of the auditorium with all the enthusiasm of a missionary. Thirty-five years old, he was dressed in a pristine white shirt and a red tie adorned with blue and white dots. He paused, one leg in the air, stable as a gymnast, and gave an effusive wave to the Soviet delegation. Chief Delegate Olag Katkov scratched his ear and declined to respond.

Ted Whittlemore had already picked him for an American when Cornell sauntered up and said, 'Hey there, buddy. Is this seat taken?'

'It is now.'

'Hey, that's really nice of you. "It is now": I like that. A bit of friendliness doesn't hurt. That Russkie fella over there, Katkov, wouldn't even say hello to me.'

'Let him be. I happen to know that he's got a whopping hangover.'

'Hey, that's too bad, but good manners stops for no man. You know what I'm saying? No man.'

They sat in convivial silence while Ted wrote in his notebook.

'What are you writing there?'

'Not much.'

'Not much: I like that. Very dry. Very English.'

'I'm an Australian.'

'Hey, never mind. There's no shame in that.' Cornell paused, then whispered conspiratorially, loud enough for most of the auditorium to hear: 'I'll tell you something for free.'

'Go on, then.'

'I hate Geneva. I absolutely hate it. Do you know what I'm say-ing?'

'*Hate* isn't quite the word I'd use.'

'Yeah, I know exactly what you mean. It's so dull. And I hate these conferences. They're just for show, everybody knows it. I mean, apartheid, Jesus, who really cares? Don't look at me like that, buddy. It's a scourge; it has no place in a civilised world. But what I mean is, if any of these government dudes really gave a shit they would do something about it other than talk about it ... wouldn't they? I'm not offending you, I hope.'

'Oh, I'm very thick-skinned.'

'That's the spirit. I know that some people swear by these talk-fests, but that's just so they can sleep at night, don't you think? I believe in telling it how it is. My name's Cornell, by the way. Cornell E. Jackson.'

'G'day. Ted Whittlemore.'

'Hey there, Ted ... No: you're Edward Whittlemore? *The* Edward Whittlemore? You write for *Radical Papers*?'

'I used to.'

'You wrote *Living with the Patriot Vietnamese*. You wrote that funny little book with Sihanouk.'

'Well, yes, I suppose I've written several funny little books.'

'I gotta ask you something. Can I? Can I? Did you really go down in the Cu Chi tunnels? Tell the truth now, buddy: you didn't, did you? You made it all up, didn't you? It's okay, I don't blame you: everybody does it if it's something they really believe in. Every-body.'

'Of course I went down the tunnels. I often moved around with the Viet Cong. That's where we went when the Americans bombed us.'

'Amazing,' Cornell said, looking Ted up and down. 'How the hell did they ever squeeze you in?'

'They're an ingenious race, the Vietnamese. Besides, I was pretty fit back then. And pretty slippery.'

'Ever get stuck down there?'

'I've been stuck many times in my life but, no, I never got stuck in the Cu Chi tunnels.'

'Hey, I know exactly what you mean.'

A smattering of half-hearted applause broke out as Nhem Kiry, dressed in a dark suit, walked up to the podium.

'Hey, this should be fun,' Cornell said. 'This dude's one crazy cat.'

Ted peered at Cornell, perplexed. 'Is that good or bad?' he asked.

Nhem Kiry lifted his eyes from his notes and slowly gazed from one side of the room to the other. Presumably, he intended it to be an inclusive act, a sweeping gesture that connected him to every person in the room. But somehow it came across like a gloat. I'm here, Kiry's look suggested, and there's not a damn thing you can do about it.

From his vantage point Kiry saw friends and enemies. Halfway back he spied Ted Whittlemore's shiny head. Kiry nodded and smiled, hoping to embarrass him. But Ted was pre-occupied and didn't notice. He had a look of stupefaction on his face as a tall young man – a new disciple? Kiry wondered – whispered urgently in his ear.

The house lights dimmed; the spotlight above Kiry's head grew bright. He shuffled his notes.

'We all agree,' he began, settling into a drone that he could not avoid, no matter how hard he tried, when reading from the page, 'that at the root of the imbroglio in South Africa is racism. The minority white government in that troubled country have rigged the political system to ensure their dominance. They maintain this dominance with politics and with fear. The world rightly condemns these actions and these abhorrent philosophies.

'In 1953 the illustrious revolutionary Nelson Mandela said this: "The racial policies of the government have pricked the conscience of all men of goodwill and have aroused their deepest indignation. The feelings of the oppressed people have never been bitterer. If the ruling circles seek to maintain their position by such inhuman methods then a clash between the forces of freedom and those of reaction is certain. The grave plight of the people compels them to resist to the death the stinking policies of the gangsters that rule our country." Let us make the crucial link: apartheid and racism. This is the heart of the situation in South Africa, and we feel for our suffering brothers and sisters.

'It is my sad duty to inform you that such a situation exists in places beyond South Africa. In Kampuchea, the imperialist Vietnamese are constructing their own version of apartheid. They continue to engage in a war of genocide and racial extermination against ordinary Kampucheans, whose resistance is reduced to attempting to survive. It is the intention of the Vietnamese not only to continue their illegal occupation – as if that were not bad enough – but also to systematically bring in Vietnamese settlers who will form a privileged permanent minority.'

In the gloom the Vietnamese envoys rose, collected their papers and strode in protest from the auditorium. Soon after, the entire Soviet bloc followed, emptying five rows. Olag Katkov held his head with one hand, his belly with the other, as he heaved himself down the steps. Then the Syrians left. Then the Ethiopians.

'The Vietnamese, of course, are hegemonic and imperialist, but only towards tiny Kampuchea,' Kiry said. 'In the global picture they themselves are puny. That is why they rely so heavily on the Soviet Union. So there it is: Mr Gorbachev's people arm the Vietnamese army and the Vietnamese army comes looking for ordinary Kampucheans, whose only crime is to want freedom in their own country.'

Ted fidgeted. He was tempted to walk out, as much out of boredom as in protest. Kiry's tone and the banality of the speech itself were making him sleepy. He closed his eyes but an instant later opened them wide and let out a little cry of dismay. He was appalled to realise that Kiry's performance wasn't enraging him. He looked up, to a spot well above Kiry's head where a giant UN symbol clasped a pair of velvet curtains together. How he hated that logo: it was like the world was wrapped up in the smug smile of forgetfulness.

Then a young Cambodian woman seated a few rows from the front stood up.

'My mother is dead, my father is dead, my brothers are dead, three of my aunts are dead, two uncles are dead, many of my friends are dead. That man standing right there – Nhem Kiry – is responsible. Do not listen to a word he says. That man is nothing but a ... but a ...' The woman dropped to one knee and began to weep.

'Finally, some action,' Cornell said.

Security guards approached the woman.

'Excuse me a moment, ladies and gentlemen,' Kiry murmured. He stepped back from the lectern while the guards removed the woman. Then he repositioned himself under the spotlight. He emitted the briefest sigh, suggesting not anger but a rueful regret that one of his compatriots could be so misguided. Then he carried on as if nothing had happened.

'If he was free to speak with candour, Nelson Mandela would no doubt shake his head in sadness at the terrible waste the Vietnamese have made of their great good fortune. He would, I am certain, reflect on the irony that he is a hero to the civilised world for his acts of resistance, whereas men and women in other places who similarly resist are branded war criminals. He would—'

'That's it. I'm off,' Ted said. 'I can't take another word of this.'

'Yeah, he's dullsville. Hey, buddy, can I come with you?'

'I'd stay put if I were you. You're meant to be on his side.'

'See you later, though? How about dinner?'

As Kiry droned on, Ted tumbled down the stairs crying out 'Remember Bun Sody, remember Bun Sody, remember Bun Sody, remember Bun Sody.' He did it for appearance's sake, so that everybody in the room would see that he was still capable of making a scene. If there'd been a back door he could have slipped through unnoticed, he would gladly have taken it.

For a moment, after Ted was gone, Kiry remained silent. Then he leant into the microphone and said, 'Bun Sody was my friend. Bun Sody was a fine man.'

Then he continued his speech. When he finished he drove straight to the airport. Within an hour, he was in the air on his way to Bangkok.

That night Ted took Cornell to an Italian restaurant on the first floor of a building near their hotel, directly above a curry house. Delicious burnt fumes – turmeric and garlic and fresh ginger – rose out of the floor.

'Can't we eat down there?' Cornell said, the curry smells having finally distracted him from extolling the virtues and the growing reputation of his think-tank, the Edgar Institute for International Democracy.

'No we can't,' Ted said, raising his glass of beer to him. 'It's dry.'

'My God. In this day and age? How very peculiar. Now, what was I saying?'

'You were telling me about yourself. *All* about yourself.'

'Hey, that's right. You don't mind, do you?'

'Know thine enemy, I reckon.'

'Right. So: as think-tanks go, we're tiny. But I'm aiming big.'

'Big for what?'

'I want to stay hands-on, I want to write the reports and direct the research, the whole thing. I have a personal vision I want to explore so I've employed an office manager and a fundraiser – that's my sister, Candy, she brings in the cash, she's a marvel. Mind you, it's not that hard: all she has to do is flash our name about and, besides, she's a bit of a looker and boy doesn't she know it ... Hey, we could use a man of your experience and knowledge. I sure would value your advice from time to time.'

'But I despise everything you believe in.'

'Could be a good thing. I've read your books, buddy. I'm telling you, we see the world exactly the same way: we just reach opposite conclusions. Whaddaya say? I pay well. Very well.'

'But why does the Edgar Institute *exist*? What is it that you actually want to say?'

'Oh, you mean the mission statement. I was just getting to that.'

Cornell took a card from his briefcase. He stood, cleared his throat and read: '"The Edgar Institute of International Democracy, founded in 1979, is a research body whose mission is to formulate and promote US bilateral and multilateral foreign policies based on the principles of upholding America's national interest, notably a robust national defence, individual freedom, trade liberalisation, and the upholding and spreading of American traditional values with the ultimate goal of furthering global democracy. Our particular focus is in the Asia-Pacific Region (APR) although we recognise the interconnectedness of other regions of import and influence." Here, you can have this one. Shall I sign it for you?'

'Isn't "global democracy" simply a euphemism for American domination?'

'Well, you can put it like that if it makes your dinner go down easier. I don't disagree. Why should I? I want to offer America to the world, honestly and without adornment. Let the people reject us if they choose, but I say nobody will dare.'

'Nobody?'

'No majority. No majority of sound mind, at least. Take Vietnam. When the shit started hitting the fan—'

'Vietnam? The Vietnam War, you mean?'

'Yeah, the war, the politics, that whole goddamned domino thing. The problem is that nobody wants to say what it was really all about. My father, for instance, knows the Vietnam War had nothing to do with Vietnam. It had everything to do with the Russkies. He'll say so at dinner, but he won't say so when it really matters: in public, on the podium, into a microphone. Don't you think that's sad?'

'But telling the truth? Really telling the naked truth? Nothing would ever be the same again.'

'I know. I *know*. That's why we'd make such a team.'

Cornell waved a waiter over. 'Do you want another beer? Of course you do ... Do you speak French, my friend?' he asked the waiter in French.

The waiter nodded, mute.

'Good. Good on you. Great language. Got me laid more than once in my life, do you hear what I'm saying? We'll have two more of these beers – what are they, Ted, German? Belgian? Two more, whatever they are, but make sure they're ice-cold this time. And I want a bottle of red wine: shiraz, the best you've got. And there's no water on the table. And Ted here dropped his fork. He needs another one.'

They started on a second bottle of wine before the food came: a pizza for Cornell – he poked it with his knife and roared, 'Where's the cheese? What a rip-off!' – and veal cannelloni for Ted.

'I have to make a confession,' Cornell said. Only the reddish tip of his nose gave away the amount of alcohol he had drunk.

'You hate and despise every ideal I've ever stood for?' Ted said. He was beginning to have trouble enunciating his words.

'Yes, of course I do, buddy, that's a given. But, no, that's not it. I'll just come out and say it, shall I?'

'Shamelessness: that's the American way. Well, let's hear it.'

'You've had some dealings with my father. You two aren't the best of friends.'

'Well, I argue with a lot of people. I won't hold it against him. Who is he?'

'My father is Senator Alexander Bernard Jackson.'

Ted roared with laughter. 'Wacko Jacko is your father? Really and truly? Of course, really and truly, you deal only with the truth, don't you, and, anyway, who would own up to such a thing unless they had to?' He peered closely at Cornell. 'Oh no: you've got Daddy's dimple on your chin, shaped like an arsehole.'

It happened one day in, I don't know, '68 maybe, whatever year it was that all of those rich kids were wandering about stoned out of their brains, trying to buy their groceries with the rows of beads they wore around their necks. Pretty brainless stuff but it scared the ordinary folk witless, which can't be a bad thing. Anyway, I went on a tour of east-coast college campuses, speaking at anti-war rallies. I had to share a campervan for a few days with a folk singer called Walt Treetrunk.

Anyway, one day I addressed a rally in Washington DC in some indoor basketball stadium. I don't remember the university, I went to so many of them back then, but I remember it was very green: rolling slopes, trees, maybe a fake pond with fish, lots of granite. Kind of reminded me of North Korea.

I did my standard spiel: Vietnam belongs to the Vietnamese, theft is theft is theft, Kissinger needs psychiatric help, Jane Fonda's a good sort and good sorts are never wrong.

When I left (the crowd stayed to listen to Walt Treetrunk do evil things to Bob Dylan's greatest hits), Senator Jackson – Cornell's daddy – was waiting with his rent-a-crowd protesters. They set out towards me chanting 'Red, red, red.' The senator took the lead. He'd been some sort of star footballer in his youth (American catch and put your feet up, not the real stuff), plus he'd seen action in a couple of wars: he was a fearsome sight as he hurtled towards me, that awful fat vein on his neck pulsating.

I didn't bother to run. If they wanted television cameras to film them making idiots of themselves, who was I to stand in their way? The senator arrived first and stood before me, silent. I stuck out my hand in greeting. 'G'day. My name's Ted.' He folded his arms. The protesters formed a circle around me. 'Mr Edward Whittlemore is drowning in the blood of American boys,' Senator Jackson told the television cameras. On cue, the protesters produced bottles of tomato ketchup and doused me in it head to toe.

While I stood there, allowing the cameras to film me from all angles,

Jackson and his lackeys dropped to their knees and prayed for the salvation of my eternally damned soul.

Ah, all those Vietnam War protests – in the US, England, across Europe, back home in Australia – happy, happy days. Great memories.

'We need more wine,' Ted said.

'How about cognac?'

'How about who's paying? The Edgar Committee for the Enforcement of American Global Domination Institute? But tell me – yes, my good man, two cognacs, the Yank's paying – you're Wacko Jacko's son and you expect me to believe that you're running an *independent* think-tank?'

'I'm not telling you, buddy: I'm promising you. We accept not one dollar of government funds.'

'Not even on the sly from Daddy?'

Cornell grinned. 'That's the great part. Father hates the whole idea but you know what? I got it started with investments he made for me.'

'He funds it and he hates it?'

'You've got it. You know what he tried to do?'

'Get the feds to take you out?'

'He tried to revoke my trust fund.'

'He sued you?' Ted was so delighted he fell off his chair. The waiter arrived, waving the bill and pointing towards the stairs. Cornell folded his napkin, pushed back his chair and sat on the ground beside Ted, holding his Diners Club card up for the waiter.

'I expect a discount,' he said. 'We haven't finished our meals.'

'Hey, Cornie?' Ted said.

'Yes, buddy?'

'Don't take this the wrong way but in my opinion – and I'm never wrong – your Hank Washington Institute for Robbing the World Blind with Honour sounds like one great big joke. Sorry.'

Cornell patted Ted on the shoulder. 'That's okay, buddy. I ought to tell you that so far as I'm concerned communism is the great plague of the twentieth century.'

'Keep your distance! I've got a disease! I've got the plague!' Ted yelled as Cornell helped him down the stairs. 'The twentieth-century plague.'

Outside, Ted sat on the curb, giggling and saying, 'Wacko Jacko, Jacko Wacko, Wacko Jacko, Wacko Wacko.'

Two men appeared, dressed in all white. Marines, Ted surmised, or maybe Cornell's personal valets.

'Cute togs, boys,' he said. 'Going my way?'

They marched Ted down the road and into the lobby of his hotel. The feeling in Ted's legs returned momentarily and he veered neatly around a Chinese dissident whom he was due to interview the next morning.

'You lost, boys? Misplaced your boat? Looking for the sea? Head that way, I reckon, via France.'

They herded him into the service elevator. 'Arr-ten-SHUN!' Ted said. He saluted, poking himself in the eye. Cornell held his elbow. 'I told him not to eat those goddamned prawns,' he said. A cleaner, whom Ted mistook for a nurse, supported him on the other side.

'If you're going to vomit,' the cleaner said, 'please do it into this bucket.'

'You're Bulgarian, aren't you?' Ted said.

'That's none of your business.'

'You're Vulg … Bulgarian, I can sense it. I can feel it. In my loins.'

'Steady on there, buddy. The nice lady's helping us out.'

'My lips have gone to sleep. Givvus a kiss to wake them up?'

'Hey, buddy, why don't you hold the bucket? It'll give you something to do with your hands.'

Finally they reached Ted's room. Cornell sat him on the end of his bed and pulled his boots off.

'Ted? Hey buddy, can you hear me? Should I call a doctor?'

'Why? Are you sick?'

'Do you want me to take your trousers off for you?'

'Why, is it something you badly want to do?'

'Not if I can help it, buddy.'

'You could get me a beer. Have one yourself if you like.'

'I don't think that's wise.'

'Beer's for rehydration. Don't they teach you that in Boston?'

'Um, Ted, fella? Your nose is running real bad.' Cornell came close, brandishing a tissue.

Ted's eyes welled up, his throat tightened, he blinked furiously.

He turned away from Cornell just as his shoulders began heaving. He might have gotten away with it if he hadn't lost his balance. Cornell caught him as he toppled off the bed. Ted bawled until the concierge rang and said the other guests were complaining. That roused him. He staggered to the shower, stripped and stood under the cold water until it hurt. He emerged happy, starving and, it appeared to Cornell, on the verge of sober.

'Let's order sandwiches. I suppose you'd rather have a hotdog, but I don't know if they stoop that low here.'

'Are you all right, buddy?'

'Yeah, no worries.'

'But what was that?'

'That? That was the effect Americans have on the rest of the world. If you're planning on doing much travelling, you're going to have to get used to it. Come on, let's order.'

*　　*　　*

I went to New York in September '83 to cover the sitting of the UN General Assembly. United? United in what? Hatred? Self-interest? Greed? That year – like the year before and the year after – they voted to keep the Khmer Rouge as the legitimate government of Cambodia, now shielded by the coalition with Sihanouk and Son Sann. Pure unadulterated immorality.

It was Sihanouk's birthday, his sixtieth I think, and ASEAN hosted a giant dinner for him at the Wiltshire Manor Hotel. In the days before the celebration I did everything I could to get myself invited. I booked a room in the hotel, a tiny square of a box that I'm fairly sure was once a service elevator: they'd added a camp bed and a bucket of water and a minibar and named it Executive Suite 2012. But no sooner was I examining the room-service menu than the manager and a goon with a gun arrived and escorted me back out into the street.

Next I phoned Sihanouk's room on the hour from 7 a.m. till 9 p.m. two days running. His aides, once loyal friends of mine, kept promising that he'd return my very important call. But he never did.

Next I sent him a long note apologising profusely. You know the sort of thing: Your Royal Highness, it has always been my honour to serve you. If I have ever inadvertently insulted you or if you imagined that I called you an apologist for any unpleasant political organisation or if I performed some perceived action that has mistakenly been taken as anything other than signifying my love and devotion blah blah blah ... *It's a great word, 'perceived': it lets you apologise without admitting a scrap of wrongdoing. It didn't stop me from feeling dirty, mind you: Sihanouk should have been grovelling for my forgiveness, not the other way around.*

On the night of the dinner I bought him a present – a silk tie and handkerchief set, pretty bloody tasteful I thought – and dressed up like a waiter. I'd got it into my head that I could serve Sihanouk a glass of champagne. I could see him clapping his hands and crying out joyfully at the success of my plan.

I slipped in through the kitchen but an over-excited assistant chef wielding a cleaver locked me in the coolroom. By the time security marched me out I was shivering, damp and dying for a pee.

I deserved to be at that dinner. I should have been standing on a table in between main course and dessert giving a speech detailing the highs and lows of Sihanouk's life. Sihanouk loved me and he needed my help to find a way out of that dirty coalition of his. He knew it, too, which I suppose is why he refused to see me.

'I have a theory that may interest you.' Nhem Kiry spoke in French to the foreign minister of Malaysia, Rajeswary Ampalavanar, on his left, and Prince Sihanouk, on his right. They sat at a table of twelve but the other people present did not interest Kiry. The light in the room was dim, despite the hovering presence, directly above Sihanouk's head, of a giant chandelier. Their table stood in the very centre of the room and was surrounded by another thirty-four tables. Although there were people everywhere, Kiry found that the continual waves of noise – the medley of voices and chewing and shuffling feet and clinking glasses – provided a quite agreeable sense of privacy.

'In America even the finest hotels with the best kitchens offer special room-service menus positively awash with fat and sugar,' Kiry said, expanding on his theory. 'I believe that this is because all Americans watch sport on television – they have a station just for sport, can you imagine it? And it is a national pastime to eat this bad food while watching their games.'

'How fascinating,' Ampalavanar said.

'I've never thought about it in those terms,' Sihanouk said. 'With insights like that, you could have been an anthropologist.'

'They are now making a concession to us Asians, or so they think,' Kiry said. 'For instance, the room-service menu in my hotel now includes spring rolls.'

'Ah, yes indeed,' Ampalavanar said. 'The ubiquitous spring roll. The all-conquering dim sim. The finger-licking-good sweet and sour pork.'

'Last night my assistant, Akor Sok—'

'What a fine fellow that Sok is,' Sihanouk said. 'A truly great Cambodian.'

'Last night Sok ordered a dozen spring rolls, as an experiment, just to see what they were like.'

'And what conclusion did he reach?'

'They were drowned in grease, he said. The insides were mashed: there was no way of telling what the filling actually consisted of. Sok rang the kitchen to find out. They claimed it was chicken but I tasted a tiny morsel myself and I've got my doubts. It came with something they called plum sauce but I dipped my finger in: it tasted like tomato ketchup with extra sugar stirred through.'

'What a finely honed palate you have,' Ampalavanar said.

'They're all going to die of heart attacks anyway ... It makes you wonder why they're so worried about Libya,' Sihanouk said.

An Indonesian general came past to wish Sihanouk happy birthday and to fawn over Kiry. When he left, Sihanouk rolled his eyes.

'That awful man reminds me of Sukarno,' Sihanouk said. 'Sukarno visited me in ... what year was it, Mr Vice President?'

'1960,' Kiry said.

'1960. Yes. He had the most oafish bodyguards I have ever encountered. They all had birth defects. They roamed around Phnom Penh as if they owned the place. All the pretty girls fled.

'As for Sukarno himself: what a crazy old man. He was absolutely obsessed with virgins ... Am I revealing too much? Should Sihanouk shhh himself? Should he clamp his mouth shut yet again? Too late now.

'And then the Cambodian Royal Ballet performed for Sukarno, led by my beautiful daughter Bopha Devi. Afterwards Sukarno held my daughter so tightly I thought she would surely break in half. He wanted to marry her ... for one night only, he didn't want to keep her. And Monique – Sihanouk's very own Monique, no less – he wanted to ravish her too. Am I being indiscreet? It's my birthday and I can tell any story I want. Anyway, he's dead, so what does it matter?'

A plate of crispy-skinned quail stuffed with figs appeared in front of Sihanouk and caused him to abandon his story. He placed a fingertip on the quail and its breast burst open. He lifted the figs one at a time towards his lips; his tongue rushed out to meet them. Only when he had eaten all the figs, leaving a purple stain around his mouth, did he begin to tear at the wet quail flesh.

'If I may change the subject, I was hoping that we might speak in a frank way, as only friends can,' Ampalavanar said to Kiry.

'It is a delicate matter,' Sihanouk added, picking at a piece of meat that was caught in his teeth.

'I wanted to take advantage of this opportunity to have an unofficial word – nothing more than friendly chit-chat, you understand – about several of your colleagues,' Ampalavanar said.

Kiry wiped his hands, took up his knife and fork and began to eat his quail from wing to wing. After a minute he set down his cutlery and indicated with open palms that Ampalavanar should proceed.

'With the greatest respect, I am hoping – my government is hoping – that you might take a moment to consider whether it might be an ideal time for Pol Pot, Ieng Sary, Nuon Chea and Ta Mok to retire. Especially Pol Pot.'

'Retire?'

'Oh what a wonderful birthday present that would be,' Sihanouk said.

'I believe it could prove to be a turning point for your country,' Ampalavanar said. 'Not to mention a very clever manoeuvre for your coalition. Many of my friends and colleagues in the ASEAN community share my views. Needless to say—'

'Needless,' Sihanouk agreed.

'Needless to say, all of us continue to support the Democratic Kampuchea movement and you personally in your honourable struggle against the imperialist Vietnamese.'

'Those ruthless bloodsuckers,' Sihanouk said.

'I'm sure you know that no one is pushing harder than ASEAN for the restoration of Cambodian self-determination. But I believe – we all believe – that collectively we could exert so much more pressure on the Vietnamese to withdraw if you considered our suggestion. It is a matter of perception. I'm sure you understand what I mean.'

'Would you like more champagne, Your Excellency?' a waiter asked Kiry. 'Or would you prefer riesling?'

'I want a glass of sauvignon blanc.'

'I'll have to check if we—'

'This is a five-star hotel, isn't it? How hard can it be to find me a glass of sauvignon blanc?'

'If, for instance, Mr Pol Pot, deploying his well-known wisdom, chose to give up his day-to-day control of the army I would be very happy to lend a hand,' Sihanouk said, a pyramid of clean bird bones drying in the centre of his plate. 'My little villa in Mougins would be his for the asking. It's very quaint.'

'I wonder if the French would embrace their new resident,' Kiry said.

'The French eat out of my hand like tame birds,' Sihanouk said. 'But if you do not think Mougins a suitable destination then Pol Pot – and Ieng Sary and Ta Mok and Nuon Chea too – could move into my palace at Pyongyang. You have seen it, what a size, almost a wonder of the world, no doubt visible from outer space. Your colleagues and their families could each take a wing and, should they desire, not see each other for weeks at a time. The amenities are first-class: an indoor swimming pool, a cinema that I had built to the exact specifications of the one in the White House, three chefs, a sanatorium, a squash court which is also suitable for badminton and volleyball, a ping-pong table. Or if *that* is unsatisfactory, I'm sure our Chinese friends would be only too delighted to find Mr Pol Pot a palatial home in Beijing. Or perhaps even in Hong Kong.'

'After the handover, of course,' Ampalavanar said.

'Really?' Sihanouk said. 'I think the British would look the other way, wouldn't they, if we asked nicely?'

Kiry pushed his plate away. He made eye contact with a young

Thai diplomat on another table, leaving the young man too discomforted to eat. Kiry opened his mouth but then pursed his lips.
Still silent, he unfolded his arms, took up his cutlery and continued to methodically de-flesh the quail.

'For us, unity is everything,' he said eventually. 'You cannot
break us into pieces with promises of squash courts or ice boxes
full of Moët. None of us concerns ourselves with insignificant
material possessions or comforts. Brother Pol Pot will never abandon Kampuchea and nor will I. We care only about retrieving the
sovereignty of our nation. That is all we have ever fought for and we
will not abandon the struggle now.'

Ampalavanar stared at his plate. Sihanouk picked at his teeth
and held his champagne flute aloft, waiting for someone to fill it.

'So much for Sukarno,' Sihanouk said. 'But have I ever told you
about the time in 1966 when I entertained Charles de Gaulle?'

1984

As he boarded the bus Cornell Jackson accepted a complimentary lunchbox from a representative of the Thai military. Having skipped breakfast, he quickly ate the shredded chicken, a hard-boiled egg and a soft, slightly stale bread roll. Cornell closed his eyes. It was hours before they would reach the Cambodian border. He figured he might as well catch up on his sleep.

When the air-conditioning forced him awake, shivering, the musty curtain was branding a diamond-shaped pattern onto his cheek. He sneezed and sneezed again. A minder materialised with a box of tissues, a bottle of water, an offer of aspirin, and a promise: 'Don't worry, Mr Jackson, we will arrive at the border very soon.' He drank two cans of warm Coke for the caffeine. He had to be on top of his game. He'd promised Ted – whose name was on a list of banned persons published by the Coalition Government of Democratic Kampuchea – that he would take in every little detail.

Soon the buses passed into Cambodia. After travelling less than a kilometre along a hard-packed dirt road they arrived at Phum Thmei. Cornell exited the bus and moved with the other visitors to a clearing. A narrow path led from a group of neat pine huts into the thick jungle. As Cornell stretched and yawned, a pair of teenagers, a svelte girl and a handsome boy, dressed in Levis and T-shirts and sandals, wandered from the huts towards the jungle. They tossed their hair in unison. As the foliage swallowed them, the girl glanced over her shoulder and smiled a smile that Cornell thought was meant especially for him.

On the far side of the clearing stood the welcoming committee, an entourage of Khmer Rouge identities. Cornell scanned their faces. He remembered a couple of political strategists from a conference he'd attended in Singapore and recognised a high-ranking military commander from a photograph Ted had shown him. But he had no idea who the others were. He wondered if that was a deliberate strategy to confuse the journalists or if he really was as plain ignorant as Ted was forever telling him.

He raised his camera but a minder appeared by his side.

'No photo. No photo: security. We give you photo later. Official photographer only.'

Cornell shrugged. In his notebook he scribbled, 'Fat man with enormous arms, thinning hair and scar under left cheek,' and 'Tallish man, very skinny, hollow eye-sockets, a couple of teeth missing when he smiles,' hoping that Ted could identify them. He looked about to see who else was trying to use a camera and noticed, back towards the buses, that the teenage lovers were repeating their stylish stroll from the huts to the jungle.

Then Nhem Kiry appeared, immaculate in a grey suit despite the heat, the heavy atmosphere, the mass of bugs in the air. He began shaking hands and offering salutations. Cornell was surprised to see Kiry so relaxed, so natural. He'd been stiff as a scarecrow when he gave his speech in Geneva. As if connected to Kiry by a switch, the younger leaders instantly adopted welcoming postures.

Journalists continued to spill out of the buses. The area was soon full of visitors murmuring 'Weird, hey' to each other, shuffling about as if to mark the ground with their discomfort, requesting water or towels or insect repellent, trying to take photographs without getting rebuked, and admiring the flowers – for, inconceivably, the path was lined with pansies.

With a smile and a wave, Kiry singled out a man standing beside Cornell.

'Do you know him?' Cornell asked the man.

'Oh no. No no no. I met him once, that's all. That's it.'

Kiry walked to them and held out his hand to Cornell, who gamely took it.

'Good afternoon, sir. My name is Cornell E. Jackson.'

'Yes, Mr Jackson,' Kiry said. 'Your reputation precedes you. I wanted to compliment you on the Edgar Institute. You're doing fine and noble work. I for one share your desire for more honesty and openness in public life.'

'Thank you, sir. You're very kind.'

'Is your father well? Do pass on my best wishes to him. Tell him I very much look forward to meeting him again one day.'

'You've met my father, sir?'

'Ah, it's probably supposed to be a secret. Ask him to tell you about me. Well, I must get on.' He took a few steps away and then turned back. 'And please give Edward Whittlemore my kindest regards.'

Cornell nodded, mute. Only now did he remember Ted's instructions: 'If you see that skinny runt, ask him where Bun Sody's body is buried.'

'Do you think you might be a little obsessed, buddy?' Cornell had replied.

The crowd followed Nhem Kiry along the path that ran through the model village to a clearing, where Prince Sihanouk and Princess Monique waited. Sihanouk clapped his hands and waved exuberantly. He attempted to include the whole crowd in a welcoming hug. Monique did her best to look interested, but Cornell could see how distasteful she found the whole event. Ted had told Cornell that Monique was nothing more than a common thief but he had not revealed how beautiful she was. She's just starting to get a bit old and wrinkled, Cornell thought, but she's still quite the looker.

Sihanouk burrowed into the crowd and fiercely embraced a friend, whose name he could not quite remember.

'My ... good man, my good, good man, I think about you so often when I read your stories. Thank you for visiting Sihanouk.'

'Thank you for the invitation, Your Majesty. This little place is very impressive,' the man replied.

'Yes it is wonderful, isn't it?' Sihanouk drew closer as if to speak discreetly. Cornell, who was twenty metres away, could hear every word. 'This is our special make-believe camp, our little fantasy. His Excellency, Nhem Kiry, doubts that it is safe for me to be at my own Funcinpec camp. And he is embarrassed by his own rough camp, just over that ridge: you'll be able to smell it if the wind changes. So we have all gathered here today to play a little game.'

'Why is your camp not safe, Your Majesty?' another journalist called out. 'Are the Vietnamese troops close by?'

For a moment Sihanouk looked annoyed, but then he saw a French journalist he knew and he rushed to embrace him.

A line of soldiers, soft-skinned boys dressed in brand-new khaki uniforms, marched out of the jungle. Their shoulders made perfect squares. Their faces were relaxed and sincere; they appeared neither to gloat nor to scowl. Their virginal weapons gleaned in the sun, which was slowly burning a hole in the back of Cornell's head.

'What do you think?' a journalist behind Cornell said. 'Whose soldiers are they? Sihanouk's? Khmer Rouge? KPNLF?'

'They can't be KPNLF,' someone else said. 'My information is that they barely have enough soldiers to field a football team.'

Sihanouk emerged from the throng, his cheeks glistening. He gathered himself into a formal pose and commenced a slow review of the soldiers. Nhem Kiry followed a few steps behind, pausing whenever Sihanouk paused. When it was done, Kiry walked to a building, opened a door and ushered forward the Yugoslavian and the Egyptian ambassadors to Thailand. Each man presented his credentials to Sihanouk and then bowed so low that Cornell stood on tippy-toes to see if their noses kissed the dirt. When the Yugoslav ambassador finally straightened, he was blinking uncontrollably. Cornell could not decide if he had sweat or dust in his eyes, or if he was overcome with emotion.

Champagne appeared on a silver tray. Cornell looked on longingly. He wondered if he could get himself a glass if he offered to make a donation to the cause.

Sihanouk raised his glass and spoke. 'My heart breaks – Sihanouk's heart breaks, I tell you all – when I see Cambodia turning into Vietnam's newest province. But we fight on. I want to take this opportunity to thank Sihanouk's special friends for the delivery of a thousand new rifles for my soldiers, although I cannot give you the specifics because these friends like their privacy. Sihanouk is obliged not to reveal the names of our donors because Singapore is so shy, tee hee. And others, too, including ... no, I cannot, I must not ... I apologise to our eminent and honoured guests, Mr Ambassador and Mr Ambassador, that I cannot currently receive you in my palace in Phnom Penh but it is, so my spies tell me, filled night and day with Vietnamese generals living the high life.' He paused and peered over his shoulder into the jungle and leaned close to the Egyptian ambassador.

'I will tell you a secret,' he whispered. 'Our enemy is not so far from this place.'

'I find this a most intriguing fact, Your Majesty. I am a former soldier, you see.'

'A military man? Oh good: if things should happen to get desperate before we depart you can defend us, tee hee.'

And then Nhem Kiry closed the meeting. The crowd turned and headed back through the village. Cornell sat on the bus, ate an orange, wiped his hands on the military-issued moist towelette and wondered what the point of all this was.

At Aranyaprathet, just inside Thailand, the buses slowed down and pulled off to the side of the road. Four black Mercedes sedans with darkened windows passed: one for Kiry, one for Sihanouk and Monique, one for the Egyptian ambassador and one for the Yugoslav ambassador. As they went by Cornell's bus erupted with claps and cheers. The bus driver, eager to please, honked his horn long and loud. He'll pay for that later, Cornell thought, which got him thinking about what he'd say to Ted.

1985

Ted Whittlemore had almost given up on ever seeing Sihanouk again when Sihanouk unexpectedly contacted him and suggested they meet in Singapore. They came together in the enormous lobby of the prince's hotel suite. Ted stood with his arm extended, offering a Western handshake. But Sihanouk rushed towards him and Ted inclined his head, bent his knees slightly and opened his arms. Sihanouk launched into the embrace but mistimed his leap. As he tumbled, Ted caught him by the collar and stopped him from careering into the door. Finally they hugged and both men noticed that their stomachs nestled together like old friends but the rest of their torsos were further apart than ever before.

'Where have you been? What have you been doing? Why didn't you ever try to contact me? Never mind, I forgive you,' Sihanouk said. 'It has been too long, my dear friend, to worry about your trivial offences.'

'It must be nearly ten years, Your Majesty.'

'Many things have changed.'

'And sadly, some things remain exactly the same.'

Sihanouk fell silent. Ted wondered if he was about to throw him out before they had even begun. Or if Sihanouk was going to tell him what he really thought of him. You've let yourself go, Ted imagined Sihanouk saying. Where is your hair? I had no idea, no idea I tell you, that your head was such an odd shape. Is that bump from birth or is it from an accident or a war wound? Why don't you try a wig? And your skin is too thin: it's not pleasant for Sihanouk to have to look at another man's veins.

Instead Sihanouk said, 'It's so good to see you. Please, let's sit. Champagne?'

'Perhaps not—'

'I see. A formal interview, is it? I was hoping that we might be two old friends renewing acquaintances.'

'Please excuse me, Your Majesty, but I haven't made myself clear: I'd rather drink beer than champagne.'

'Tee hee: the Aussie wants a beer.' Sihanouk pushed the coffee table aside and pulled his chair forward. He indicated that Ted should sit. 'I think that you are disappointed in Sihanouk.'

'May I be frank, Your Majesty? I am more than disappointed: I am distraught.'

'Hmm. The Aussie speaks his mind. You want me to become a Vietnamese king, is that it? Like you are a Vietnamese Aussie? You understand, surely, that I cannot allow foreigners to tramp around Cambodia as if they own it. Cambodia is Sihanouk's – and nobody else's – to plunder. Why are the Vietnamese still in my country? In my palace? What do you say, Ted? Do you know? Will they ever leave or will they stay forever? Well? What do you say?'

'But you are allied with the Khmer Rouge again, Your Majesty. After everything that has happened, after they fooled us, you are letting them use your name again. The world thinks that you and Nhem Kiry are the best of friends.'

'Really, Ted. Nobody believes that. Nobody who matters, anyway. Nhem Kiry does what Sihanouk tells him to do.'

'That's what I believed last time because you assured me it was so, Your Majesty. Look where that left us.'

'No: that will not do. If you think you made an error don't go blaming Sihanouk for your bad judgment. Have the Vietnamese poisoned your mind? Or the Americans? I order you to recant your dirty accusation.'

'I apologise, Your Majesty, for any perceived insult. I forgot my place.'

'Are you unwell? I hear your bills are being paid by a right-wing American think-tank.'

'That's a dirty lie. But, Your Majesty, as for Nhem Kiry—'

'Nhem Kiry's life is written on his wrist: do this, do that, stand up, lie down, eat, drink, blink, breathe. Nhem Kiry is a harlot: he'll spread his legs for anybody. He is irrelevant.'

'I believe that you underestimate him. I'm worried that you are helping Pol Pot prepare to take charge of Cambodia once more.'

'No. No no no. Sihanouk is doing what is right. *You* disappoint *me*, Mr Aussie. There was a time when you would have understood. There was a time when I could have counted on your help.'

'The price is too high, Your Majesty.'

'The price of what? Whittlemore's reputation? You used to be fearless.'

'But you can change all this. You have the power now to achieve great things, and to sway world opinion, without the Khmer Rouge.'

'Me? Sihanouk is as irrelevant as Nhem Kiry. Sihanouk is nothing.'

'Your Majesty, you have never been nothing.'

'I have a new coat of paint but I am still a condemned house.'

'Then why not accept the inevitable? Retire, go to France.'

'I wish I could, of course I do. Monique would be ecstatic. She might even let poor parched Sihanouk drink more often from her well: ooh la la, she plays so hard to get these days. But it is not possible for me to retire. Yes, I am nothing, I am jaded, I am wretched, but I must still do what I can for Cambodia. After everything I have endured, I cannot allow Cambodia to become a province of Vietnam. And when the superpowers decide Cambodia's fate, I will be ready to take charge once more ... But, anyway, Sihanouk does not want to retire. He would shrivel up. But I will do it – believe me, I am serious – if, but only if, a Cambodian leader arises who is better and more worthy than Sihanouk. If only my boy would grow up.'

'Ranariddh? With respect, Your Majesty, I hear that he and his brothers keep setting their private militias on each other.'

'Ah well, boys will be boys.'

'Your Majesty, if I may say so, I know you think you have your reasons, but surely you understand that people become confused when you ally yourself with the Khmer Rouge.'

'Tee hee, I confuse them, I know it. And I confuse you, too, yes, don't I? And do you know how I do it? Can you keep a secret? I tell the truth. Everybody says that Sihanouk changes his mind. Mr Flip-Flop, you called me that yourself, don't deny it, you naughty rude Aussie. Monique was so angry with you when she read that awful article ... I tell the truth and nobody believes me. Sometimes I need to be the president of the Coalition Government of Democratic

Kampuchea. Sometimes I have to give Mr Nhem Kiry a great big sloppy kiss. Sometimes I am Prince Norodom Sihanouk, private citizen. But every day I tell the truth as I know it on that day. Is it Sihanouk's fault that the truth changes every time the sun rises? Ah, here are the drinks.'

A waiter, dressed in a red dinner suit, set down a silver ice bucket containing a bottle of Moët and half a dozen bottles of Stella Artois. While the waiter wrestled with the champagne cork, Ted flicked the top off a beer with his pocketknife and swigged straight from the bottle. The waiter looked at him disdainfully then withdrew, taking an ice-frosted glass with him.

'You're not going to assassinate me, are you?' Sihanouk asked, eyeing Ted's pocketknife.

'Kill my gracious host? Of course not.'

'We still have one thing in common, I think: we avoid violence ourselves, we would not even know how to hit a man, as opposed to how to caress a woman. But as for our friends, there is nothing that they are not capable of.'

'Yes, well ...' Ted said, momentarily lost for words. 'But in military terms, Your Majesty, the situation for your coalition is grave.'

'Not at all. Your friends the Vietnamese are expert at propaganda. And they have a knack of appearing to win insignificant battles close to the Thai border. When journalists see battles with their own ears, when they see men lying in pieces, they take photographs, they collect newsreels and, alas, they think that what they witness is the key to understanding the world. You do it too, my friend, you are one of the worst. But I tell you that when it really matters – when there is nobody around to see – Sihanouk's soldiers hold their positions. And our allies in the coalition are also doing very well.'

'Even if that was true, how can it make you happy? Your allies are mass murderers.'

'Do not speak to me as if I am a child. I do not need someone who watches and never acts to tell me things I have always known. You explain that Mr Pol Pot is a criminal, you say he is demented, you tell me he is a devil, and you expect me to look at you in wonder as if these things have never occurred to me before. Sihanouk is no dunce, Ted.'

'Please excuse me, Your Majesty, I mean you no offence, of course. But if you know—'

'If I know? *If?* They killed my family. How about yours? I sat in my prison-palace for three years while they massacred my people, hundreds and thousands of my little children. Sihanouk and Monique sat there like leaves on a tree, praying for cool weather and a wind to blow us off the branch.'

'But with the greatest respect, Your Majesty, if you know all this—'

'If, if, if.'

'If you know this then how can you live with yourself for helping them? Why not abandon them? You can do it, the politics allow it now, surely you know that.'

'Sihanouk's world does not revolve around making friends with the Vietnamese.'

'More's the pity. But even the Americans, even ASEAN, are beginning to notice how badly the Khmer Rouge smell.'

An aide entered and reminded Sihanouk he had an appointment in half an hour.

'Who is it? No, don't tell me, I don't care. Cancel it.'

'But Your Majesty, it's the American ambassador.'

'Too bad. Tell him I have heard bad news from the war zone. Tell him I am awash with pain and guilt like at no other time in my long and distinguished life and that I cannot possibly see him until lunchtime tomorrow. Come on, old friend, drink up: so much earnest talking. You worry too much these days. You used to know how to enjoy yourself.'

'I am sorry, Your Majesty, but—'

'I know, you are frustrated. Well too bad: Sihanouk wants to have fun. I want to play music. You will accompany me, yes? See, I had them bring a piano especially.'

'But Your Majesty, it has been years since I last played.'

'And I blame the Vietnamese for that too. Is there a properly tuned Steinway anywhere in Indochina? Come, fix yourself another beer. I will prepare myself.'

Sihanouk sucked a reed, assembled his clarinet and wiped it reverently with a soft cloth.

'What shall we play, Your Majesty?'

'Oh, Ted, surely you don't need to ask.'

Ted's fingers hovered above the keys for a moment, then eased down and held a muted chord. Sihanouk closed his eyes, rested the clarinet on his trembling lower lip, and launched into his very own version of Acker Bilk's 'Stranger on the Shore.' Ted watched Sihanouk's face as he turned the old standard into a whole new composition. His enthusiasm infected Ted. As Sihanouk's clarinet swept high and low, Ted's chords echoed the warble and occasionally led the way.

When they finished the song, Sihanouk stood silent and immobile, transported to a higher consciousness. Ted watched him and, just for a moment, could not help but fall in love with him all over again.

As he stood to leave, Sihanouk embraced him and whispered in his ear, 'Come back to me: all is forgiven.'

'I'm honoured, Your Majesty. I'll consider it,' Ted said.

Ted left on a high, but by the time he found a bar and perched himself on a stool, he felt as if Sihanouk had jumped on his back and was crushing him with his weight. Ted jerked his shoulders and shook his head, drawing a sharp stare from the barman. Ted pondered Sihanouk's offer and quickly dismissed it: his job was to carry on being the voice of reason, the voice against cant. It wasn't his fault if nobody was listening.

1988

It is difficult to believe that the Jakarta Informal Meeting has furthered the cause of Cambodian peace, if indeed that was ever its true purpose. At Bogor, former Indonesian president Sukarno's getaway palace, sworn enemies sipped cocktails and pretended that they could stand each other's company. They may have engaged in so-called dialogue, but it is highly unlikely that they allowed themselves to do what normal people do at cocktail parties: have spontaneous conversations. In all likelihood, they stood about reciting carefully crafted scripts. All very predictable. All very pointless.

The content of the dialogue gives no cause for optimism. One example will suffice: the Vietnamese delegation, led by the redoubtable Nguyen Co Thach, reiterated that Hanoi is in the process of withdrawing all of its troops from Cambodia. Everybody knows that the soldiers really are leaving, but Vietnam's opponents persist in pretending it isn't true.

This observer sensed an even more worrying trend. Calls from various parties for some type of UN peacekeeping force are wrongheaded and even pernicious. This conflict has never been a civil war – or, at least, never solely a civil war. The Cambodian people are not to blame for prolonging this war or for the continued presence of the Khmer Rouge as a guerrilla force. The principal combatants in Cambodia have always been China, the Americans and – as a defensive measure and against their personal wishes – the Soviet Union. Ask yourself this: when the UN arrives to make peace, whose interests will they truly be serving?

—Edward Whittlemore, 'As I See It,' syndicated column

'This suit is a disaster,' Nhem Kiry said. 'And I hold you responsible.' He tried to smooth the wrinkled white linen. 'Oh, I give up.'

'You look suave,' Akor Sok said, 'and *so* statesmanlike.'

'I look like a tennis player sent out to save the world.'

Kiry took the paper orchid from his lapel – the purple dye was beginning to run – and threw it into the gutter. He acknowledged but waved away several reporters loitering in front of the hotel.

'No, it's too hot today. I will talk to you tomorrow.'

Two Cambodian monks, dressed in saffron robes and holding umbrellas to protect their shaved heads from the sun, stood waiting for traffic to pass so they could cross the road. Kiry's bodyguards stepped forward and one of them yelled, 'Stay away,' but Kiry held up his hand.

'It's all right. I want to speak with them,' he said.

'But we're late, Your Excellency,' Sok said. 'It will take at least an hour to reach the palace.'

'Late? *Late?* I can't imagine what we're going to miss.'

'You cannot trust monks. Talking only encourages them.'

'When peace comes we must be a party for all Kampucheans. How do you propose I lay the groundwork for this if I cannot speak with the people who will spread the word on our behalf?'

'It could be a dirty trick. They may want to yell at you. They may pressure you to make promises that they will then hold against you. Check their sleeves for recording devices. And for knives: they could be here to assassinate you.'

'They are monks. I read about them in the newspaper: they have come to promote the cause of peace.'

'They look like monks, but looks can be deceiving. I heard about a mass murderer in Japan. He shaved his head and wore robes and nobody suspected him. He killed twenty-eight women before they caught him. When the police asked him why he did it he said, "The Buddha made me do it."'

'Do you know your problem? You have no empathy for everyday people. It makes me sad.'

'Wait for your guards, Your Excellency.'

'If I do that then there's no point in me going at all.'

'Please, Your Excellency, be careful crossing the road. Remember the golden rule: look to the left, look to the right, look to the left again.'

As Kiry stepped onto the road Sok ran ahead, waving the traffic to a halt. As Kiry walked past Sok he hissed, 'Get back over there.'

The monks clasped their hands together in greeting. Kiry stooped as low as his travel-weary knees permitted. One of the monks sprinkled water from a plastic bottle over Kiry's head and blessed him.

'Thank you, Venerable Ones,' Kiry said, 'and thank you for travelling such a long way.'

'No distance is too great in the cause of peace.'

'I agree fully. Please know that I am genuine in my efforts to find a solution. I believe with all my heart in reconciliation and in forgiveness. But please be patient with me. Peace may not come today. It may not come tomorrow. But it will come soon. Do you have any advice for me?'

'Might we remind you that you should always choose non-violent rather than violent methods?'

'Of course that is the ideal. But, regrettably, the ideal is not always possible. A monk I once knew used to say, "When I swallow a glass of water I kill microscopic living creatures. I admit it. But I do not consciously set out to kill. My act of will is concerned only with staving off dehydration." I feel as though I have been drinking from that glass of water for decades, all the time trying to end the fighting. My actions these past decades have always been in the service of the sovereignty of my country and the wellbeing of its people. It has never been my intention to harm a living thing.'

'Please remember that to search for peace is not the same as to push for victory.'

'Wise men do not desire victory or defeat. He who thinks he has won has lost. Didn't the Buddha say that?'

'Yes. He was talking about—'

'Thank you again. I am moved and inspired by your devotion to our country. My heart will remain heavy until Cambodia is at peace.'

Kiry took his money clip from his pocket and handed fifty US dollars to each of the monks. Then he crossed the road and got into the back seat of a long black car.

'There now, that wasn't so terrible, was it?' he said to Sok.

'It was a waste of time. It was dangerous.'

'It was a glimpse of our future, if things go well. You must prepare yourself. You must be ready to adapt. Come on, hurry up. The cocktail hour is upon us.'

1989

At 2 a.m., some time in the middle of August, in a box of a room in the heart of Paris, Nhem Kiry sat at one end of a long conference table, resting his forehead on his wrist while the fingers of his other hand rapped a thesaurus. A mess of papers lay before him. Akor Sok sat to Kiry's right. The rest of the Khmer Rouge entourage were spread out, some working alone at smaller, odd-shaped desks, some huddling in twos and threes having debates about draft documents which dealt with the terms and conditions of a possible interim government or the practicalities of repatriation for refugees or the rules of engagement for UN peacekeepers or the possible content of a sparkling new constitution. A cloud of cigarette smoke hung low.

Son Sen, who had hardly slept for a week, lay on a couch, a newspaper on his stomach, staring at a hook that protruded from the bare wall (when the French had assigned Kiry this room he had demanded that they remove the portraits of former trade ministers from the walls). Ol stood by the door to the corridor reading Book One of *Learn English Now!*

Akor Sok read to Kiry from a handwritten draft of a document entitled *Draft Agreements on a Comprehensive Settlement of the Cambodian Conflict*: '"The existence of Vietnamese settlers in Cambodia is a violation of—"'

'No,' Kiry interrupted. 'Change it to "is in flagrant violation of."'

'"... is in flagrant violation of the *Geneva Convention on the Protection of Civilian Persons in Time of War of 12 August 1948*."'

'1949.'

'Yes. Sorry. "The most troubling aspect about the settlers is that they are part of a Vietnamese plan of continued occupation—"'

'Stop. I want to quote the Convention after the first sentence.

Otherwise our point will be lost. Who has a copy of the *Geneva Convention on the Protection of Civilian Persons in Time of War?* Anybody?'

Vireak, a Beijing-trained lawyer skilled in international law and euphemisms, leant down and shuffled the papers on the floor beside his desk. 'Here, I have it.'

Kiry read for a moment. 'Insert this after the first sentence: "In fact, the final paragraph of Article 49 of the Convention states that *the occupying power shall not proceed to the deportation or the transfer of a part of its civilian population into the territory occupied by it.*"'

Sok continued reading: '"The most troubling aspect about the settlers is that they are part of a Vietnamese plan of continued occupation, a systematic attempt to Vietnamatise Kampuchea. In other places around the world the presence of illegal settlers is always condemned but in Kampuchea, where there are a million or more Vietnamese, as much a part of the invading force as any battalion of soldiers, the situation—"'

'No,' Kiry interrupted. 'Too vague. Sharpen it. And be specific.'

Underneath a mound of papers a telephone rang.

'Yes?' Sok said. He handed the receiver to Kiry. 'It's Nuon Chea.'

'Yes? … Are you sure? But I think that language is too strong. For now we need only to reiterate that we require a genuinely quadripartite interim administration and … I don't agree … Why? … Yes … I have Hun Sen's position on the Supreme National Council right here. They say I am not acceptable as a member … No, *not* acceptable. They say they will reluctantly agree to a moderate member of the Khmer Rouge being on the Supreme National Council if and only if … No, I don't know what that means either if it doesn't mean me … No, that's unhelpful … No, that's too antagonistic … Because they're just posturing. Let me send a memo pointing out that Hun Sen's position amounts to the Cambodian People's Party maintaining effective control right through the election campaign, which is clearly unacceptable, and that the so-called solutions by third parties is … Yes, by 'third parties' I do mean the French but I don't want to name and shame them right now … Well, I'm posturing too, of course I am … All I want to say at the moment is that so-called quadripartite solutions by third parties amount to a bipartite arrangement between Hun Sen and

Sihanouk, which we cannot agree to … No, I don't want to say that … No! … All right … Yes, all right.' Kiry hung up. 'I want coffee.'

'Sir, Tony Birde is outside. He's one of the Australian foreign minister's aides. He wonders if he might make a suggestion with regards to the genocide question.'

'Ask him to wait. Who has the last Vietnamese statement on Vietnamisation? Anyone? Read it aloud, whoever has it. Where's my coffee?'

'They say, "The alleged question of so-called Vietnamese settlers is nothing but a fantasy. The sole purpose of linking this non-existent problem of Vietnamese settlers to the repatriation of Cambodian refugees and displaced persons from the Thai border areas is to pave the way for a return to the genocidal policies and practices previously inflicted on the long-suffering Cambodian people, including repatriated refugees, and on foreign nationals in Cambodia."'

'Irrelevant. Ignore it. Make it clear that "to settle" is no different than "to invade." Therefore "Vietnamese armed forces" is a term that must be given the widest possible application, and must include any Vietnamese national who is living in Cambodia for any reason whatsoever,' he told Sok. 'This coffee is old. Somebody ring for another pot. And sandwiches. I don't care what's in them so long as they're fresh … But no more ham.'

'Sir, what about Mr Birde?'

'Who?'

'The Australian. Might I admit him now?'

'What does he want?'

'He wants to talk about genocide.'

'Poor fellow: what did he do to deserve that? All right. Let him in.'

Son Sen lifted himself off the sofa and disappeared into the bathroom. Technically not a part of the delegation, he tended to make himself scarce when certain foreigners came calling. Kiry suspected he was only there to spy on him; to make sure he wasn't going soft or conceding too much or straying from the one true path.

Ol opened the door. Nhem Kiry shook hands and exchanged pleasantries with Tony Birde, a tall man with a gently curved hint of a beer gut and a bright red face. He'll be dead from a heart attack within two years, Kiry thought.

'Come and sit down,' Kiry said, leading Birde to the sofa. 'I have fresh coffee on the way.'

'Thank you, Your Excellency. I hope it's not a bad time. I do not wish to impose.'

'It is no imposition at all. I remain deeply grateful for the heroic efforts of all our friends in the international community. A cup of coffee – even the muck they serve here – is the least I can do.'

'Thank you indeed. But on the question of the use of certain words, we are hoping we can find some way forward so that meaningful progress on other issues is not stymied.'

'Of course, although I must repeat – and I have already made this point more than once to your minister – that this is not a peripheral issue for us. I simply cannot agree to support any document that has, as its defining spirit, an expression such as "the genocidal Pol Pot regime."'

'I understand your position.'

'It is an insult, especially coming from the Vietnamese, who are the root cause of the tragedy of Kampuchea.'

'Well, you understand, at the moment I do not wish to make any comment one way or the other about root causes. I am focused on the use of the disputed phrase. I am attempting to find an accommodation that allows us to move forward in the drafting process. What I would like to propose is that you consider agreeing to the use of an asterisk.'

'If I may, I will ask one of my legal colleagues to join us.'

'By all means.'

'Ah, here's the coffee. Vireak, Mr Birde is proposing an asterisk solution to the genocide issue.'

'I'm not sure I follow,' Vireak said.

'If I might explain,' the Australian said. 'We include this disputed phrase but we put an asterisk beside it and with a note at the bottom, in bold perhaps, which says, "The use of the word *genocide* is contested by some signatories to the communiqué, and indicates no criticism, real or implied, towards any involved party." I welcome your thoughts.'

'Well now ... We will consider your suggestion, of course, and we are grateful indeed for your efforts to deal with this matter,' Kiry said. 'But it seems to me that this approach will still allow the offending phrase to appear in black and white for all time. I also wonder if adorning the word "genocide" in such a way – with a star, of all things – might actually accentuate its presence.'

'What if we were to adorn *all* disputed phrases with an asterisk? Or a cube, if you prefer. For example, the Vietnamese are gravely concerned that the words "colonialism" and "imperialism" appear in draft documents as descriptions of their occupation,' Birde said.

'But those words are statements of fact,' Vireak said. 'There can be no comparison with this genocide matter.'

'Really, I would prefer that we arrive at an alternative wording less offensive to the long struggle of the Kampuchean people,' Kiry said. 'Less offensive and more accurate.'

'Such as?'

'Perhaps something akin to "steps to avoid any return to the dangers of the past."'

'What about "incidents and outcomes that gravely imperilled the Cambodian nation and its people between the years 1975 and 1979?"'

'Really, Mr Birde, you know better than that. Was there no American occupation, no war, from 1970 to 1975? Did the Americans not prop up Lon Nol and did they not drop more bombs on the defenceless Kampuchean people than were dropped on the whole of Europe in World War Two? Have the Vietnamese, on behalf of the Soviet Union, not waged war on Cambodia every day from 1979 up to and including this very day? Vireak, what was it that His Excellency, Mr Raoux, said when he opened the conference?'

'I believe he said "it should now be possible and urgent to put an end to one of the bloodiest and most unjust conflicts in history."'

'Yes. We will accept some version of that,' Kiry said.

'How about "the future absence of universally condemned policies and practices of the past"?' Birde said.

'Not ideal. I would prefer, simply, "the policies and practices of the past."'

'Excuse me, Your Excellency,' Sok said, holding up a telephone.

'The French have a question: will you accept a seating plan at tomorrow's afternoon session based on seniority? They are asking because it means you will sit beside Mr Hun Sen.'

'Does Hun Sen agree?'

'He does, apparently.'

'Oh very well, if I must. Now where were we? Oh yes: asterisks. We will consider your proposal, Mr Birde. That is the best I can do for you right now. But I commend you for your ingenuity. You do your country proud.'

1991

I was passing through London in '91 when I heard that peace was about to break out in Cambodia. The sky was blue, the sun shone soft and warm, but it was the blackest of days. I felt as if a great thundercloud was dumping lunatics of every nationality down on me and that my only choice was to cower and prepare to drown.

The talks had been going on in Paris for weeks. I'd dropped in once or twice for a look and a sneer. I was certain that the whole thing would unravel sooner or later. But the world had changed and I was the last to notice. The Soviet Union collapsed in a heap and suddenly nobody could be bothered propping up the different Cambodian groups anymore. And Vietnam wanted out.

But this Comprehensive Settlement they came up with was nothing more than a washing away of the blood so that we could pretend the whole thing was a dream. All of them – the Cambodians, the countries who helped draft the settlement, and even the Vietnamese – were going to sign it in Paris. The Khmer Rouge too. Afterwards, the French were going to host a grand reception: another dirty, squalid celebration. At first I planned to boycott it. But then I wondered, What if I refuse to go to Paris and nobody notices?

'Whittlemore: how dare you show your face here?' a distinguished-looking man, a relic of the fifties, snarled.

'Hello, Mac: my very favourite enemy,' Ted said. 'How long has it been? It must be at least twenty years.'

'That's because I can live at home. I'm not an outcast. I'm not a traitor. I get to write for the *Sydney Morning Herald* without half the country sending in complaints.'

'Come on, Mac, that happened a decade ago. And you know as well as I do that you wrote most of those complaints yourself. I could tell, see, the spelling was awful. But jeez, mate, you're looking fit. Just look at those shoulders.'

'You look old. Sick. Fat. Broken-down.'

'And you should donate that moustache of yours to the Museum of Antiquities. But, hey, you know what they say about the size of a man's moustache. Still got the wife and the mistress, have you? Still keeping 'em both satisfied? How is that secret apartment in Wansea, by the way?'

'You shut your mouth. And piss off quick or I'll call security. Your type isn't welcome here.'

'Sorry, mate, seems like everybody's legal these days.' Ted held open his jacket to reveal an accreditation card pinned to his shirt. 'Anyway, what's your problem? Haven't you read your press release? Today is a great day. Today we are collectively ushering in Cambodia's new era of peace. Today we're offering hope for war-ravaged people everywhere. Today we're flying over Cambodia in a fleet of B-52s and pissing down on the peasants. I thought you'd be happy.'

'You've got an ocean of blood on your hands and I for one will never forget it.'

'You mean you hold me personally responsible for all your South Vietnamese cronies getting it in '75?' Ted said.

'Feeling guilty?'

'Don't make me laugh: corrupt, murderous thugs, the lot of them. They deserved everything they got. Don't look at me like that – deep down you know I'm right. Anyway, I had nothing to do with any of it. I just told it how I saw it: *South Vietnamese Criminals Pay for Their Crimes.*'

Mac's eyes narrowed. His hands became fists. He adopted a boxer's pose, slightly crouched, perfectly still, ready to pounce. '*Whittlemore Endorses Khmer Rouge,*' he hissed.

Mac's hand shot out and shoved Ted's shoulder. Then, tears in his eyes, his hands still clenched, he backed away.

'*Massacre at My Lai,*' Ted called out. He felt a tinge of regret as he watched Mac disappear. He was possessed by an urge to grab him by the arm and lead him through the kitchen to a dark alley, where they would rip their shirts off and square up. Ted wasn't under any illusions: he knew that Mac would have finished him off in seconds. But he was attracted to the idea of nursing a bloodied nose and a couple of bruised ribs.

Ted moved towards the centre of the room until he came to a roped-off area. A Frenchman in a grey suit and with a radio jammed in one ear barred his way: 'No further please, Mr Whittlemore.' Ted leaned against the rope and watched Nhem Kiry and Son Sann and Hun Sen and Prince Sihanouk's son, Prince Ranariddh, as they posed for photographs and groped each other. Sihanouk stood close by, applauding, staring longingly at the leaders. Finally he could not bear it any longer: he barged in, stomach-first, broke them up and dispensed royal cuddles one at a time.

Ted had waded through the Comprehensive Settlement on the plane to Paris. It was plain to him that poor Sihanouk had been used up and spat out. Ted couldn't believe that he'd voluntarily handed leadership of Funcinpec to Ranariddh and agreed to become king again.

Sihanouk caught Ted's eye, raised his glass of champagne and mouthed, 'Neutral at last!' Ted bowed low. By the time he raised his head Sihanouk had disappeared.

Surrounding the Cambodian peacemakers stood foreign-affairs specialists and UN functionaries of all nationalities. They clutched champagne and horded finger food. They congregated in groups of three or four to congratulate themselves and to break off and stare in wonder at the Cambodians, who continued to stand in the very middle of the room embracing.

'Lots of baby steps are better than one giant stride,' Ted heard an English diplomat remark.

'This is a victory for saying "Yes,"' his Chinese counterpart replied. 'When a person says "No" and really means it, he is doing a great deal more than uttering a tiny word. His entire being, his entire organism – glandular, nervous, muscular – merges into rejection. Then follows a physical withdrawal, or at least a readiness for withdrawal.'

The Englishman, a convivial diplomat who occasionally leaked documents about Vietnam to Ted, came across to the rope.

'Did you hear what that Chinese chap just said to me? Who was he quoting? Was it Mao?'

'Possibly Chou En-lai,' Ted said, 'but more likely Deng Xiaoping.'

'But don't you know? You of all people?'

'I must be overcome – I should say, I must be influenced – by the moment. Hey, you couldn't get me some of that skewered squid, could you? There's nothing decent to eat back here. Grab the whole plate.'

As he ate, Ted leant against a pillar and watched the Khmer Rouge delegation. Son Sen retreated to a corner with his aides, where they sculled their beers and giggled. Nhem Kiry stood with his back to Son Sen and listened intently to the French deputy prime minister, who waved his arms about a lot as he spoke. Kiry nodded occasionally, smiled and made a point of inclining his head to demonstrate his intense satisfaction. Ted grabbed the elbow of a waiter who held a tray of drinks and stole two glasses of beer. He sipped from one and sat the other one between his feet. He scanned the room for security; the place, he saw, was crawling with goons of all nationalities. Still, he calculated the distance that separated him from Nhem Kiry and decided that it might just be possible to slip under the rope and pour his spare beer all over Kiry's head. Was stealth the way to go, he wondered? Should he use the Japanese foreign minister then the Soviet ambassador then that drinks waiter for cover? Or should he sprint straight at Kiry and hope for the best?

Ted's scheming was interrupted by the Australian foreign minister, a short man with a red face and a stomach that had dropped as if he were eight months pregnant. He vaulted the rope and thrust a piece of paper and a green texta at Ted. It was a press release – *Foreign Minister Slattery Hails Signing of Cambodian Peace Deal* – on which there was a mass of signatures.

'Mr Ted Whittlemore: hello. Nice to see you still alive. What a glorious day. Even you must think so. Sign here, please,' Slattery said, thrusting the press release at Ted.

'Only if you give me a quick interview,' Ted said.

'No problem. Fire away,' Slattery wheezed. He was having trouble catching his breath and he was perspiring heavily.

'How does it feel to be part of one of the great whitewashes in modern history?'

'Ha ha ha. Next question.'

Ted inclined his head towards Kiry, who was posing for a photograph with Sihanouk. 'Seriously, you've legitimised – you've rewarded – one of the most horrid regimes in history: how can you bear it?'

'Mate: off the record, it's called getting the job done. It's called baking bread using whatever ingredients you're lumbered with. It's called living in the real world.'

On the press release, Ted scribbled, 'To withdraw in disgust is to win' and signed it 'Ho Chi Minh.' Slattery skipped back into the VIP area, surprisingly light on his feet. 'You bloody ripper!' he yelled, embracing someone with one arm while waving the piece of paper above his head with the other. When he disengaged and pushed through the throng – 'Gotta get the Russians to sign' – he left Cornell Jackson standing in the afterglow of his affection. Ted waved and called out, 'Over here, comrade.'

Cornell vaulted the rope and lifted Ted off the ground. 'Hi there, buddy. Come on, givvus a squeeze. Everybody else is. Hey, who's the fat guy with the sunburn? He sounds like one of your tribe.'

'No idea. Look at you, all grown up and dressed in a suit. How'd you get into the VIP area?'

'We did it. We've finally broken through.'

'We?'

'I can hardly believe it, buddy. You can't doubt our *bona fides* now.'

'Can't I?'

'You can't tell me that America doesn't keep its promises. The Vietnam War is finally over and guess what? After all these years, we won! Peace in our time: who was it who said that?'

'Jack the Ripper?'

'Who's he, buddy?'

'Just another English diplomat. Before your time.'

'Do you know what I just heard?'

'That some people don't like America?'

'I know that already, buddy. I don't get it but believe me, I know it. No, listen: apparently Pol Pot was at that Supreme National Council gathering in Pattaya a couple of months back. Actually there. Can you believe it?'

'That's hardly news. My information is that he's been going back and forth to Thailand for years.'

'The word is he stayed in his hotel room and the Khmer Rouge delegation had to keep breaking off negotiations to go and get his approval. Isn't that a riot?'

'I think it's despicable.'

'Oh, come on, buddy, lighten up. Enjoy the moment. But get this: apparently Pol Pot got bored sitting around in his room. He wanted to go for a swim. So they cleared the pool, he put a towel over his head and staff lined up all along the route – with their backs turned, can you believe it? – so nobody – you know, like Siha-nouk or Hun Sen or the Vietnamese – would accidentally bump into him. Do you wanna know the best thing?'

'I'm dying to.'

'He got an ear infection. From the crappy water.'

'Oh joy.'

'Cheer up, buddy. Why do you have to be such a sore loser? This is what we at the Edgar Institute call a classic CPL situation.'

'Cesspool, eh? *The Cambodian Comprehensive Settlement and Other Cesspools of Our Time.*'

'Don't you read the stuff I send you? CPL: Can't Possibly Lose. Listen, if the Khmer Rouge stick with the Comprehensive Settle-ment, we've delivered peace.'

'We?'

'Grow up, buddy: no America means no peace. And the beauti-ful thing is, there's no risk. If the Khmer Rouge do the wrong thing, if they keep fighting, we can now take all necessary measures. And it's the US of A talking: when we say "all necessary measures" you know we're not messing about. Even the Chinese are happy. Come on, drink up, I'll get you another one.'

'This whole thing disgusts me. You disgust me.'

'Come on, givvus a smile. Let me see your happy face. Don't make me tickle you ... Goddammit, buddy, you've got to shape up: peace is peace, no matter how bad it smells.'

But Ted was staring beyond Cornell. He watched, aghast, as Sihanouk led the Vietnamese foreign minister by the hand towards Nhem Kiry. 'Oh no,' Ted said, grasping Cornell's shoulder. 'No, not that ... Please, don't do it. Don't ...' Ted flung his hands over his eyes but it was too late: the image of the three men clinking glasses and toasting each other's health embedded itself in his mind.

Part 3

1991

Ted Whittlemore loved the Núi Café in Ho Chi Minh City so much that he had moved into the apartment upstairs. One Wednesday morning, Ted descended the outside stairs. He felt unsettled and heavy-headed, as if he'd slept all night hanging by his ankles. But he gripped the handrail and inched towards the bowl of coffee that would restore his equilibrium.

Ted entered the café and slumped into a chair at his regular table near the window and beside a wall of tatty-spined French and English paperbacks, most of which were his. Deep breaths, he told himself. From the bottom shelf of the bookcase he pulled a fat manuscript of unbound pages, *Ho Chi Minh: A New and True Biography of a Great Man by Edward Whittlemore*, single-space typed and annotated in his ugly hand. From his top pocket he took a blue ballpoint pen, the end of which he chewed as he scanned the pages looking for sentences to rewrite.

Hieu arrived with coffee. Without looking up, Ted murmured his thanks.

'You all right, Ted?' Hieu asked.

'Fine. Why?'

'Your skin is yellow.'

'Hmm, really?' Ted held his arm out in front of him. His fat fingers pushed together; his hand trembled slightly; his wrist seemed smaller than he remembered. 'That's not yellow. I call that a healthy glow.'

'You want food. Beef noodle soup?'

'Maybe later.'

Ted sipped his coffee and pored over his Ho Chi Minh manuscript. It was nearly ready to be retyped and sent away. He just wanted to add a few concluding thoughts, although at 874 pages he supposed it was probably already too long. Although Ted had access to a virgin cache of papers in the Hanoi archives, his book was mostly a series of personal reminiscences. For instance, he'd taken forty-two pages to recall lovingly the time he and Ho had been stuck in a cave while US bombs landed all around them. To pass the time, Ho had explained to Ted just where Stalin had gone wrong. 'He lost sight of the people,' Ted quoted Ho saying, 'and then quickly, no surprise, he cared nothing about life.' Ho was no Pol Pot, no Stalin, no Mao, Ted wanted to tell the world. Ho epitomised everything communism could and should have been.

Hieu brought Ted a pot of jasmine tea. 'Later you want beer, Ted?' he asked in English.

'Yes, of course.'

'Good, good. I have very excellent news for you. I have cleaned the basement.'

'Drained it, you mean. Last time I went down there I ruined a perfectly good pair of boots.'

'I have found beer especially for you. Two bottles of Victoria Bitter.'

'VB? You've got VB?'

'This is your national beer?'

'Close enough. Bring them over, I want them.'

'No no no. You are very busy. You want to finish your working first?'

'Bring them now.'

'But don't forget your writing. Uncle Ho needs your help. You need Uncle Ho's help. You and Uncle Ho can save each other. But only if you concentrate.'

'I want that beer. Now.'

'But Ted, they are not cold. I put ice with them, yes?'

'No!'

'My ice is clean, very clean, from a good factory. We collect it ourselves, no worries, ha ha ha, no worries mate. You have my ice many times. You don't get sick, not once even.'

'Never – *never* – serve beer with ice. My father taught me that when I was fourteen years old.'

'Surely that is a personal opinion. Surely it is a matter of taste.'

'Don't get all high and mighty and freedom of expression on

me, mate, I've heard it all before. No ice with beer: it's a fundamental truth.'

'Please, Ted, please let me ice them.'

'You can put them in an ice bucket. That'll cool them nicely.'

'No ice bucket.'

'Why not?'

'Waste ice, too much ice.'

'You can still use it afterwards.'

'Will melt. Ice ix-pen-hive. I poor, so poor. You not understand. You fat rich carpetelism en-tree-pree-neur from Aust-raa-lee.' A smile broke onto Hieu's face, which he quickly suppressed. 'Ice, yes, I think so.'

'I'll buy you some more ice.'

'Burr-ket for clean all onto floor. Burr-ket dir-tee.'

'Your English is deteriorating,' Ted remarked in Vietnamese.

Hieu doubled over, beat his hand on his knee, and exploded with laughter. 'Me no underhand you, Mister Aust-raa-lee, me no underhand YOU.'

The door opened, admitting a beautiful woman in a dress of blue sequins. Ted fleetingly wondered how she possibly squeezed into the dress – and, less fleetingly, what gymnastics she engaged in to extricate herself. Hieu watched Ted staring openly at the woman. 'Don't dribble on my tablecloth,' he said, not because he much cared but because he knew that Ted liked it when people noticed how much he loved women.

Later, Ted claimed to Hieu that the woman's exquisite curves caused the dizziness that suddenly overcame him. His head sagged between his knees. He vomited on his sandals. His knee knocked the table and warm tea ran into his lap. He closed his eyes, thereby avoiding the spectacle of an unconscious man slowly sliding off a chair.

After Hieu doused him with water, Ted lay on his stomach and listened to Hieu and his family debate whether to lay him on his side or his back, whether to massage his neck or to slap his face. When they made preparations to soak Ted again, he turned himself over and said, 'Could everyone please just shut up?' He fanned himself with the introduction of his Ho Chi Minh manuscript, disappointed that the beautiful woman, now nowhere to be seen, had not rushed forward to cradle him in her arms. 'Late for school, was she?' he asked Hieu, who stared back uncomprehendingly.

Ted sat cross-legged on the ground and refused to budge until Hieu agreed to serve him a VB. Hieu muttered about crazy foreigners all the way to and from the basement, and pursed his lips as he poured the golden liquid into a glass.

Ted rinsed his mouth with VB, grimaced and spat between his feet.

'It's hot,' he said.

'I warned you,' Hieu said.

'It's stale. And flat. When did you open it, '65?'

'If you don't like it, give it back.'

'Oh no,' Ted said. He sipped another mouthful and this time swallowed. 'It's awful. It's ... heavenly.'

Hieu wheeled his Vespa out from the kitchen. Ted rode in the middle. Hieu's son sat perched on the back to make sure Ted didn't fall off. They flirted with Saigon's traffic, reaching out to touch bikes and cars and trucks and pedestrians. Somehow, they arrived unscathed at the doctor's rooms. Hieu sent Ted inside with smiles and consoling thoughts. But Ted could tell that Hieu was worried that his weight had cracked the Vespa's axle.

Hanh Nguyen had been Ted's doctor since they'd met in a Viet Cong sanctuary in 1966. Twenty-six years old then, she was already a widow, and – though she didn't know it at the time – two of her four siblings were dead. Ted was thirty-four, and dividing his time between Vietnam and Cambodia. Reporting on the war from the North Vietnamese perspective – 'sleeping with the enemy,' his critics said – he was at the height of his fame and influence. He arrived at the sanctuary filthy, high from snorting war pollution up his nostrils, and with several tiny pieces of shrapnel embedded in his thigh.

'I can't spare you any drugs,' Hanh politely told him as she cleaned his leg of mud and metal.

Then a crowd of wounded soldiers and civilians arrived. Ted watched Hanh dig for bullets and seal holes and remove limbs and drag bodies away. He wrote about her in *Living with the Patriot Vietnamese*, a book he was particularly proud of: *To say she works in tough conditions is an understatement. Somehow, perhaps through willpower alone, she maintains a sense of sterilisation, even though her operating theatre is in a swamp. She works without pause for several hours. Most of her face is hidden behind a mud-spotted surgical mask, so I watch her eyes. I have never seen such resolve. During an amputation, in the fifteen minutes that she works on the brave youth before he bleeds out, she doesn't blink once. She saves more patients than she loses, though she impassively informs me that some of the wounded will die in the coming days. Then she takes her mask off and I try to comprehend how someone who has endured such a day can be so young.*

Now, a couple of hours after Ted had collapsed in the Núi Café, Hanh scolded him as she helped him into the examining room. 'Were you planning to tell me? Or were you just going to mention in your will that you were sick?'

'I don't feel *that* bad,' Ted said. She handed him a mirror and he stared, shocked, at his yellow skin and bulbous, bloodshot eyes.

Hanh stuck thermometers into him like acupuncture needles. She stared at his tongue for a very long time: 'I'm reading your fortune. Shut up and let me do it.' She laid him on his back and massaged his side until he laughed so hard she worried he would crack a rib. She swabbed his cheek, stole blood, pointed an arrowhead light into his ear canals: 'Disgusting.' She prodded his testicles: 'Take that smirk off your face.' She made him touch his toes and then followed him as he floated around the room fighting the urge to faint.

Ted gave vague answers to her questions. He tiptoed around the truth. But he must have been resigned to hearing bad news or he would have found a stranger to examine him.

'So what's the diagnosis? It's the napalm, isn't it, finally catching up with me?'

'No.'

'It's napalm. It must be, I know it is. Just promise me one thing: when I die make sure you write "American imperialism" on my death certificate.'

Hanh didn't smile.

'Come on then: what's wrong with me?'

'Lots of things. You're old, for one thing. You're wearing out.'

'You're not so young yourself.'

'I act my age.'

'Poor you.'

'Ted, I can't really say. You need better tests than I can give you here. You must—'

'But it's nothing terminal, right?'

'You could have diabetes. There's something wrong with your heart. Have you noticed that your left hand shakes sometimes? Your skin is yellow. You're too fat. One of your balls is twice the size of the other one. Your liver—'

'I'm flying to Phnom Penh on Tuesday. That's okay, isn't it?'

'No.'

'I've got to go. I've got a contract, and Cornell's promised to cover my costs. Nhem Kiry's flying in, I've got to see him, the word is there's going to be a demonstration, I'm going to try to interview him, it's—'

'You're going to have to stop.'

'Stop? Stop what?'

'Everything. No more travel. No more wars, Ted … You know, maybe it's time you went home.'

'Home?'

'And no drinking.'

'Home? What do you mean, home? I mean … Where, go where?'

'Australia.'

'*Australia?* Have you lost your bloody mind?'

'Wherever you want then. Wherever you think is best. Moscow. England. New York. France.'

'But I want to stay here. Fair go. How would you feel if I told you that you had to leave?'

Hanh sat down and stared at the floor between her feet. When she looked up she had tears in her eyes. She opened her mouth but a long moment passed before she spoke.

'If I could get out of here, just like that,' she said eventually. 'If I could pack a bag and leave and never come back, I'd be gone before dark.'

*   *   *

Cornell was there that day in '91 when the people of Phnom Penh attacked Nhem Kiry. Lucky bastard. He'd booked me five-star accommodation and in return I'd promised to critique some god-awful manuscript he wanted to publish about America's triumph in Indochina, written by one of his fuck-wit neo-liberal mates. But then I collapsed in Ho Chi Minh City and that was that. Forever, as it turned out.

When I asked him what the demonstration was like, he said, 'I don't mind telling you, buddy, I was so scared I nearly shitted myself. And my shirt got ripped: two hundred bucks down the drain.'

'What do you reckon: was it staged or was it real?' I asked him.

'What's the difference?' Cornell asked.

Nhem Kiry blinked – once, twice – to clear the blood from his eyes. The man wielding the iron bar swung it at him again but he was drunk on tenacity – or just plain drunk, Kiry suspected – and he lurched forward and swiped the air. Kiry wished for a calmer, more rational atmosphere. He felt sure he needed only to sit the poor misguided fellow down, share a pot of tea, or a bottle of beer if that's what it took, and remind him that he – Nhem Kiry – had sacrificed his whole life to improve the circumstances of the ordinary people. 'Nothing is more important,' Kiry would have counselled, 'than the fact that we are both patriots. And, by the way, please vote for me next year.'

As the man took aim at him again, Kiry dropped to all fours and scuttled like a cockroach into a wardrobe. Akor Sok jumped in too and pulled the door shut.

'I'll save you, Your Excellency,' he said.

'Really? Who's going to save you?' Kiry replied.

The mob opened the doors of the wardrobe. 'Kill him,' they chanted, 'Kill him, kill him, kill him.' Someone threw Sok into a corner as if he was Kiry's dirty laundry. They dragged Kiry into the middle of the room. Concrete thoughts eluded him. Later, when he tried to recall the moment, all he could conjure in his mind was the sensation of multiple hands yanking at his collar to expose his neck.

Then someone lifted him off the ground – later he learned that it was Ol – and threw him into the bathroom. One of the French photographers was already in there: aren't women brave, Kiry thought. Her camera hung from her hip, its lens peering up at him. He turned his back on her and pressed a towel against the wound above his eye.

When Ol opened the door, the room had miraculously cleared of rioters. That's when Kiry lost all feeling in his legs. His minders led him to the bed. He lay on his side and bloodied a pillow.

Son Sen entered the room. He was shaken. His hair, usually immaculate, took off in all directions.

'Oh dear. You've got a thumbprint on your glasses,' Kiry said.

Without knocking, government officials entered the room.

'You must go. You must go now,' one official said, waving a walkie-talkie around as if that was proof of something.

'We have every right to be here,' Kiry said. 'Mr Son Sen and I have come to Phnom Penh in our official capacity as members of the Supreme National Council. We have the legitimacy of the United Nations behind us and the support of the international community.'

'Yes, Your Excellency, forgive me, you are correct in every sense. Now you must go to the airport.'

They bundled Kiry into an armoured personnel carrier and jammed a blue UN helmet onto his head, an outcome he found almost as shameful as the beating he'd just endured.

Kiry could barely breathe, even before they started jamming bodies around him. His staff threw their elbows about and complained or whimpered or compared bruises in what Kiry considered a most unseemly way. He felt like crying out, 'Be proud.'

As the personnel carrier rumbled out of the city, Kiry closed his eyes and pretended he was alone in an open field: the soft light of dawn, fresh air, a log to sit on, a mango and a knife. Sok thought Kiry had fainted and shook him. Kiry's helmet – made for a larger head – banged against his wound and he started bleeding again.

At the airport he sat on the tarmac. Sok held an umbrella over his head to keep the sun away, but his hands still shook with fear. Kiry made him hand the umbrella to Ol. Sok, who hated to have his limitations exposed, became sullen and resorted to acute politeness: 'Would Your Excellency care for a glass of iced water?' and 'Does Your Excellency require a trip to the toilet before we leave?' and 'Are you hungry, Your Excellency? Perhaps something sweet: a banana or a Mars Bar? At times like this it is important to remember to eat.'

The commercial flight they took to Bangkok was only half full. Son Sen sat across the aisle from Kiry and fell asleep immediately. His arm dropped into the aisle. His glasses slipped to the end of his nose, where they balanced precariously but did not fall, even though several people bumped his arm on their way to the restroom (Akor Sok made a point of hitting him at pace).

Kiry had heard rumours that Pol Pot, on Nuon Chea's urging, was planning to cut back Son Sen's responsibilities as defence minister. Kiry thought that that was probably for the best. He seems so easily tired, Kiry thought, so readily distracted. He's not good for much anymore other than ordering people about. Why not let him retire to Beijing so he can read those military histories he's so fond of?

Kiry failed to sleep. He thought about how close the mob had come to killing him. In his mind, death – like malaria, like bad press, like stale food on an aeroplane – was an ever-present possibility. The thought of it bothered him, but what he feared more was losing control of himself: drinking tainted water and soiling himself because he could not drop his trousers and squat fast enough; being harangued by Nuon Chea or bullied by Ta Mok in front of a room full of witnesses; getting the shakes while waiting in an anteroom to meet Chairman Mao. These moments – today's attack was another one – never left him. They made him stronger. Except that Kiry wasn't sure how much more toughening up he needed.

At Bangkok airport, Kiry was irritated to find there was a helicopter waiting to fly Son Sen to Pattaya. What about me, he thought, but he said nothing.

'See a doctor,' Son Sen said as he departed. 'Try to rest.'

'Yes, yes.'

Sok read Kiry's complaint in his tone and spoke out on his behalf: 'You were the one who was nearly killed. Surely you're the one who should be rushed to the beach.'

'Oh well.'

'Didn't you say your wife was going to be in Pattaya? And your girls? How long is it since you last saw them? How many weeks?'

'That is irrelevant. Anyway, I need to be available.'

'Who to? German tourists?'

'Don't be petulant. We will have a beach holiday another day.'

Airline officials herded Kiry and his entourage onto a rusting red bus that smelt so heavily of gasoline that Kiry told Ol not to smoke. The bus deposited them beside a building. A security officer led them along a winding concrete corridor and through a door that slammed behind them. They found themselves inside the main terminal, but when they turned to retreat the door would not open.

'You imbecile. You stupid monkey,' Sok yelled at the security officer, who tried to salvage the situation by leading them towards the safety of the Qantas Golden Club lounge. But in the distance, several waiting journalists saw Kiry and came running.

'Quickly, Your Excellency, this way,' Sok said.

'No. I want to talk to them.'

'I beg you, Your Excellency, not today. You have not been briefed. You are not ready, after such a shock, to know what it is best to say.'

'I will speak to them.'

'Please, Your Excellency, you are a mess.'

'Exactly.'

Sok ran ahead to brief the reporters, the same faces who had farewelled Kiry at dawn.

'Please do not crowd in. His Excellency Nhem Kiry has suffered a terrible shock. He is not so well. No photos.'

'That's not up to you,' one reporter said.

'If you take photos, His Excellency will not speak.'

Sok positioned himself at Kiry's right shoulder. Kiry blamed himself for this: as the peace negotiations had dragged on for months and years, he had set Sok the task of monitoring the public statements of the US administration. It was important work and it gave Sok something to do in the world's hotel rooms other than watch pornography. But clearly, Kiry now saw, Sok had watched too many CNN news conferences during which brash American politicians were incapable of answering questions unless they had a row of faces – people, farm animals, cardboard cut-outs, it didn't seem to matter – standing behind to nod and bray in unison.

'Stand back there. I won't be long,' Kiry told Sok, who looked aggrieved.

Kiry knew these reporters. They reminded him of a pack of stray dogs roaming the streets at night, frothing at the mouth and baring their teeth at passers-by, scavenging and, come morning, slinking under houses or behind garbage bins. Their predicament amused Kiry: they were desperate to damn him in print but they tied themselves in knots feigning objectivity.

'How are you feeling?' a fat American man asked.

'Fine, all things considered. I have no serious injuries. I thank you for your concern.'

The corners of the American's mouth were flickering and his blue eyes gleamed. He could barely contain his amusement at Kiry's predicament.

'Who did this? Who is responsible?'

'Who? You ask *me* who? How would I possibly know? All I can do is ask questions of my own: is this an act perpetrated by Cambodians or is this the work of foreigners? Is this the behaviour of locals and lovers of peace or is this the behaviour of visitors, of those lovers of imperialist mayhem who hate the very excellent Paris Peace Agreement?'

'Are you suggesting that the demonstration was staged?' asked a wiry Italian woman. As Kiry had come to expect, she addressed him in a derisive tone, choosing to disbelieve him even before he opened his mouth. He peered down at her and wondered, not for the first time, why she bothered to be so aggressive in person when her articles were so tame and lacking in insight.

'Of course it was staged, and more than that I—'

'But surely the Cambodian people have the right to reject the Khmer Rouge? Surely this protest represents the very essence of the democratic reforms the world is giving Cambodia?' an Irish woman interrupted.

'If I might be allowed to finish: of course it was staged. Because the Cambodian people would never participate in such a low and misguided act. The Cambodian people understand and respect me. They know that I love Cambodia. And they rely on my party – and my party alone – to resist the Vietnamese, who everybody knows have not really withdrawn from Cambodia. We believe that

Cambodians of all stripes should not quarrel or fight each other any longer. We should forget the past, which after all was not caused by Cambodians ... It's quite similar to the situation in Belfast, now that I think of it.'

The Irish woman persisted. 'Prime Minister Hun Sen says he urged you to take certain precautions for your own security but you refused.'

'What is your question?'

'Doesn't he have a point? Didn't you bring this upon yourself?'

'No. And no.'

'But what about—'

'Does anybody have a relevant question?'

'What broader ramifications does the attack on you have for the peace process?' a thin Australian man asked. Beside him, the Irish woman, aghast at a question that she considered too friendly, hopped from foot to foot.

'I do not want to say anything concrete about that right now. But you must understand that it is not just me who has been shamed today. The United Nations has been shamed too, for if the Supreme National Council, of which I am a rightful member according to all the nations of the world, cannot meet in Phnom Penh, then there can be no peace process. Still, I am an optimist. I believe that we should maintain a mature and mild attitude to such setbacks, however troubling, and not give in to those who hate peace.'

'It is irony on a grand scale, don't you think,' the Irish woman said, 'for the Khmer Rouge to demand early deployment of the UN forces?'

'That is not a helpful question.' Kiry paused, and with self-restraint avoided scratching the scab on his forehead, which had begun to itch and ooze. 'I'm terribly sorry, but that's all I can manage today. I'm sure you understand.'

By the time Kiry retreated to the privacy of his hotel suite he felt drained – literally bereft of fluids that might allow his brain not to scratch and bump against the inside of his skull. He needed silence and solitude to retrieve his bearings and his self-control. But Sok, himself tired and tense, irritating but somehow comforting, refused to budge.

'The medic said not to leave you alone.'

So while Kiry showered, Sok stood by the towel rack holding a pillow, ready to dive forward and cushion Kiry should he slip or faint. Then, as Kiry prepared to rest, Sok admitted a succession of visitors.

First came a mournful, fidgety Thai doctor. He'd been treating Kiry on and off for years, and had delivered his second daughter into the world.

'What's your name?' the doctor asked, shining a pen torch in Kiry's eyes.

'Doctor Henry Kissinger.'

'What day is it?'

'It's my day of great triumph. It's a day when all Cambodians can finally and truly believe that peace has broken like the first rains in May.'

'Er—'

'Oh, for goodness' sake, it's Tuesday.'

'Where are you now?'

'Purgatory.'

'*Where?*'

'Room 877, executive suite, Lotus Hotel, Bangkok.'

As the doctor left the hotel manager arrived. He presented Kiry with a bowl of fruit, a get-well card on behalf of the citizens of the Kingdom of Thailand and a heavy hint that he could arrange for a 'lovely lady' to come and comfort Kiry.

'Maybe later,' Kiry said. Sok nodded eagerly.

As the manager left a UN delegation arrived.

'Please stay calm,' their spokesman said. 'The situation is being actively attended to.'

'Please accept this fruit bowl as a token of my goodwill,' Kiry said. He kept the mango, but when he later cut it open it was bruised and soft all the way to the seed.

As soon as Kiry lay down, the telephone rang. Sok answered. 'It's your wife,' he mouthed. Kiry shook his head and closed his eyes. 'He'll ring you back,' Sok said and hung up. Almost immediately, the phone rang again. Kiry faked a snore but Sok shook his elbow.

'Your Excellency, you must take this.'

'Unless it's Nelson Mandela I'm not interested.'

'Please, Your Excellency.'

Kiry lay on the bed and half-listened as Nuon Chea harangued him for being a victim: 'How can you have been so careless? And why on earth did you speak to those reporters? You might have said anything.'

It was close to midnight before Kiry was finally alone. But by then sleep seemed impossible. He was unable to prevent waves of fear from passing through him. So he dressed and took the glass elevator – another opportunity, he thought, to watch the ground disappear beneath his feet – to the Wild Rice Restaurant and Piano Bar.

He sat at a large table in the farthest corner of the restaurant and scattered the world's newspapers around him. Before dawn he had sat at this same table, with the same newspapers, and prepared himself for the day ahead with black coffee and papaya. Since then, he had drunk nothing but water and eaten nothing but paracetamol.

The restaurant was nearly empty. A Chinese-Malaysian business-man sat in a corner. Like Kiry, he could not avoid listening to a young Australian couple recounting their expedition to the red-light district of Patpong, where they had photographed each other in front of a long line of school-uniformed prostitutes. At the street market they had bought Calvin Klein underwear. 'Cotton is cotton,' they decided, although the material was scratchy. 'It probably came from the same factory as the real stuff,' they agreed, although the labels read 'Kelvin Clein.' Clutching their new knickers in a plastic bag, they had found themselves in a subterranean bar where they watched a naked teenager shoot ping-pong balls from between her legs into a half-drunk glass of beer on the far side of a stage.

Ol and one of the other bodyguards entered the restaurant. Ol's frown disappeared when he located Kiry. Kiry waved them to a table halfway between him and the Australians. They immediately ordered steak and beer and recommenced their endless card game. One day, stuck in transit in an airport lounge, Ol had tried to explain the rules of the game to Kiry. But Kiry could not grasp the game's purpose. He had lost badly, an outcome that stunned Ol.

Beside Kiry's table stood a large, bubbling fish tank. He tapped the glass. A decorative school of fish veered away but a fatalistic lobster held his gaze. It looked healthy, but Kiry didn't think he could be bothered hacking into the hard shell of the tail, although he was tempted to send Ol to find Sok to do it for him.

'I want a plate of Singapore sambal prawns and a bottle of Moët.'

'An excellent choice,' the waiter said.

'Don't go skimping on the prawns. And I want a jug of cold water with lime, no ice.'

Kiry picked up a newspaper: 'Nhem Kiry is widely considered a puppet of the notorious Pol Pot, but one unnamed UN source also described him as a "savvy and dangerous political operator with his eyes firmly on the prize." On his first evening in Phnom Penh Nhem Kiry is scheduled to attend a private meeting with Prince Norodom Sihanouk before attending a cocktail reception being held in his honour.'

Kiry let the paper fall and closed his eyes. The champagne came.

'It says here I am made of wood,' Kiry said to the waiter.

'Oh no, sir, I don't agree. Not at all.'

'Neither do I. Wood doesn't bleed.'

The prawns and the rice came.

'According to this I have my eyes firmly on the prize,' he told the waiter.

'Oh yes, sir. I'm sure you do.'

The prawns were juicy and sweet. He ate them in a rush. His stomach was bloated but he finished the rice, as was his habit. He departed for his room with a stomach ache, which he cured with a glass of Glenlivet.

At 1 a.m., lying in bed, the lights dimmed, the television on CNN with the sound low, he remembered with a groan that he hadn't rung his wife.

*   *   *

Two weeks after he collapsed in the Núi Café, dispirited and nervous, and feeling thoroughly defeated, Ted encountered an officious customs officer at Adelaide airport. He ached everywhere and his

ankles were bloated with the bottle of shiraz he had drunk on the
plane to help smooth the transition from East to West. All he
wanted was to get processed and retreat to the suburbs before the
sun came up.

Although Ted's legs felt heavy as concrete, he shuffled forward
and forced a smile. He carried nothing illegal and he had passed
through such checkpoints thousands of times, yet he felt oddly
nervous. Perhaps, he thought, this customs officer was really an
intelligence officer. But then he admitted to himself, with a tinge
of regret, that ASIO had probably archived his file a decade or
more ago. Or worse, pulped it.

He declared a set of teak chopsticks. That didn't seem to help.
He removed his boots and declared the dried Mekong Delta mud
embedded in the tread. A gleam appeared in the customs officer's
eyes. He unzipped Ted's case and fingered everything – books,
papers, his giant unfinished manuscript on the life of Ho ('Great
man,' Ted couldn't help himself from murmuring), dirty underwear, sweat-stained shirts – as if rubbing the items might reveal
some criminal purpose. He found nothing incriminating: no
marijuana brick, no asylum seekers, nothing but a half bottle of
Mekong whisky, which he sniffed and returned. 'That's probably a
waterways hazard,' Ted said. The customs officer half-smiled but
said nothing, for which Ted was grateful: he wasn't sure he could
survive any banter about having your life in a suitcase.

Ted paused before the doors that led to the arrival lounge,
unfolded a photograph and studied his family: his middle-aged
son, Michael, and his daughter-in-law, Anne. He was determined to
avoid the embarrassment of walking straight past them.

Michael was a lawyer. Ted knew that much. Anne too, apparently. Ted didn't much trust lawyers but he was willing to give them
a go.

The doors opened. Ted stepped onto concrete-hard carpet and
into harsh light. Michael walked towards him. Ted identified his
single arrowhead eyebrow from the photo, but mostly he recognised him because they looked so alike. Michael smiled broadly,
letting his mild gingivitis show.

Ted knew immediately, and with relief, that this encounter
would not resemble the time Mary had brought Michael to India.

He couldn't remember now what he was doing in Bombay or why he had imagined it was a suitable place for a family reunion; he supposed it was something about last chances. Four years old, Michael had leaned against his mother, folded his arms and stared at Ted as if he had stolen his lunch. When the train had pulled away, leaving a large and attentive audience on the platform, he screamed, 'You told me that my daddy was handsome.'

The last time I'd seen Michael was in London in '69. It must have been July because we watched the moon landing together. I thought that would be a bonding experience, father and son seeing history unfold before us. How wrong I was.

What was Michael: twenty, twenty-one? Maybe older, but he seemed like a boy still, all earnest and awkward and shy. He was on one of those year-long sojourns to England that Aussie youngsters – at least the ones with cashed-up parents (that's his mother I'm talking about!) – are obliged to undertake. They still do it to this day. What's the point? None that I can see, other than to keep faking some ludicrous link with the 'old country' (old and senile, I say) and to help Australians pretend that the Yanks don't own us.

Michael was studying at some university: one of the posh ones. Or was he working at a law firm by then? Anyway, I made a huge effort to go and see him in his tiny little room. Postponed a trip to Moscow, even. I bought a television for him (it cost a bloody fortune) and lugged it down a flight of stairs all by myself. And we sat there, me drinking beer and him nursing a glass of white wine, watching the Americans claim the moon as their own. But just as Neil Armstrong was delivering to the world his 'one step for mankind' line, his foot hovering over the surface, something went terribly wrong and he floated, like a balloon, up into the air and out of sight. 'What's he doing? What's happening?' the television commentator cried out. 'Armstrong is flying through the air like a bird. Is that right? Is that how it's supposed to be? What the ... He's gone, he's gone, Armstrong's gone.' He was, too: never to be seen again, although if you believe the conspiracy theorists he defected to the Soviet Union.

Poor Buzz Aldrin didn't know whether to launch himself off in pursuit of Armstrong or to take advantage of the accident. And, of course, he didn't have a line of his own ready to deliver. So Buzz stood clutching the ladder, and by the time he finally took that famous step – having finally thought to shout out 'This step's for you, Neil, and for all who came before you' – all hell had broken loose on Earth and nobody really noticed. So he stuck his flag in the sand and he hopped back on board and he helped carry the empty coffin at Armstrong's funeral.

In Michael's tiny basement, watching all this unfold, I fell off the couch I was laughing so hard. 'America the brave,' I cried out. 'America the bold. America the innovative. God bless America the bloody useless.'

But Michael was staring at the television screen, his eyes moist, his lips quivering.

'Come on, mate: you reap what you sow in this world,' I said.

'Grow up, Dad,' he replied. He grabbed his coat and swept out the door and up the stairs, leaving me, like Buzz, staring about and terribly confused as to what had just happened.

That time in Bombay was the last time Ted ever saw Mary. She decided that nine months of cohabitation spread across seven years of marriage wasn't worth the fuss. And she decided that Ted thought so too, except he was too lazy to call it off. Decades later, Michael rang Ted to tell him that Mary had died. She had gone to the doctor to get her cholesterol checked; three months later she was dead of liver cancer. Ted was on holiday in Russia and Michael had a dreadful time locating him. Ted clumsily expressed his sympathy but the truth was – why deny it? he asked himself – that he had to pause and think before his throat tightened and sadness took hold.

Grateful that Michael was not going to lecture him on the responsibilities of fatherhood, Ted dropped his bag on Michael's toes and, surprising himself, lowered his head onto his shoulder. Michael wrapped an arm around him and said, 'Hello, Dad.'

Ted sniffed his response.

'This is Anne, my wife.'

'Welcome to Adelaide,' Anne said. 'Welcome home.'

Ted nodded. Anne was taller than the photograph suggested. Her hair had shortened and turned auburn. Ted felt lucky that he didn't have to pick her out of a line-up.

'And our daughter, Leonara.'

'I'm so pleased to finally meet you, Grandpa. Dad's told me all sorts of things about you,' said a young woman. She kissed his cheek and Ted saw that she had Mary's wonderful clear eyes. 'I can't wait to find out if any of them are true.'

Ted finally spoke. 'Grandpa: bloody hell.'

'One thing: my name's Lea. If you ever – *ever* – call me Leonara I'll send the heavies around to rough you up.'

'The heavies?' Ted asked.

'The heavies!' Lea said ominously, then winked.

Ted felt stripped bare. All the props of his life, all the elements of the persona he'd cultivated so lovingly for decades, were useless now. Although he knew this moment had been coming for months, probably for years, it seemed like in an instant he'd lost the moniker 'Ted Whittlemore: radical reporter' and become 'Ted Whittlemore: grandpa.' He was too tired, and his limbs ached too much, for him to do anything other than submit to this new reality. He'd told Michael that he just needed a few weeks' rest and then he'd be on his way. But he knew it wasn't true.

They drove through wide manicured streets – there's so many straight lines, Ted thought despondently, it's so flat, so neat – to a suburb called Kensington and to a house with a four-sided veranda. Ted's home was the granny flat, out the back beyond the swimming pool. 'What, no granny?' he complained when Michael and Anne showed him through, but it was freshly painted and the bathtub doubled as a jet spa. Ted felt like Ho Chi Minh in Hanoi: with victory came retirement, a simple house by a lake, daytime strolls if his wonky legs permitted, weeding the garden, afternoon retreats to the bomb shelter (Ted, like Ho, found he often needed a post-lunch nap) and, Ted hoped, a steady trickle of devout visitors.

Ted adjusted as best he could to the relentless quiet, the remoteness of this city he'd fled as a nineteen-year-old. He soaked up the love and attention that Michael and Anne offered. They brought him food and clothes and brochures about healthy living for seniors. They introduced him to their friends and neighbours. Sometimes he ate meals with them in the house, sometimes he stayed in the flat and kept company with the newspaper and the radio.

But tired as Ted was, his new sedentary life was agony. Adelaide was about as far away from the action as he could imagine. He soon found himself faking cheerfulness for Michael and Anne's sake. He pretended not to mind that he could barely walk around the block unaided or that they meted out wine to him one standard drink at a time. He knew he was still breathing but he wasn't certain he was still alive. Some days he wanted to run at the walls of the granny flat and break every bone in his body so at least he could excuse himself this awful new do-nothing, be-nothing existence.

Ted found himself pining constantly for Lea, who two or three times a week blew through bearing library books and international newspapers and the oddest ideas about life. Each time, she brought a longneck of Coopers Sparkling Ale for them to share out of glasses Ted kept frosted in the top of his tiny refrigerator.

One sunny morning, a few months after he'd arrived in Adelaide, Ted and Lea sat on fold-up chairs in the shade of an oak tree watching Anne pull weeds from the herb garden.

'Did I ever tell you about the time Simone de Beauvoir mistook me for Bob Menzies?' Ted said.

'Come on, Grandpa.'

'What do you mean, come on?'

'I just don't believe you. I doubt that de Beauvoir would even have known who Menzies was.'

'All right, all right, it was Anäis Nin. We were friends. The best of friends, if you take my meaning, and ... and ... and ... '

'Grandpa? What's wrong? GRANDPA?'

Suddenly Ted could barely breath. His head felt so heavy that it flopped forward. His chin bounced off his chest. He clawed at his face and opened up a cut on his cheek. Then everything went black.

When Ted regained consciousness he was lying in the dirt (the grass grew sparsely under the oak tree) with an oxygen mask over his nose and mouth. An ambulance officer hovered over him. Ted wanted to tell her that she was pretty even if she was dressed like a man. He wanted to tell her that the smell of her latex gloves aroused him. But Anne, who was holding his hand, said, 'Don't try to talk now. Relax, everything's going to be fine.'

Anne had painted a look of reassurance on her face: trust me, her crinkly eyes said, I know what I'm saying. But she was the worst liar Ted had ever come across. He knew he was in trouble. He felt as if his illness was sweating out of every pore in his body, covering him in a sticky layer of agony. The heat in his head was excruciating.

Lea didn't believe Anne either. As Ted's vision returned fully, he saw her crouched behind Anne, her face as pale as flour. He reached up and pulled the mask off long enough to say, 'Get yourself a drink of water, love, and have a bit of a sit down.'

Ted stayed in hospital for a week, educating the hospital staff in the evils of napalm, even convincing one intern to read up on it to see if it might be the cause of Ted's myriad afflictions. Then he packed a small suitcase of clothes, a box of books, his Ho manuscript, a 34-centimetre television set, a ream of clean paper and an electric typewriter. Michael delivered Ted via the wheelchair access doors to Room 17 of the Concertina Rest Home. Ted considered kicking and screaming in protest but he didn't have the fight for it. And he knew he wouldn't have fooled anybody, least of all himself.

1992

A few weeks after the crowd nearly killed Nhem Kiry, he returned again to Phnom Penh. This time he stepped from the chartered plane onto a set of aluminium stairs. Below him, standing at the end of five feet of red carpet, stood Roberto Gallasi, an Italian career diplomat. Gallasi's right shoe covered up a small perfect circle which allowed the carpet, when it wasn't serving as a welcome mat, to double as a practice putting green.

Kiry had met Gallasi before. He thought that he was adept at standing on the fringes of cocktail parties, shuffling his feet and looking lost but all the while listening intently and taking mental notes. He was, Kiry thought, a great deal better than most of the UN fools he had to deal with.

The two men shook hands and agreed what a fine thing it was to meet again. Gallasi's palm was sweaty, his face a mass of tiny red dots. His white shirt was creased and sodden. Its top two buttons were askew, revealing a hairy black and grey chest, pink skin and a silver crucifix. The ornament looked so heavy that Kiry wondered how the poor man kept his head upright. The power of prayer, he supposed. Gallasi's wedding ring bit deep into a swollen finger. Grey trousers – polyester? Surely not, Kiry thought – clung to his thighs. An abandoned necktie spilled from his trouser pocket.

In honour of Italy, Kiry considered dropping to his knees and kissing the ground. While watching the television news he'd seen the Pope do it on his arrival in Africa, although Akor Sok claimed that he was demonstrating some new Catholic birth-control technique. But, Kiry thought, what if his lips stuck to the tacky tarmac? What if he was forced to crouch there, enduring the roar of the planes ferrying all those foreign soldiers in to keep the peace? What if he was still there when the same soldiers departed with the undignified haste that invariably accompanies Westerners being shot at?

'Welcome to Phnom Penh,' Gallasi told Kiry in Calabrian-accented French.

'*I* welcome *you* to *my* city,' Kiry said. 'But I had hoped that the peacekeepers would have been fully deployed by now. I want to emphasise how displeased I am. What justification can there be for the delay?'

'Yes, you are no doubt correct. The wheels of world government do indeed turn slowly.'

'I have known them to turn backwards,' Kiry said. He gave the Italian's elbow a quick massage, implying that he trusted him like a brother. 'But if they don't begin to turn faster then there may well be no peace left to keep.'

'I venture to say that these things are complicated. But might I respectfully suggest that you speak to my superiors with regards to the amended timetable for troop arrival.'

'Yes, yes. It is an issue for tomorrow,' Kiry said, allowing Gallasi to lead him to a waiting car.

'But please understand that the whole Comprehensive Settlement is predicated on the Supreme National Council being able to meet in Phnom Penh. You will be safe here ... this time.'

'For that to be true you must deploy the peacekeepers without delay. And not just in Phnom Penh. The people still need protection from the Vietnamese aggressors or they will not be free to vote as they choose.'

The motorcade – a car for Kiry and Gallasi, minivans for Kiry's entourage and luggage – moved through Phnom Penh without incident. As the two men chatted about where to get the best pizza in town – 'Everywhere, the crusts are too thick,' Gallasi complained – Kiry felt safe. The situation simply did not allow for any more lynch mobs.

'If I may say so, I feel that you and I are of one mind on many issues,' Kiry said. 'I sense that we are kindred spirits.'

Gallasi looked slightly alarmed. 'Well, no doubt we share a desire for peace.'

'I sense that you have seen a great deal of how the world really works and that you understand the root causes of suffering and hardship for the oppressed peoples of the world.'

'Well, I like to think so. Although I would perhaps suggest that the expression "less privileged" – rather than "oppressed" – better reflects the progress and the positivity of human history.'

'In my opinion, only privileged people are free to dismiss the word "oppression."'

'Please, I intend no offence. I meant only that I believe life is always improving, slowly but inexorably.'

'May I tell you a story about being "less privileged"? One day in 1974, in Takeo Province in the south of my country, in our Liberated Zone, in an era during which we were supposedly good friends with our Vietnamese brothers, three of our young freedom fighters came across a Vietnamese patrol. Our poor Kampucheans offered to pool their meagre supplies and the Vietnamese said, "Yes, let us eat together but, first, let us share tea." The Kampuchean boys ran about and collected wood for this purpose. "We are sorry but we have not found rocks big enough to rest the teapot on. What do you suggest we do?" they asked the Vietnamese captain. "The solution is so simple that I cannot believe you did not think of it yourselves: perhaps you are stupid? Well, no matter: before we make our tea we must finish the day's work. Will you help us? I want you each to dig a hole, not too far apart, deep and narrow," the Vietnamese captain said – I will not identify this captain, diplomatic niceties do not permit it, but suffice to say he is now a prominent figure in Hanoi.

'The Kampuchean lads assumed that the holes were to bury ammunition. They eagerly commenced digging. They worked very hard and soon finished the holes. "Just stand in your holes so we can check the depth," the Vietnamese captain said. As soon as they did so the Vietnamese soldiers began shovelling dirt into the holes. When the three Cambodians were buried all the way to their necks, the Vietnamese soldiers piled the wood in the space between them. While the naïve young patriots looked at each other and finally sensed trouble, the Vietnamese captain lit a match and dropped it between them. Soon the woodpile was ablaze and as the Cambodians burned alive the Vietnamese captain balanced a pot on their heads and said, "Do not spill my tea." Soon the kettle boiled and then all was quiet.'

Gallasi unfolded his arms and scratched his chest. 'But I have heard this story before. It is a fable, yes?'

They set off along the corridor. After a few metres, Ted began to fake a limp. He didn't want to disappoint her by seeming too healthy and, besides, it was a pleasure for him to have a lady on his arm, even one dressed like a Hiroshima wasp. But suddenly Ted's other leg turned as heavy and fixed as concrete. By the time they reached the far end of the corridor he was panting. The publisher put her arm firmly around his waist and steered him to the hand-rail.

The sunroom was empty except for Marjorie Tabbener, who said to the publisher, 'Hello, Lea.'

'Hello, dear,' the publisher said, accepting a sugar-speckled jube despite Ted's chivalrous warning: 'Don't chew it.'

'How's the photography going, sweetheart?'

'This isn't Lea, Marjorie. Lea comes on Wednesdays.'

'No. That can't be right,' Marjorie said. She squinted at the publisher, then abruptly dropped her head as if in prayer.

Ted eased onto a two-seater and patted the cushion beside him but the publisher chose to sit opposite on a straight-backed chair, allowing her a view of the rose garden.

'Well, now,' she said. 'Your name is still quite well known in Australia—'

'Quite well known? Only quite well known?'

'Still quite well known, at least amongst the older generation.' She handed Ted a paltry advance cheque. 'It'd be ten times as big if you'd been a cricketer.'

The publisher paused to extricate the jube from her back teeth with her tongue. Ted watched her neck muscles contract as she forced the whole thing down her throat. She coughed once, then said, 'I'd like you to call it *The Confessions of Edward Whittlemore*.'

'You make it sound like I've got some explaining to do.'

'I certainly hope so. I want you to spill the beans on yourself. What did you get up to on all those trips to Russia? And did you really write propaganda for the North Koreans?'

'That wasn't me. That was Wally Ball. And Wally wasn't into propaganda. He told the truth.'

'Ah, yes, Ball, what's the goss on him? Was he really KGB? That's the sort of thing I'd like you to go into. Was Ho Chi Minh gay? What was Mao like? As a leader, certainly, but also as a man? Did

'A story based on true events.'

'I must confess I find nothing constructive about it.'

'I am illustrating a point.'

'With the greatest respect, I do not think it helps your cause to tell it.'

'Perhaps. But the Vietnamese remain in my country in vast numbers. Of course, you cannot agree with me out loud, but I think you know that Vietnam's desire to conquer continues unabated. But when I express concerns – and I have specific, documented complaints – the world turns away from me and mutters "xenophobe." So why not tell my fable, as you call it?'

They sat silently now as the city traffic thickened. Too late, Gallasi realised they were passing Kiry's villa, where two months earlier the mob had beaten him. The driver slowed behind a pack of Hondas, giving Kiry a clear view of the bolted gates, the boarded-up windows and the graffitied walls.

'My apologies,' Gallasi said. 'It was thoughtless of me to take this route.'

'Yes, yes, apology accepted,' Kiry said. He folded his arms and stared out the window. 'The past is gone. Just to be in Phnom Penh again, I feel as if I am waking from a coma and that my skin is discovering sunlight all over again.'

They pulled into a quiet compound which sat in the shadow of the Royal Palace and was protected from the world by tall white walls and an entrance with a manual boom gate and a sentry box.

'Is this it?' Kiry said.

'Yes, Your Excellency. I very much hope you will find it satisfactory.'

'Oh dear. I'll be able to hear Sihanouk snoring. And fornicating,' Kiry said in Khmer to the driver, who laughed. Gallasi, who only knew two Cambodian phrases – 'Do you sell red wine?' and 'Can I smell it first?' – grinned and nodded.

Gallasi rushed around to open Kiry's door. Kiry set off across the sparse garden towards the main building, a two-storey colonial mansion behind which several squat buildings lay. When Gallasi made to follow, Kiry turned and said, 'This is all most agreeable. Thank you again.'

'But I haven't shown you inside yet.'

'I would be most grateful if you would collect me in time for tonight's reception at the Royal Palace.'

'Very well.'

The garden was sparse. There was a green tinge on some areas of the ground, several mango trees and a pond that was home to a family of enormous catfish. A gardener, raking dirt, was watched by several security guards. A single lost duck, desperate for a swim but petrified of the catfish, wandered about aimlessly.

Kiry greeted the gardener, who bowed so low that he needed help getting up.

'Please feel free, Uncle, to take that duck home for your family's dinner,' Kiry told the gardener, whose hands shook with what Kiry felt sure was gratitude.

Today while I was eating my prescription breakfast – raw muesli with cashews and sun-dried prunes and something called lecithin, all of it softened (that's overstating it) with soy milk – I saw a photograph of Nhem Kiry. He was standing on a carpet at Pochentong airport, shaking hands and smiling with some bloke from the UN. Kiry had hold of the other bloke's elbow with his spare hand. Poor bastard probably never even saw it coming: he'll get grief for weeks about being so nice. I almost feel sorry for him.

If the photo is anything to go by, Kiry is ageing gracefully. The shit. He looks fit, wiry. He could have been a boxer if he wasn't such a coward. He's still got that wavy hair and it doesn't look like there's any grey: that's thanks to a bottle, probably.

It's so unfair. How come he's still in the centre of the action? I should be feted in Phnom Penh. He should be here at the arse end of the Earth trying to avoid going to bingo and mulling over whether for lunch tomorrow to eat the ham steak with pineapple rings or the lamb's fry with bacon.

*   *   *

Ted shook hands with the woman from the publishing company. He didn't understand modern women at the best of times but this one petrified him. She had shimmering black hair and matching eyelashes. She wore red-framed glasses, a black shirt set off by a red

bra strap, a red skirt, black stockings and red shoes with thick black heels. She gripped a bulging black leather briefcase.

They stood in the foyer of the Concertina Rest Home – 'Our shopfront to the world,' as Ted once overheard the CEO describe it to a politician, an ex-trade unionist with gouged wrinkles, sculptured white hair, aftershave perspiration and hands that slapped men on the back and women on the arse. The pollie had come to open the revamped high-dependency wing. After he cut the ribbon and pledged his government would solve all problems geriatric (he stopped just short of promising to cure old age), he spent twenty minutes pretending to drink tea and calling everybody either 'love' or 'mate.' Ted circled but the politician avoided him with such finesse that Ted soon realised that he was doing it deliberately. He wasn't offended. He knew that free-market lefties had to be careful who they fraternised with. And he was quite chuffed to discover that he still had a noxious reputation.

The publisher was not diverted by the Concertina Rest Home's soothing apricot-coloured wallpaper or by the row of watercolour vistas on the far wall: wildflowers, vineyards and treeless green hills curved like buttocks. Neither was she lulled by the lavender-soaked air, which masked the smell of antiseptic and boiled broccoli. She focused exclusively on her task, which, so far as Ted could tell, was to ensure that he did not collapse and die in her presence.

She steered Ted to an ergonomic couch. 'Do you need to down? Here, take my arm, ease yourself down here. Are you right? ARE YOU COMFORTABLE?'

'I'm not deaf.'

'No, of course you're not. I'll sit over here, shall I?'

'No, no,' Ted said, lifting himself off the couch with difficulty don't want to conduct my business in full view of the front Geraldine – over there, answering the phones – already know much about too many people. Come this way. I thought w sit in the sunroom.'

'Well, I don't know.'

'Or we could go to my room.'

'The sunroom sounds pleasant, very pleasant indeed. it's not too far away.'

'Why don't you take my arm?'

Kissinger really have a crush on Pat Nixon? And I'd like a full chapter on Pol Pot.'

'But I never met Pol Pot. I never even laid eyes on him.'

'Are you sure?' She shuffled her notes, peered at a page. 'It says here that the two of you were quite close for a time.'

'Absolutely not. Of course I met some of the Khmer Rouge in the early days. The very early days, before they turned bad. Bun Sody was my friend.'

'Bung who?'

'Bun Sody. He was murdered for being such a fine fellow. And it's a matter of public record that I knew Nhem Kiry.'

'Never heard of him.'

'I never really warmed to him, though. He was too pious for my taste.'

'Can you write about Pol Pot by writing about these others?'

'Of course,' Ted said, holding tight to the cheque. 'And I did know Kissinger. And Ho Chi Minh. And Mao. And Brezhnev. And Castro.'

'All right, then.'

Marjorie shifted in her seat and let out a long slow fart. Only when she opened her eyes did she remember that Ted and the publisher were in the room. 'Oh my,' she said, hauling herself out of the chair. With surprising purpose, she turned on her flat-soled shoes and bolted.

'I also intend to offer my views on the United Nations peace plan for Cambodia: why it's a sham, why it's bound to fail,' Ted said.

'Oh no, you—'

'*No?*'

'You don't want to write something that might be proved wrong two weeks after it's released. Or worse, something that's out of date. Remember, you're not writing journalism anymore: you can't change your facts day in day out.'

'But I've got important thi—'

'Really, I do think it would be best if you concentrated on the past. Focus on the juicy stuff. Is it true you had an affair with Martha Gellhorn?'

'Me and Marty? I'll never tell.'

'That's a pity. But you used to be quite the ladies' man, right?'

'Used to be? *Used to be?*'

Ted tried to wink but the whole side of his face contorted. The publisher eased her knees together and lifted her shoulders slightly.

'Of course, and I realise this might be painful for you, I want you to include a chapter on your journalistic philosophy.'

'I'd rather not.'

'People like that sort of thing these days. And in your case, of course, it's essential: you'll never get away with it if you don't justify your personal politics.'

'My ... justify, what do you mean, *justify*? What do you mean, *get away with it*?'

'You'll have to explain your attraction to communism. You'll have to offer some sort of defence. That's the whole point of the book, obviously.'

'I'll tell you what I told Lewis Dellmann when he wanted me to write a philosophical appraisal of the American War in Vietnam: I don't do philosophy. I chase stories.'

'Oh, I had no idea you knew Dirty Dellmann. That's a stroke of luck. And there's your hook: you can reflect on the terrible trouble he had abandoning Stalinism, despite everything, and compare it with your own slow awakening to the truth.'

'My slow awakening?'

'To the truth, yes.'

'But what if I'm still asleep?'

She stared at Ted, aghast, and then she smiled for the first time since she'd put the jube in her mouth.

'Oh, Edward, are you? Are you still asleep? But that's simply wonderful.'

I'm famous, infamous really, for my reporting on the American War in Vietnam (as anyone who knows their history calls it) and on the Cambodian conflict. But before Indochina came Korea. My first war exposed me to the simplicities of the world and to the reality that, for men and for nations, a bare-faced lack of integrity can be a great asset. The whole event seemed like a badly organised agricultural fair – confused exhibitors, animals roaming free, far too many loud speakers – but I suppose that's only because I had no idea what was really happening. When I wasn't crippled by fear, I spent my days faithfully recording whatever moments the authorities allowed me to see.

I was barely trained: my editor, Clarrie Jenkins, had waved me off with this advice: 'Commie propaganda is a woman, my lad, a woman with red lipstick. Need I say more? And don't go getting killed. If you die you become the story and that's sloppy reporting.'

So I did what I believed to be the right thing. I took UN transport to set-piece battles. I attended official news conferences as if my life depended on it. I scribbled down the creative interpretations and the bare-faced lies of officials and I wired them home. I called absolutely everybody 'sir.'

I was deeply impressed with myself.

My smugness – not to mention my view of the world – came crashing down during the drawn-out peace negotiations of 1953. At first I got into a good routine. I went to the daily news conference of the UN spokesman. I copied down what he said, his complaints and expectations, his forlorn hopes, his artful alliteration. I took him at his word because he was negotiating peace, a laudable aim after all, and because I understood that he was the sort of person who Clarrie considered sound. Besides, my mother raised me to respect authority.

One day, behind the shed that was the foreign correspondents' bar, I stumbled upon a different news conference. It was being held by the legendary Australian journalist Wally Ball – 'Aussie Pinko,' as the Americans called him. Wal was a true rebel. He had reported the whole war from the North Korean side, offering up a wholly distinct version of events. Now he was offering a radically different version of the peace negotiations. I listened to him and I began to think that we had been watching different wars. From that moment my routine changed: first I attended the daily UN briefing and then I sought out Wal, who told me the truth.

Less than ten years my senior, Wal was a veteran. In 1945 he had taken the train to Hiroshima and broken the story of radiation sickness: A WARNING TO THE WORLD, his famous headline screamed.

'You know what?' Wal told me. 'I got back to Tokyo and the Americans still called me a liar. Since that day, I haven't taken anybody's word for anything.'

'I asked Clarrie about you. He says you're not a reporter. He says you're a partisan, a propagandist.'

'He's right, mate, but think about it: I'm hardly alone. Clarrie's a partisan, too, because he believes, at least he tries his hardest to believe, that *there's a difference between independent experts and Western apologists. You're a partisan, too. Listen, here's the truth: objectivity exists so reporters can claim they don't have opinions and so people who only have a spare fifteen minutes a day can pretend that they are informed. Balance is for acrobats. Look around you: do you see anyone, can you find me one person, who is neutral? The only difference is that I don't mind admitting it.'*

Filling in gaps – that's what Wally Ball did. And that's what I've devoted my life to doing, upending headlines and seeking out the treasures – the hard and awful truths – that lie underneath. The world is constructed by – no, the world has become – a series of episodes, snapshots, clichés, slogans, triumphs and tragedies, assumptions. Everybody has their own history of the world, their own personal history. Everybody has their own history of Angola, of Korea, of Iraq, of Vietnam, of every war zone and holiday getaway on earth.

Take Cambodia. Your history of Cambodia is probably a few lines, regurgitated simplicities and absolutes, boxed-in summaries written by play-by-the-rules journalists. You might be content that these 'simple facts' tell you everything you'll ever need to know. But my history of Cambodia has lasted a lifetime. I have tried and tried to explain the messy truth but you have hugged your headlines and let your minds stray. Shame on you.

All my life I took sides, just like Wal taught me. You think you're being neutral by living in a world of headlines? Think again: you have as much blood on your hands as the leader of any army.

People say I chose to support communism. But all I really ever did was ally myself with the underdog. In Cambodia, in the 1960s, I believed in Sihanouk and, yes, I believed in the Khmer Rouge. How was I to know what Pol Pot's mob would become?

*　　*　　*

Ready to mingle, keen to be seen, Nhem Kiry arrived early at the International Conference on the Rehabilitation and Reconstruction of Cambodia. When he entered the room – a spacious hall in an exclusive Tokyo hotel – the crowd spread. Even his friends and allies stared at him with open contempt. Kiry had expected as much. It was obvious that the world was ganging up on the Khmer Rouge. But Kiry knew his mission.

Behind him Akor Sok hissed and moaned about their reception.

'Control yourself,' Kiry said.

'But—'

'We are the one clothed man who is inevitably shunned by the naked mob. But it doesn't matter anymore. Take your seat and wait for me.'

Kiry smiled at an Englishman, one of those officials who met him frequently in private but refused to shake his hand before witnesses. The Englishman bared his teeth like he was a dog then looked around to make sure his peers had noted his display of loathing.

Kiry gazed intently at Wang Jen-chung from the Chinese foreign ministry. He considered standing in front of Wang until he acknowledged him. After all, they had shared food and showed each other their family snapshots more than once. But then he decided that Wang, who was suddenly fascinated by his brogues, was only following orders. Instead, Kiry caught the eye of a Romanian fellow who had once said to Kiry, admittedly under the influence of vodka, 'You're just about the most impressive men I've ever met.' Today the Romanian shook Kiry's hand and said hello but declined to stop and chat.

Next Kiry entrapped General Tran Quang Hai from Vietnam in a staring competition. Eventually Kiry blinked and nodded his head in defeat. But he had played to lose. He hadn't found the general to be at all frightening. He was podgy and what teeth remained in his mouth were green. He squirmed and itched like a child in his business suit.

Then Kiry attached himself to a circle of delegates. He stood by as the Singaporean head of a Christian aid agency shook hands with the New Zealand minister for defence and international development, who squeezed the shoulder of the leader of the Mozambique delegation ('As if *they* have money to spare *us*,' Kiry thought) who offered to show the deputy director of the WHO the sights of Maputo when she was next in town. 'Yes, you must go. It's a fine city,' Kiry said. 'Make sure you visit the Bazaar Central. And the Museum of the Revolution is an absolute must.' The circle splintered, leaving Kiry standing alone.

The organisers placed Kiry next to Prince Ranariddh, Sihanouk's son, who sat next to Hun Sen who sat next to Son Sann of the KPNLF. The leaders all embraced. And Kiry raced across in front of the lectern to genuflect with such gusto before Sihanouk that even Sihanouk knew that Kiry was making fun of him.

The Japanese minister for overseas aid, Hiroshi Yamaguchi, beckoned Kiry to come to him. Kiry nodded, then turned and spoke to Akor Sok for a full minute before he approached Yamaguchi, who set about politely haranguing him.

'Please think hard about the merits of giving up your weapons. This is the only way for you now, I repeat, the only way.'

'Can you guarantee me that the Paris Agreements will be fully implemented by all parties? *Fully* implemented, do you understand? Because you know as well as I do that this is not yet the case.'

'This is a marvellous occasion for you to atone. To rehabilitate.'

'Atonement is irrelevant. I am about justice.'

'Please: might I announce that the Khmer Rouge have agreed to disarm? It would set a wonderful example for the remainder of the conference.'

'You may report what a fine city I think Tokyo is. Beyond that, what you ask is impossible.'

Yamaguchi sighed. He turned and walked to the podium and stood waiting for the room to settle and for Kiry to take his seat. Then he began to speak.

'This is a golden chance for all of us to do something concrete rather than to talk vaguely about a better future for Cambodia. Cambodians have suffered egregiously for many decades ... but especially in the mid to late 1970s. It is time for the international community to do what it can to help fix these problems. Today we talk of practical responses: the challenge of effective health programs, clean water, the eradication of land mines, the development of essential infrastructure. But as we all know, one of the Cambodian parties still refuses to comply with the disarmament timetable. That same party is not allowing UN personnel to access areas of land still under its control. Let none of us forget what is at stake here on a day when I ask the global community to affirm its commitment to Cambodia.'

Kiry leant past Ranariddh. 'What's the Japanese word for egregious?' he whispered in Son Sann's ear.

'I think it's *daisoreta*, but don't quote me on that.'

'I never do,' Kiry said.

'Stop playing around,' Prince Ranariddh hissed.

'Please don't concern yourself, Your Majesty,' Kiry said. 'We are four partners in peace sharing a joke. Surely that is good for business.'

'It's all very well for you, but after the election I expect to be prime minister.'

A hint of a smile appeared on Hun Sen's lips. He folded his hands neatly in his lap. Kiry took note.

'I grant you,' Kiry said, 'that a road built by Japanese engineers, with all the extra business for that new Australian brewery and for the brothels, is better than no road. Fine. Good. But Your Majesty, today is cosmetic. First the French, then the Americans, then the Russians, then the Vietnamese butchered us. Now they gang up to taunt us, while claiming they are helping us. We four sit here for their benefit; do not fool yourself that it is the other way around. In a few years' time, when our economy is still shambolic and our people are still impoverished, these people will tell us it is all our own fault because they gave us peace and, what's more, one day in Tokyo they gave us a great big pile of money.'

Ranariddh fidgeted. Son Sann's eyelids flickered – the stuffy room and his arthritis medicine were making him drowsy. Hun Sen licked the faint smile from his lips and assumed a neutral gaze. He looked like a schoolboy, Kiry thought: innocent and eager to learn. But he was as hard as a diamond.

'You want Cambodia to be like France or like America, Your Majesty?' Kiry said. 'That is impossible, I tell you, because the West has built its glory on the systematic abuse of the rest of us.'

'But still, today is a day for getting what we can,' Ranariddh said. 'Today we are in a shopping arcade with another man's Visa card. And we will get a great deal more for a great deal less if you tell them what they want to hear.'

'You may well be right, Your Majesty,' Kiry said.

As speeches came and went, as grand promises and fine intentions heavied the air, Kiry imagined that a cloud might form up in the ceiling, amongst the lights hanging from silver threads, and that a thunderstorm might wash all the hypocrisy away. Build new roads, someone said ... so Thai trucks can import vegetables, Kiry thought. Rehabilitate the agricultural infrastructure ... plant more rice. Take note of this malaria-modelling software ... some laboratory in Oxford wants its research funding doubled. Contribute to the easing of the global epidemic of anti-personnel ordnances ... there are already so many landmines in the ground that manufacturers are being forced into stockpiling: dig 'em up so we can plant some more. Improve sanitation infrastructure and engage in educational programs ... Cambodians shit into holes and wipe their arses with their hands and then wonder why they get sick. Improve basic literacy ... children should be able to read all about the meritorious work of the United Nations. Kiry sat seething, outwardly calm.

After lunch, a nuggety American man rose to speak. Franklin Faludi was a deputy to the deputy secretary of state, which Kiry supposed made him the most important – and definitely the loudest – person in the room.

Faludi began his speech by making what Kiry considered a spurious connection between literacy and nutrition and democratic change. He made no mention, Kiry noted, of blanket bombing or of the crimes of the CIA or of napalm. Then Deputy Deputy Faludi paused for effect, folded his prepared speech into a square and jammed it into his inside coat pocket.

'The time for airy-fairy chat is over. We all know that we are here today to repair the damage – to infrastructure, of course, but more so to the very fabric and to the collective psyche – inflicted upon the Cambodian people by the past genocidal behaviour of the Khmer Rouge, that same group who today do most to obstruct our efforts to bring a lasting and comprehensive peace to this country.'

'I'm all in favour of exuberant fundraising, but this is too much,' Kiry whispered.

'Don't do anything rash,' Prince Ranariddh said.

Kiry let out a full-throttled yawn. He swivelled in his chair. 'It's true what people say,' he told Sok loudly. 'Americans do make the best evangelists.'

After Faludi finished, Sihanouk rose to speak. Emboldened by the American, his whole body was so energised that his movements became jerky. His face shone: too much moisturiser, Kiry thought. From time to time he'd been guilty of the same crime himself (he knew he'd done it whenever Akor Sok came at him brandishing a damp towel).

'I love my beautiful, beautiful children, all eight million of them. And they love Sihanouk back, every single one of them. They have deep faith in his capacity to fulfil their every need, to keep them safe and warm. It is this love that keeps Sihanouk virile and keeps him searching for a peaceful and prosperous outcome to my country's woes. So let us face facts: it is impossible for us to meet the various demands of the Khmer Rouge. It is ridiculous for us to try to accommodate them because they hate peace. Mr Pol Pot, via his puppet-men, tells all of us – from the mighty United Nations of America to tiny insignificant Sihanouk – that we must do this, do that, climb a mountain, dig a hole, fly to the moon on an elephant. We try our hardest because we decide that we need Mr Pol Pot and his friends to achieve peace. Tee hee, can you imagine the irony? But all we want is peace so we say, "Thank you, Mr Pol Pot, we agree with everything you say. What a decent fellow you are. Handsome too." Then Mr Pol Pot's slaves put a screen in front of his mouth so he can laugh at us. And then he thinks up a new set of rules so he can accuse us of not keeping our promises. Don't misunderstand me: Sihanouk barely knows Mr Saloth Sar, who you know as Mr Pol Pot. But Sihanouk knows how Mr Pol Pot's people – his immaculately dressed lackeys – behave. Sihanouk has seen all this before and he doubts that we will ever be able to fix their bad behaviour because they cannot change and they do not want to change. They will talk sweetly and when that doesn't work they will start the killing all over again.'

The next morning Nhem Kiry woke at dawn and quickly packed. In a soft towelling dressing gown and with a plunger of sludgy coffee by his side, he shredded a dozen or so documents. He made a few phone calls, showered, dressed and waited.

Around 7.30 a.m., one of the conference organisers rang to speak to Kiry about seating arrangements. Kiry had Ol tell the organiser that he was busy speaking to Boutros Boutros-Ghali on another line.

At 8 a.m., Hiroshi Yamaguchi arrived in the hotel lobby for a pre-arranged meeting to try to broker a deal with Kiry about disarmament. Kiry sent Akor Sok down to tell him Kiry had slept in.

At 8.40 a.m., Kiry gathered his aides and his luggage and left his room. The entourage walked slowly through the lobby, Kiry ahead of the others, relaxed, arms clasped behind his back. He might have been looking for a soft patch of grass onto which to throw a picnic rug.

He paused when he saw Akor Sok sitting with Yamaguchi. When he had both men's attention he nodded once to Sok, who stood, shook hands with Yamaguchi and handed him a press release which was headed 'Nhem Kiry Rejects False UN "Peace" Plan.'

By 11 a.m. Kiry sat in the first-class section of a Qantas jumbo. Waiting for the rest of the plane to board, he sipped iced water and chewed Juicy Fruit gum: he was a little worried about his ears, which had been playing up recently, and not only when he flew. Some nights, while he slept, a thin stream of watery wax ran down his jaw and stained his pillow.

When Kiry had signed the Comprehensive Settlement – with a commemorative gold Parker pen that he gave to Ol, who carried it everywhere, even after it leaked and left an ugly blue stain on his favourite shirt – he had dared to imagine himself minister for foreign affairs in a coalition government. And then, one day – after Prince Ranariddh had tried and failed, after Hun Sen had crashed and burned – maybe even prime minister. But now? Now he was fleeing to the jungle as if it was 1967 all over again.

* * *

One damp afternoon in June, Lea drove Ted to the Cabbage & Slug, a traditional English theme pub that sat in an alley off North Terrace in the city centre. As she held the heavy wooden doors open for Ted, he recoiled, horrified, at the interior: imitation wood panelling, plush red carpet designed to hide ale stains and the blood of soccer hooligans, a framed copy of an eighteenth-century map of Lincolnshire, a red telephone box complete with an 'Out of Order' sign, and a portrait of W.G. Grace above the fake fireplace.

'What's this, Disneyland-on-Avon? Can't we go to a real pub?'

'It's got twenty-seven beers on tap,' Lea said. 'And my friends from the newspaper come here sometimes. They're all dying to meet you. Especially Tim.'

'I thought your boy's name was Randy.'

'Ralph, not Randy. And he's a man, not a boy. Tim's a colleague.'

'A colleague, eh? Is *he* a man or a boy?'

'He's a journalist.'

'I already don't trust him.'

'Well, I told him we'd be here. He said he'd try to drop in.'

Lea had chosen the Cabbage & Slug carefully. It had leather couches, firm yet springy. It had a disabled toilet at ground level. Although it was raucous at night, it was quiet in the afternoons, which, to Ted's dismay, he found he desperately needed. And it had a publican called Marcia, a shapely fiftyish brunette. Marcia inspired Ted to perch on top of a barstool, in contravention of several medical directives, so he could learn the art of pouring a perfect Guinness while simultaneously staring into her green-black eyes and then down her low-slung white tanktop.

'You know what?' Ted said to Lea, trying to ignore the deer-head trophy that kept watch over them. 'I don't think I've enjoyed a beer in my whole life as much as this one.'

'Terrific. Now how are your memoirs going? How about showing me some of what you've written?'

'No, I don't think so. Not right now.'

'That's what you said last time. You've got writer's block, haven't you?'

'Certainly not. I've never had writer's block in my whole life. I don't believe in it.'

'I don't believe you.'

'As if I'd lie to my own granddaughter. My own flesh and blood.'

'You know what you should do?'

'I'm sure you're going to tell me.'

'You should write whatever you want. If no one wants to publish it, that's their problem.'

'Enough: I'm writing the truth. The bloody awful truth, which is precisely the reason why you're the last person I want to see it. We're getting on so well and I'd like to keep it that way. I suggest you wait to read it until I'm dead.'

'But I can help you. I could ask you questions and that might help you remember things.'

'Remembering things is not my problem, love. I wish it was.' Ted sipped his beer and smacked his lips. 'Your dad wants me to talk to you about going back to law school next year. He's got it in his head that I might wield some influence.'

'Once I've got this "ridiculous photography diversion" out of my system?'

'I think that's the expression he used, yes. So let's agree that I lectured you severely but unsuccessfully for, say, half an hour. Sound okay?'

'Fine. But don't think I'm letting you off the hook. I want to see your memoirs.'

'I'm too busy right now.'

'Doing what?'

'Getting myself another drink.'

'You've hardly touched that one.'

'It takes forever to pour a Guinness. Trust me, I've seen it done.'

'It's a pity that you didn't know me when I was a baby.'

Ted reared back. 'Well, I'm truly sorry, love, but … Are you upset about that? You're not, are you? I chose to live a certain sort of life and there's no point getting all soppy about it now. Move on, girl, that's my advice.'

'It's not that. I was just thinking of the women you could have pulled if you'd had me to carry around as a baby.'

'Pulled? What do you mean, pulled? *Pulled?* I never would have used you in that way.'

'If you'd been around at all, you mean?'

'Exactly.'

'I was a cute baby.'

'I've seen the photographs. You were somewhat cute.'

'Maybe you should get a puppy.'

'I don't think the nursing home would be too impressed.'

'For the pulling power. And I read somewhere that old people—'

'Careful.'

'I read that old people find pets to be excellent therapy.'

'I don't need therapy. I'm not a bloody nutcase.'

'Don't try and wriggle your way out of it, Grandpa. You're dis-associating yourself from those aspects of your past that embarrass you. It's not healthy.'

'Disassociating myself? *Disassociating?* Do you think you'll ever recover from your education?'

'My point exactly: the last thing I need is any more of it. But look, Grandpa, from what Dad has been telling me—'

'You shouldn't believe a word he says. He's a lawyer.'

'He says you've spent your whole life upsetting people.'

'That's never been my intention. It's just been an added bonus.'

'Well, why stop now?'

'It's not that, it's—'

'You doubt your own beliefs. You've gone all timid.'

'*Timid?* You're joking, right? Just because I choose not to show you my draft.'

'Take America—'

'I've never been able to stomach the place. Why start now?'

'What happens if America stops doing all those terrible things you say they do? What happens to the world?'

'Peace and harmony and goodwill in our times.' Ted licked at the froth on his glass. He wasn't sure where Lea was taking this dis-cussion. She was setting him up and he couldn't follow her moves.

'Why aren't you married?' he said.

'Why aren't you?'

'A-ha. Got you. I—'

'Hey: you've got Dad's grin.'

'No, no, he's got my grin. I'm the senior partner, remember?'

'Well, whatever, no wonder you've irritated so many people in your life, if every time someone catches you out you flash that "I'm still smarter than you and there's nothing you can do about it" look.'

'Don't change the subject. I *was* married once, to your grand-mother, which is why you exist. What have you got to say about that?'

'I say you should see a therapist about your writer's block. And get yourself a puppy.'

'I say I'm getting us another drink.'

'I say that woman behind the bar is half your age.'

'I say you'll make a great lawyer.'

'I say that you should write your book as if you're telling *me* the story of your life.'

'That's the last thing I'll be doing. But, listen, when I die—'

'When you die? Oh, Grandpa, don't be piss-weak.'

'I'm just saying, when I die—'

'When you die.'

'Stop interrupting. When I die I want you to cremate me.'

'Me, personally? I'd really rather not. I might set the whole nursing home on fire. I couldn't live with the guilt.'

'When I die, have me cremated. Okay?'

'What you should do is arrange to see a funeral director. Lots of old people—'

'Whoa there.'

'Lots of people in the sunset of their lives are planning their own funerals, did you know that?'

'Excellent. Let's plan it now.'

'No.'

'I want the Internationale.'

'Not that you were ever a signed-up communist.'

'That's right, I wasn't. But I had a lot of friends, so I want you to sing the Internationale. Solo. Unaccompanied. And—'

'Do you want me to sing it in Russian? In Chinese?'

'Stop interrupting. I want you to get me cremated. I want you to take my ashes for a drive around the city. Then I want you to find a monstrously expensive sports car – a Ferrari, a Lamborghini, something like that – and pour my ashes into its petrol tank.'

'Can't we throw you off the end of the Brighton jetty?'

'You know how much I hate the ocean.'

'If you're lucky, you might float all the way to Vietnam.'

'I'll probably get eaten by a jellyfish. It's been happening all my life.'

'Very appropriate, too, seeing you're too scared to write your memoirs. Oh, there's Tim,' Lea said, waving at a young man in a navy-blue suit, his tie yanked down and his top button askew.

'Great.'

'Behave yourself, Grandpa: Tim knows all about you. He's a bit of a fan, so be nice ... Hi, Tim, how's it going?'

'Great, great. Hello, Mr Whittlemore, my name is Tim Jones. It's a great honour to meet you. A real highlight. Thanks for the opportunity.'

'G'day, mate. Pull up a pew. And call me Ted.'

'Excellent, excellent.' Tim took a tiny tape recorder from his inside pocket. 'With your permission, Ted, I thought we'd make a start today. We'll keep it informal of course, just a get-to-know-you chat. Then I'll do a bit of research and we'll get down to the nitty-gritty next time.'

Ted peered at Lea. 'What's the boy on about?'

'I'm sure I mentioned it, Grandpa: honestly, your memory is just shot to pieces. Tim wants to write a profile on you.'

'He wants to put my voice on that thing? No chance, girlie.'

'Come on, it'll be interesting. And good PR. And it might help you get going on your memoirs.'

'I told you, the memoir's going just fine.' Ted leaned forward and grabbed the recorder. 'You're welcome to stay for a drink, sonny. But I'll just keep hold of this for a while.'

'Grandpa: that's so rude.'

'Really? Sorry, lad, let me make it up to you. You look like a Heineken man, right?'

Breathing heavily, Ted dragged himself to the bar. 'Where's Marcia gone?' he said to the young woman who was serving.

'She's on her break. What can I get you?'

'A pint of Heineken and two pints of Guinness.'

'Are you okay? You don't look so good,' the woman said. She reached out to pat his arm but thought better of it and pulled back.

Ted knew for certain that she was flirting with him. She'd wanted to touch him but she was too shy. As she pulled the handles and poured the beers, the tip of her moist tongue appeared between her lips and her cleavage beckoned to him. Ted leaned as far across the bar as he could manage, clutched his side in pain and gasped, 'I ... just ... love ... your ... bahoonies.'

Reaching for the beers, he panted like a dog and then commenced a coughing fit, spraying an earthy mist all over the beer taps and the woman's singlet.

Lea grabbed Ted's elbow and yanked him towards the door. 'He's not well,' she told the woman. 'He gets so confused in the afternoons. It's very sad.'

'But what about the beers?' Ted said.

'Leave them.'

'I need to pee.'

'Not here, you don't.'

'Goodbye, Tom. We're leaving, I think.'

'Tim. I hope to see you again, Mr Whittlemore.'

'Call me Ted.'

'Bahoonies,' Ted yelled as Lea shunted him away, 'is an old-fashioned word for earrings.'

The door closed. Tim raised his eyebrows at the barmaid, who shrugged and dabbed her front with a sponge. Then the door opened and Ted's head reappeared. 'That's all off the record, Tom, if you don't mind.'

Lea's a good girl but she's got it all wrong. Do what you've always done, she says. But what I'm writing is completely new for me. I've never written a word of history in my life – the past is the past – and it's no fun trying now. I'm getting on with it, I'm making progress, but it's not my forte.

I've always written about the here and now. I've always dressed and shaved and gone out and witnessed some great event and then come home and written it up and then gone for a drink. But now I've got nothing to say about the present, unless I describe what Mrs Marsh ate for dinner last night or how no one ever visits Charlie Watkins or how Essie Burke takes eleven different pills every day only she's hoarding the little blue ones so she can do herself in before she goes gaga. I've got no idea what's been happening in Vietnam since I left. I can tell you that Hieu's wife has been ill but she's all right now; that Hanh and her husband have to move to Hanoi and don't want to go; that Tran's daughter is thinking of going to Moscow to study. It's not that I don't care about what's happening in my friends' lives. But it's not news. It's gossip.

1993

Ted Whittlemore was asleep in the chair by his bed when the phone rang. He came to on the ninth ring, his eyes blinking in the light. Just as he made sense of the noise, the ringing stopped. He folded his arms and adjusted the blanket that lay across his knees. He was cold, but if he put on a jumper he knew an acrid smell would rise out and shame him.

As he closed his eyes and settled, the phone started up again.

'Hello? Yes?'

'Ted? … Ted, buddy, is that you?'

'Speak up, for Chrissakes.'

'Ted, it's me. It's Cornell.'

'Michael? Is that you, Michael?'

'HEY BIG TED, IT'S CORNELL SPEAKING. CAN YOU HEAR ME?'

'Cornell?'

'It's me, buddy, it's me. Turn your hearing aids on … How are you?'

'I'm fucked, mate. Really rooted.'

'Hey, that's too bad. But, listen, guess where I am.'

'Jesus, mate, how should I know?

'Come on, guess.'

'Up Abraham Lincoln's nostril at Mount Rushmore?'

'Phnom Penh. Can you believe it? I got a junket with Senator Kemp's fact-finding mission. We went to Battambang for the election. You been to Battambang? Nothing but mud. Do you know Kemp?'

'I'm not sure. I don't think so.'

'He sure remembers you: something about you claiming he was on the payroll of Handby Electronics? They make bombs, buddy, ring any bells? No? Well, he's taken quite a shine to me, the senator.

I can't quite work out whether he's doing it as a favour to Daddy or if he's doing it to spite Daddy. Anyway, it's all expenses paid.'

'Lucky you.'

'You got that right. I gotta tell you, it's a beautiful thing, watching a whole nation discover democracy.'

'Apart from the mud.'

'I don't mind telling you, I stood there watching all them people lined up in their Sunday best and I wept. But listen, buddy, this whole country's a dump, even Phnom Penh. It's nothing like how you described it, I'll tell you that for free.'

'Well, it's been through a bit.'

'Hey, haven't we all. It still doesn't hurt to spruce yourself up when you're expecting visitors: put a clean shirt on, you know, comb your hair, maybe do the dishes, clean up the dog shit.'

'When's the last time you did the dishes?'

'That's not the point I'm making, now is it? So I've got a maid? So what? The dishwasher gets stacked three times a day and that's all that matters. I tell you, I'll be pleased to get home and get myself a decent feed.'

'I'd do just about anything for a plate of chicken amok.'

'Are you kidding? When they say it's chicken who really knows? I had a pizza on the main street last night. Awful. "Just because it's yellow doesn't make it cheese," I told the waitress, and do you know what she said? "You want happy herb? You pay extra?" "I don't want happy herbs," I told her. "I want pepperoni." But listen, buddy, how'd you like a job?'

'It depends—'

'How'd you like to write it up for me? Give me your impressions, you know, Big Picture, just the way you like it.'

'Of what, mate?'

'The Cambodian elections. Come on, Ted, haven't you heard? Prince Ranariddh won but Hun Sen wouldn't accept the result. So the UN made them both prime minister.'

'That's the stupidest bloody thing I've ever heard in my life.'

'Sihanouk's king again, only he's pissed off to France for medical tests, and the Khmer Rouge are licking their wounds. All in all, it's a damned fine result, I reckon. What do you say, buddy: give me a few thousand words on the whole brilliant mess.'

'Yeah, thanks but ... I don't really get what you're saying. Two PMs? Two? How does that even ... No, thanks mate, but I'd better say no.'

'Don't be hasty, buddy. Have you got some coffee there? Call room service. Take a moment to wake yourself up. I'm telling you that you can write whatever you want. I'm giving you complete editorial freedom. No swear words, mind, and no God jokes.'

'Why? Are you running for office?'

'My subscribers are very broad-minded, very open to new ideas, even to your brand of craziness, but there's only so much I can ask of them. Of course, I'll write a separate piece explaining, point by point, why you're wrong, why you're fundamentally misguided, but—'

'But you haven't a clue what I'm going to write.'

'Buddy, we both know that isn't true. So you'll do it, then?'

'No, mate. I'm a long way out of it now.'

'Bullcrap. Thirty years of insight. Misguided insight, of course, weirdo commie claptrap, but thirty years of it just the same. Come on, buddy. You know I pay well.'

'Mate, that sounds like charity.'

'Philanthropy: that's a whole different deal.'

'My son's helping me out now with the bills. I'm not sure I really need the hassle.'

'I'm paying for your experience, for your opinions. You're worth every penny. Give it a go at least, won't you? Think about it. In the meantime, I'll wire you the cash.'

This is surely the UN's finest hour. I say this because the recent election typifies everything about the UN's many years of abject failure towards Cambodia. Remember this: after Vietnam entered Cambodia and defeated the Khmer Rouge, who had tried to kill off Cambodia's whole population, the UN, in its wisdom, chose to punish Vietnam for invading Cambodia. They allowed the Khmer Rouge to regroup – hell, they more or less funded them – and so the war inside Cambodia carried on for another decade. Has there been a more awful sight in the last few years than Mr Nhem Kiry, as conniving a politician as I have ever met, once again strutting the world stage? The UN claims the Khmer Rouge are terminally weak, but I for one have heard it all before.

As for the election itself: what a shambles; what a joke. The UN does not care about Cambodian democracy. They care only that there was an election and that the Khmer Rouge did not disrupt it with violence. Now they can pretend that they – the UN, I mean – did a great job. Their equation is simple: election plus the façade of democracy equals Cambodia must now sort out its own problems. Including the Khmer Rouge. The international community has spent a fortune absolving itself from its shonky and bloody past practices. The UN is like a mafia assassin, cleaning up after itself. And now the poor, desperate, war-weary Cambodians will have to fend for themselves. And what's more,

Ted tried hard to give Cornell what he wanted. He forced a few lines out, but after that the page sat in his typewriter for a week. Every time he sat down to work his mind rebelled. But each time he turned away, regret washed through him. He desperately missed the cut and thrust of it all but he knew that a reporter with old news was irrelevant.

Ted had never worried about what other people thought of his journalism. In fact, he was honoured by the number of people – prominent people – who hated him. But now he recognised that he had nothing to say. Nothing new, at least. And so he stopped bothering to fill in gaps.

He knew he owed Cornell a letter, but he didn't want to explain himself. And the more he thought about it, the more he didn't see why he should have to, just because Cornell had done so much for him, just because he threw money around. He wasn't being generous. He just had too much of the stuff.

1996

'Do you need me?' Nhem Kiry asked Ta Mok.

'I have everything under control. If I can think of anything I want you to do, I will certainly call for you,' Ta Mok replied.

Kiry stood outside, under a tree, while Mok went inside Pol Pot's hut to tell him that Ieng Sary had taken a thousand or more troops and supporters and defected to the government, who had rewarded him by letting them take over Pailin.

Ta Mok and Pol Pot spoke for less than ten minutes. Pol Pot occasionally asked a question in his quiet, calm tone, but Mok did almost all of the talking. Kiry could hear their voices but could not make out what they said. When Mok emerged his mouth was set grim yet Kiry detected a sparkle of amusement in his eyes.

'That shook him up,' Mok said.

'Oh, for goodness' sake. The last thing he needs is shaking up,' Kiry said. 'Did you at least break it to him gently?'

'Gently? *Gently?* What is he, a baby duck? "Let me stroke you, dear duckling, while I inform you that everything you hold dear and have sacrificed your life for is crashing down around you. A terrible thing, terrible, what with you too lame to fly, but don't let's worry about it, don't be concerned, dear duckling, everything will be okay." No: I told him plainly. He would expect nothing else. Anyway, it doesn't matter.'

'Doesn't matter? How can you say that?'

'I will take a battalion and we will retrieve Pailin. And then I will have some fun with Ieng Sary.'

'I'm not sure that's wise.'

'I don't care what you think.'

For several hours after Mok delivered the news of Ieng Sary's defection Pol Pot stayed alone inside his hut. His young wife, Mea, spent the afternoon washing clothes at the river. His daughter,

Sisopha, old enough to know to make herself scarce but too filled with joy to be fussed by the tension, wandered around the village chattering to anybody willing to listen. Kiry walked about too, waiting for Pol Pot to call for him, trying to think about something other than the implications of these latest defections. He wished Kolab did not insist on going to the fields every day. He needed her and he could not imagine what point she thought she was making. He wished his daughters were not studying in Bangkok, buying clothes and eating Big Macs or however it was that they spent their time.

Sisopha and Kiry sat down together – she was bored, he was tired – close enough to Pol Pot's hut that they could hear him moving about inside. His movements had always been characterised by a slow evenness, but these days they were laborious and punctuated by worrisome pauses. The stroke, a year before, had affected his left side, a fact that Mok made a constant joke about: 'He's lost his left side, who would have ever imagined it after all this time? His left side: do you get it?'

'I understand. It's not funny.'

'He has abandoned the left and collapsed to the right, ha ha ha.'

Kiry had noticed that when circumstances warranted it, Mok could act as if he was gentle and kind, in amateurish but passable imitation of Pol Pot. But at other times he filled his followers with terror. And Kiry, too.

While they sat there, Kiry taught Sisopha to count to ten in French. She especially liked 'one.' She was running around in a circle with her hands lost inside her flapping shirtsleeves, calling out 'oughn, oughn' to great guttural effect, when Pol Pot appeared in the doorway of his hut.

He blinked in the harsh light. 'Hello, my sweet darling,' he said to Sisopha softly. As she ran to him and wrapped her arms around his legs, he wedged himself in the doorframe so that she would not knock him down. A month earlier he had slipped on a rock while washing in the river. It had taken two weeks for his swollen buttocks to return to their normal size. He still had a scab on one elbow, to which Mea administered an antiseptic powder twice daily. But the powder came from Tá Mok's supplies, and since he had started using it Pol Pot's hut was often overrun with giant red ants. Kiry suspected that its principal ingredient was castor sugar.

'What are you up to, little bird?' Pol Pot said.

'Oughn, oughn, oughn.'

'Oh my goodness. Are you a monster? Do you live in a cave?'

'Oughn, Pa, oughn,' she admonished him. 'Oughn, duh, twah, qwat-r-r-row ...'

'Very clever, my precious darling. Off you go now so I can talk to Grandfather Kiry.'

'Perhaps, Sisopha, you can go to Aunty Sisi and ask her to bring us ginseng tea,' Kiry said.

'Yes. That's what we need. Can you manage that, do you think?'

'Of course, Pa.'

Pol Pot motioned Kiry inside and onto a wooden stool on the plastic mat in the middle of the room. He sat on a straight-backed chair, the only one in the room.

'I have bottled water. Have one while we wait for the tea,' he said. 'My little girl is beautiful, but speed is not her greatest asset. So, for now, you will have water?'

'Thank you, Big Brother. Please let me fetch it.'

'Don't be silly. Sit. Sit, I say.'

Pol Pot did not walk easily but neither did he seem to be on the verge of collapse. He carried himself a few steps to a cardboard box with Nestlé stamped on its side that sat beside the wooden wall. He stayed bent over the box for so long, hands connected to a couple of plastic bottles, that Kiry rose to help.

'No, I am fine. No, I say,' Pol Pot said. He straightened and faced Kiry, one eye squeezed shut. 'It makes it easier to focus, some-times,' he said as he peered at one bottle, then the other. 'I always check, always: sometimes the bottles are filled with river water and the caps have been burned to the seals. Such unscrupulous behav-iour, all for the sake of a little profit. So sad.'

He sat, grappled momentarily with the seal on his bottle and then handed it to Kiry to open for him. Kiry drank silently. Pol Pot made sloshing noises and let out a tiny gasp when he swallowed too quickly. He righted his head and waited for the gurgling to cease.

'I suppose we must denounce Ieng Sary, him and his no-good wife and their cronies.'

'Mok has somebody attending to it, Big Brother. There is no need to trouble yourself with such details.'

'I want to trouble myself. Do not order me about.'

'I did not mean to, Big Brother. I just wanted you to know that Mok is preparing a formal response.'

'What good is friendship – a lifetime of friendship – if it does not last until death? Of what value is the history of a friendship, let alone the history of shared experiences, shared sacrifices? What good is—'

'Pa? Hello, Pa?'

'Hello, my sweet one. What is it? I am quite busy at the moment.'

'I brought tea.'

'Oh yes. Thank you, darling. Leave it by the door, that's a good girl.'

Pol Pot deposited the teapot on the mat. He took several deep breaths and said, 'Perhaps you wouldn't mind doing the pouring.'

'Of course.'

'But leave it to brew a minute or two longer, won't you? Unless you would prefer it weak?'

'I prefer it strong.'

'Good. Me too. You pour it when the time is right for you, then.' He paused. 'But, tell me, how are you feeling about all this business? Are you angry?'

'I am disappointed, Big Brother, but not angry. Not surprised, either.'

'Good. Anger is beside the point, no matter the depths of the betrayal. It serves no useful purpose, once an event has passed. And it clouds the mind. I prefer to try to understand.'

'I agree.'

'Somewhere on our journey, I think Ieng Sary became too attached to a life of comfort.' Pol Pot paused and sighed. 'But that cannot be the whole story, surely? A soft mattress, is that it?'

'I think he prefers a firm mattress. He has terrible trouble with his neck.'

'What a lot of carry-on for the sake of one man's neck. Why could he not endure the pain? Anyway, if he wants a firm mattress, he can get that here. My own bedding is as hard as concrete. An electric refrigerator, is that what he craves? A restaurant that serves frogs' legs, is that all he strives for now? After all we've been through, can he be reduced to that?'

'He's been preaching surrender, quietly, for two years or more.'

'Yes. I heard all that rubbish. I still have eyes and ears everywhere. He stopped believing that there was any point to winning. Should we have given him more to do? Paid him more attention?'

'Perhaps.'

'He missed the attention, don't you think? He missed being pompous. There's not much call for it around here.'

'I suspect he would like to retire to New York. He's always loved it there. I think they reward pompous behaviour there.'

'I was complimenting him when I called him pompous. You, also, can be pompous when the circumstances demand it ... Why did he have to take Pailin from us? Why didn't he go to China? Surely they would have granted him entry? Why not just slip away? Why did he have to take so many with him?'

'They were going anyway, I think. There are many more who want to follow, I suspect.'

'You are right. They were lost to us and we can do without them.'

'Big Brother, I wanted to tell you that Ieng Sary has taken Akor Sok with him.'

'But ... Surely not.'

'Recently I suggested that he give his motorbike back to the community. He wasn't happy. I suppose he doesn't have the stomach for the fight anymore.'

'You shouldn't blame yourself. You taught him well. He failed to learn.'

'He was so itching for the challenge when you first sent him to me. Do you remember? We sat in a clearing and he condemned Lon Nol because he thought that's what I expected. I told him to think big. I quoted Liu Shao-chi: "The average party comrade is far from possessing the great gifts and profound scientific knowledge of the founders of Marxism-Leninism, and most of our comrades cannot attain their deep and broad erudition in the theory of proletarian revolution. But it is perfectly possible for our comrades to grasp the theory and method of Marxism-Leninism, cultivate the style of Marx and Lenin in work and struggle, constantly heighten their revolutionary quality and become statesmen of the type of

Marx and Lenin, if they really have the will, take a really conscious and consistent stand as vanguard fighters of the proletariat, really acquire the communist world outlook ... and exert themselves in study, self-tempering and self-cultivation." I told him that I did not believe in fate any more than I believed that this life is predetermined by the last. I told him that there are key moments in a man's life: whether you grasp these moments or mess them up or carry on oblivious that they have even occurred depends on preparation and hard work and clarity of thought. It seems he never learnt that lesson.'

'Perhaps he learnt it too well. Tell me ... and be honest: are you sorry that you did not go too?'

'Of course not, Big Brother. I will never abandon the struggle. I will never surrender.'

'What do you still hope for?'

'Negotiation is always possible, I suppose. The world is full of rehabilitated politicians. Why not me?'

'And me? Could I be a future leader of a reconciled Kampuchea?'

'Perhaps not, Big Brother. Not directly, at least.'

'Not even if I change my name?'

'Don't tease me, Big Brother, it makes me sad.'

'But we are still a fighting chance, don't you think?'

'No, Big Brother. I am sorry to say that I believe we are as exposed as a monkey in a minefield.'

'Don't be sorry. I'm not blind. Not completely, anyway. I'm not stupid.'

'Mok wants to fight for Pailin.'

'Ha. Mok lives in a tiny world. It always involves war.'

Pol Pot rose unsteadily.

'Are you all right, Big Brother?'

'Sometimes I feel better if I stand up for a while.'

Pol Pot went to the Nestlé box and pulled out a bottle of Jim Beam bourbon. 'A gift from Mok. It came with the truck that brought his beer. He's *such* a kind man, isn't he? We will toast Ieng Sary, our old friend, and Akor Sok, your former protégé, and we will wish them as much luck in the future as they deserve.'

'Are you sure that's wise?'

'They deserve no luck at all. That is exactly what we will wish for them.'

'Is it wise to take a drink, I mean?'

'One sip won't kill me. And what if it does?' Pol Pot poured the liquor and handed Kiry an ample serve. 'Perhaps you should consider offering yourself completely to Mok.'

'Mok knows nothing of the world beyond the brothels in Aranyapathet. He's never set foot in Paris or Geneva. I doubt he could even find Washington on a map. I'm pretty sure he thinks Korea and China are one big country. And he lacks taste. He has the ugliest house in the whole country.'

Pol Pot smiled a black-gummed smile and held aloft his glass. 'To absent friends,' he said, 'and to friends we wish were absent.'

*　　　*　　　*

'In my day football was kick and catch, kick and catch. Handball was a last resort … like drinking your own urine on a desert island,' Ted said.

'Here it comes: "When I was a boy, blah blah blah,"' Lea said.

'Did you ever play?' Lea's colleague Bazza, a sports reporter, asked Ted.

'Oh, don't go asking him stuff like that, Bazza, it only encourages him.'

'As it happens, I did play for a few years. Showed some potential. But I had to choose between footy and seeing the world. I chose the world.'

'Yeah, yeah, but did you ever drink your own urine?' Lea said. 'Hold still, Grandpa.' She pinned an 'Official SANFL Photographer' badge to Ted's chest. 'There, you're legal.'

'In my day, when the coach told me to play at full-back that's where I stayed. I did not "run off" – that's the right expression, isn't it, that's what the TV commentators go on about? I never, not once, left my man and sprinted to the forward pocket as a loose man looking to kick a goal. That would have been sacrilege.' Ted paused and winked. 'Of course, in my life I've often been accused of being a loose man. But that's a whole other story.'

'Bazza doesn't need to hear your fantasies, Grandpa. Come on, let's go.'

Lea and Ted sat on low fold-up chairs, hard against the boundary line, careful not to obscure a beer advertisement that was painted on the fence. 'Are you comfortable, Grandpa? You'll tell me if you're not, won't you? Are you all right with your legs squashed under like that?'

'I'm fine. Don't fuss, love. Just do your job and pretend I'm not here.'

'Don't get too comfortable. We'll have to move in a little while. I prefer to watch the match from different angles. All right?'

'Fine.'

There was a smattering of applause and some good-natured heckling as the Port players came onto the ground.

'There aren't many people here,' Ted said.

'Three and a half thousand, maybe four: that's a pretty decent turnout these days, since the big league went national.'

Lea hung a camera around Ted's neck, a tiny silver box that Ted was disconcerted to find beeped like a kidney machine. It was a brand Ted had never heard of and couldn't pronounce. He pushed a button and a zoom lens unfurled itself. He peered through the viewfinder and was stunned by the magnification.

'Not bad,' he said.

'It's the latest,' Lea said.

'Even so, it's not bad.'

Lea brought out a camera with the biggest lens Ted had ever seen and screwed it onto a tripod.

'When I was in Vietnam and Cambodia I used nothing but a tiny little Canon Regulator. Did I ever tell you that?'

'I think you might have, maybe a hundred, a hundred and fifty times.'

Once the game started, Ted watched Lea working almost as much as he watched the game, which at ground level moved too quickly for him to follow. Mostly she stayed hunched over the camera, staring through the peephole. Occasionally she leant back and reminded herself of the bigger picture. Ted thought it was a whole lot of effort for the single photograph that would make it into the next day's newspaper.

'Cricket must be easier,' Ted said. 'At least you can rest up between balls.'

'Cricket goes on and on and on.'

'But if you did the cricket you could travel all over the world.'

Late in the first quarter, his knees aching, his roll of film all used up, Ted leant back against the fence, watching Lea. Hunched over her camera, staring through the peephole, she was as still as a sniper. He followed the line of her lens back onto the field. A Port player, tackled as he kicked, slewed the ball from the centre towards the wing.

Another Port player reached the bouncing ball first and soccered it straight towards Ted. A Port and a Norwood player sprinted after the ball. Close to the boundary line the Port player pulled up. But the Norwood player – a compact, hairy mass of muscle – realised too late that the ball would beat him out of bounds. He narrowly missed decapitating a boundary umpire and ran into the fence beside Ted, who ended up on his buttocks. The Norwood player gave Ted's shoulder a tap of apology as he stepped back onto the field. 'Well done, Scotty,' someone in the crowd called out. 'Keep at it. Show 'em who's in charge.'

Scotty pushed past several players and shoved the Port player who had soccered the ball. 'Hear the footsteps, eh?' Scotty yelled and shoved him again. The Port player collapsed as if he had been shot in the heart. He lay motionless. When he understood that the umpire would not award him a free kick he miraculously recovered. 'If you're gonna hit him, Scotty, make sure he doesn't get up,' someone in the crowd hollered.

Lea helped Ted get back onto his stool. 'Are you all right, Grandpa?'

'All right? I'm wonderful. This is what I came for, the biffo. I like that Scotland fellow. He should be playing in the national league.'

'He's too slow,' Lea said. 'Everybody says so. He says so himself.'

From the boundary throw-in, the Port ruckman dropped the ball in front of his feet. A scramble ensued. Scotty was the fifth man to jump into the pack. Ted couldn't imagine what he hoped to achieve other than to inflict more hurt. The umpire was about to halt play when, miraculously, the ball came free. A Norwood player, already running at full pace, scooped the ball up without breaking stride and wrong-footed a Port player, who turned and chased hard. After the Norwood player had bounced the ball twice, and as the Port player was about to catch him, he kicked. Ahead, a curly-headed lump of a lad, his imposing physique emerging from young fat, ran forward. He arrived too late to mark the ball but he crashed the pack, thumping his knee into the shoulder of one of his opponents. His fist connected with the ball, which fell at the feet of a tiny Norwood bloke who scooped it up, ran forward, looped a handball over a defender's head to a team mate who turned and kicked an easy goal.

'Good onya, Scotty,' a voice in the crowd called.

'Your goal, Scotty.'

Ted was perplexed. Gary Scotland was a hundred and fifty metres away, closer to Ted than to the goals. 'What's it got to do with him?' Ted asked Lea.

'Brilliant,' she said, leaving Ted no wiser.

By half-time Ted's legs were cramping. Lea had planned ahead. She settled him into a seat in the grandstand, fortified with a couple of cushions and a meat pie. She coerced a ground attendant to bring him a light beer – 'Only one, mind you!' – and, later, to help him to the toilet.

Ted was disappointed with his photos. He had tried to capture players kicking goals: impossible. He tried to convey how the lump of a lad – 'Destined for greatness,' Lea said – dictated the movement of every other player on the field, depending on whether he ran left, right or 'down the guts,' but his photograph revealed nothing other than distant statues standing motionless on the muddy, green-tinged field.

One of Lea's photographs – not the one of a smiling winner they put in the newspaper – was a revelation to Ted. It captured the moment when the pack of players formed directly in front of them, just after Scotty had leapt onto the others and at the exact moment that the ball came free. In the centre of the frame, emerging from limbs and torsos and flying green mud, was a hairy, tattooed arm, unmistakably Scotty's. The ball lay on a direct trajectory from his fist to the feet of his team mate who, running past, had swept it up.

'It's a brilliant photo, love,' Ted said. 'You should have it framed.'

So she did. She blew it up, inserted it in a silver frame and hung it on a wall in a café in Norwood. A businessman bought it for four hundred and fifty dollars. When Lea rang to tell Ted she was more excited than he'd ever known her to be.

'He asked me if I had any more,' she said, her voice quivering in triumph.

1997

The commotion woke Nhem Kiry. He lay in the dark, momentarily confused. But then he heard Son Sen's voice protesting his innocence. Kiry knew that Pol Pot had long suspected his defence minister of disloyalty. He knew what must be happening.

Kiry squinted at Kolab. She lay with her back to him, breathing evenly. He knew that she was feigning sleep. And who could blame her, he thought. The girls were somewhere else, as usual, at one of the border towns, or in Bangkok again. These days Kiry never knew exactly what they were up to but he was relieved that they weren't here for this.

He sat up, cross-legged. From the cluster of huts fifty metres away, he heard a soldier barking instructions. He heard Son Sen cry out, angry and desperate. Kiry closed his eyes and listened as Son Sen pleaded for his life, his wife's life, for the life of his elderly aunt, his soldier sons, his grandchildren, the youngest barely walking.

The executioners walked them down the path towards the road. When the voices grew more distant Kiry got up and stood outside his hut. He saw a flash of light. They shot Son Sen first, probably to shut him up. Then, one by one, they shot his family. Soon it was quiet. Kiry vomited in the doorway of his hut, wiped his mouth and then went inside and lay down.

'Why?' Kolab whispered.

'You know why. Because he has gone soft. Because he is treacherous,' Kiry said. 'He has been talking to Hun Sen about a possible ceasefire, completely undermining my delicate negotiations with Prince Ranariddh.'

'So you are in on this?'

'Certainly not. My hands are clean.'

'Are we next?'

'No, of course not,' Kiry said. 'Big Brother must have been certain in his mind that Son Sen was betraying him or he would not have done it.'

'So he deserved to die? And all of them with him? The children too?'

'I don't know. Probably not. But people die. It's a fact. My mother never got to celebrate the liberation of Phnom Penh. My brother died, so far as I know. My aunty died, cousins, friends. To focus on one family's death is to distort reality.'

'Don't lecture me about death. About killing.'

Suddenly the door of the hut burst open. Brandishing a torch, Ta Mok grabbed Kiry by the neck and shoved him up against a wall.

'This time he's gone too far! Too far, I say. He has no authority now. He has no right to choose who lives and who dies.'

'Please, Mok, you're hurting me.'

'Did you know this would happen? Did you? Answer me: DID YOU? He tells you everything, he's always asking your opinion, he consults you before he eats, before he dresses, before—'

'Of course I didn't know. I was asleep.'

'It's time he learnt who's in charge around here,' Mok said. He shoved Kiry onto the bed. 'He's a spent force, no matter how many idiots he kills.'

Mok left, screaming at the night.

'In the morning, first thing, you must go away,' Kiry said to Kolab. 'Go to Bangkok. I will tell Mok that you are ill again.'

'What's going to happen? What are you going to do?'

'I don't know. Maybe nothing.'

A few days later Nhem Kiry, Pol Pot and their small entourage fled Anlong Veng. Before dawn they pushed a four-wheel drive the first couple of kilometres until Kiry decided it was safe to start the engine. Then they drove along a track that seemed to grow bumpier, windier and narrower the further west they travelled. The young driver, Charya, gripped the wheel tightly. Every time he turned his head to stare at Pol Pot, who sat beside him wheezing and grunting and slowly turning grey, he clipped a jutting rock or bounced off a tree root.

Pol Pot gritted his teeth. He reached out to pat Charya reassuringly on the arm, but his touch caused Charya to run off the track onto a narrow patch of soft dirt. The wheels spun for a long moment. Then Pol Pot took his hand off Charya, placed it on the wheel and eased the vehicle back into the centre of the track.

There was a hint of morning light in the sky when Charya pulled over. After they unpacked, Kiry ordered Charya to turn the vehicle around. Back and forth he spun the wheel, braking and accelerating, increasingly desperate to complete the manoeuvre. Revs like coughs filled the air. Finally, having created a minor dust storm, he faced back in the direction they had come from.

'Stay on this road,' Kiry said. 'There are government soldiers patrolling the end of it. Give yourself up to them. Offer them the car as a peace offering.'

They took to the wilds, walking in single file around the base of a mountain. Bonarith, Pol Pot's sole remaining bodyguard, led the way. He wore two backpacks. In one hand he held a long knife for hacking at encroaching foliage. In his other hand he carried Kiry's black suitcase, the one he took on all his overseas trips. It was full of US dollars.

Following Bonarith came Pol Pot's wife, Mea, and their daughter, Sisopha. Mea shouldered both their packs. She murmured never-ending encouragement to the girl, who was already complaining about the heat and the insects. Pol Pot came next. He used a tall bamboo pole to drag himself forward. He panted like a dog. He shuffled, as if lifting his feet off the ground would signify a terrible defeat.

Kiry followed close behind Pol Pot, carrying Pol Pot's pack as well as his own. They were not too heavy, though, because Ol had insisted on taking the bulk of the load. Kiry had tried to protest but even now his shoulders felt as though Prince Sihanouk was lounging across them. Soon Kiry snagged his shirt sleeve on a branch. He had a spare shirt in his pack, but he wanted to save it for when he was negotiating with the Thais to gain safe passage to the Chinese embassy in Bangkok. Within an hour he had split the webbing between two toes. Each time he planted his foot a searing pain shot up his leg.

Ol and Vireak walked behind Kiry. Ol carried two backpacks,

one of which contained a portable radio, and, under one arm, a collapsed camp stretcher. Vireak dragged a second suitcase of money; the case had wheels, which he insisted on trying to roll over the rough terrain.

Vireak had only come, Kiry suspected, because Ol had pleaded with him. Not that Kiry thought Vireak disloyal. He was devoted to Pol Pot and revered Ol like a father. But he had a dejected air about him. His grim expression told Kiry that he did not think they had any chance of reaching the border.

As they pushed up a slope that looked gentle but seemed never to level out, Pol Pot veered off the path and collapsed into a bush. When Kiry turned him over his eyes, his mouth, his nostrils, were open wide in a desperate effort to draw in oxygen. His skin was yellow and black blotches graffitied his forehead.

'Can you hear me, Big Brother?' Kiry said.

When Pol Pot did not reply they laid him on the stretcher. He opened his eyes and his breathing became a little more steady. He smiled. Ol loaded the suitcases on top of him. Pol Pot groaned feebly and tried to push them away.

'I'm sorry, Big Brother, but there is no other way to carry everything,' Kiry said. 'Just imagine what the newspapers would say if they saw this. Pol Pot in the middle of nowhere, grasping suitcases full of money.'

Pol Pot opened his eyes. 'Ha … ha … ha,' he moaned.

Ol and Vireak carried Pol Pot. Kiry walked beside him. Occasionally Kiry used his *krama* to wipe the puddles of perspiration that formed in the depressions on either side of Pol Pot's body. Pol Pot groaned every time one of the suitcases thumped against him.

'All you need is a decent doctor, medicine, an oxygen cylinder. A bit of R and R under an umbrella on Phuket beach. A lobster dinner or two.'

'Yum,' Pol Pot said.

'Don't worry, we are making excellent progress. Any moment now you will open your eyes and we will be in Beijing. You'll be in your very own palace, a tranquil place with hunting woods and a vast lake with ducks on top and fat trout below. You will eat pork dim sims whenever you want: hundreds a day if you choose. And rice wine and as much beer as you want. And do you know the best thing? You will eat and drink to your heart's content and all the while you will be sitting on Vietnam's head. How they will hate having Pol Pot as a hat.'

Sisopha came up beside Kiry and peered incredulously at Pol Pot.

'Who painted your face? I want my face painted too. My feet hurt, Pa. Can't we stop now?'

'Pa's busy thinking right now,' Kiry said. 'Do you know what? We're going to China. You'll love it there. There are a billion little girls and boys to play with. That is such a lot of girls and boys.'

'Maybe more boys than girls,' Vireak muttered.

'Are we nearly there, Pa? How long till we get to China? *Pa?* Ma, why doesn't Pa answer me?'

'You know that Pa likes to have a rest in the afternoon.'

'It doesn't look good. He's barely conscious,' Ol whispered to Kiry.

'I know. But we must keep going. We must try to keep him awake.'

Pol Pot opened his eyes. 'My daughter wants to have a rest.'

'But we are so close to our destination, Beloved Uncle,' Ol said. 'Can you smell how close we are?'

'I smell something.'

'I've been doing some thinking, Big Brother,' Kiry said. 'I believe I might have found the solution to our problem, right here, right now, while we have been walking. I'm going to tell you about it, Big Brother, for although it is unformed in my mind I trust your judgment and I hope you will think it is a grand scheme.

'Here it is, Big Brother, my new idea: guided tours of the Dangrek Mountains. Authentic treks with real-life guerrillas. What do you say? The tourists will come from everywhere for this. They'll pay a premium for it, too, so long as we feed them properly. They call it "Adventure Tourism." Our country will fill with Europeans eager for some adventure in their lives. Imagine this: "Come and get your feet muddy in pristine wilderness, with authentic mud, and your choice of Soviet, Chinese or American minefields. See the actual site where Son Sen and his family were slaughtered. See headless statues at Angkor temples, then visit Ta Mok's villa at

Anlong Veng to find the heads. Meet real-live Khmer Rouge soldiers. Clean and fire their rifles. Work in the fields for a day just
like a real Cambodian peasant. Hide in a shallow bunker and enjoy
a simulated attack by President Richard Nixon's B-52s. Best of all,
be stimulated by a one-hour lecture in a genuine grass-roofed hut
by the famous revolutionary, Mr Pol Pot." What do you think of my
tourism plans, Big Brother?'

Ol half turned his head. 'He's passed out.'

'Why didn't you say so?'

'I wanted to hear your plans for the future.'

'I wanted to keep him conscious. I was making a joke.'

'Really? Are you sure?'

They stopped for the day near Kbal Ansom, east of the Chrork
Choam Pass. Ol and Bonarith carried Pol Pot into a cave. Kiry
kicked rocks aside and they set him down. Mea and Kiry propped
him up and helped him drink. His skin sparkled in the gloom. Mea
wiped his brow with a *krama* and said, 'Everything is going to be
just fine.'

'Have we crossed the border yet? Is this Thailand?'

'Not yet. But we are very close.'

Ol and Mea went to look for leaves to boil for a soup. Little Sisopha lay wedged between two rocks, as if a swollen river had
dumped her there. Kiry started telling her a story about a frog who
got sick of waiting for the rains and abandoned its pond. But the
effort of listening to him made her burst into tears.

'Take the radio up that hill,' Kiry told Bonarith and Vireak.
'Find out if they are chasing us. Find out how close they are.'

Kiry took off his boots and socks. As he stretched his feet, the
blood blisters on his heels split open. He dressed Sisopha's feet as
best he could. She screamed for a while and then fell quiet. Kiry
closed his eyes. Ol woke him up a couple of hours later to tell him
that dinner was ready and that Bonarith and Vireak had fled with
the hand radio and all the money.

At dawn, Kiry removed a wad of US dollars that he had strapped to
his stomach.

'You must keep going,' he told Ol. 'Go to the border and get
help. When you reach Ubon Ratchathani ask to speak to Captain

Subramanian. Give him all of the money. *All of it*, Ol, do you understand me? Forget everything Sok ever told you: this is no time for
skimming. Tell Subramanian there is more if he helps us. If he
wavers, tell him I have been negotiating with Prince Ranariddh.
Tell him that our talks are so advanced that I am effectively an
unofficial member of the Cambodian government.'

'But ... is that true? Have you been talking to Ranariddh?'

'Just tell him. Go on now, you're our last chance. Go, I say ...
What? What is it?'

'Thank you for teaching me everything,' Ol said. Before Kiry
could reply Ol turned and ran away.

Soon after, Ta Mok's soldiers found them, announcing themselves like visitors standing in a street unable to remember which
house they should enter. Kiry sent Mea and Sisopha to the very rear
of the cave.

'I'm sorry, Big Brother, but we need to go outside now,' Kiry said
to Pol Pot.

Pol Pot turned to the wall of the cave. Kiry was momentarily
confused, thinking that he was refusing to go. But Pol Pot placed
his hands on the wall of the cave and painstakingly dragged himself upright.

'I feel much better for the sleep,' he said.

'I'm pleased, Big Brother.'

Kiry took two handguns from his backpack. Together he and
Pol Pot stepped from darkness into light. Both men stood straight
and proud, although Kiry could see that Pol Pot's whole body was
shaking with the effort. As they came out from the cave's opening,
Kiry pointed one gun at Pol Pot's ear and one at his own chest.

Samnang – a senior officer Kiry knew well and admired for his
courage and fairness, even though he had aligned himself with Ta
Mok – stepped forward.

'There is no sense in this,' Samnang said in a kind tone, as if he
was explaining to a child that if you leap from a roof while holding
a chicken you will not be able to fly. 'Please surrender, Brother
Kiry.'

'What do you want to do?' Kiry said in French to Pol Pot. 'What
do you want me to do?'

'Who are all these people? Am I supposed to address them?'

Pol Pot said. 'Greetings, comrades. Today we are going to learn about ... about ...'

'Don't trouble yourself, Big Brother. Everything is okay. We're in Beijing now. Here comes Mao himself to welcome us.'

Kiry dropped the guns at his feet. Samnang came forward and picked them up.

'You should be proud of yourself. True loyalty takes no account of circumstances,' Samnang said, embracing Kiry. 'Are you hungry?'

Kiry hung his head in shame. He had failed. To surrender so easily, with so much relief, made him a fool and a coward.

Samnang aimed one of the guns at a tree trunk and squeezed the trigger. Nothing happened. He examined the weapon.

'This chamber is empty.'

'I have no bullets. I have no idea how to load such a gun.' Kiry dropped to his haunches and accepted a bottle of water. He took a swig and poured a little over his exposed neck.

Samnang recognised the other gun. It was Ta Mok's Luger, circa 1930. Mok claimed it was worth a fortune. He only ever brought it out when he was drinking. Samnang slowly raised his arm and pointed the gun at the bridge of Kiry's nose. Kiry forced a weak smile. Samnang squeezed the trigger. A tiny blue flame appeared. A soldier stepped forward and lit his Marlboro.

*   *   *

Ted Whittlemore wanted desperately to skip the opening of Lea's latest photography exhibition. The thought of a room full of people petrified him. But he knew he had to go. He'd missed the last one, Lea's first-ever solo exhibition. He'd been holed up in bed, the whole right side of his body quaking. It was a pretty decent excuse, he thought, but Lea only forgave him once she spoke to Nurse Wendy, who had wasted most of the afternoon trying to help Ted get dressed.

Ted was waiting in the lobby when Michael arrived at five-thirty to collect him.

'Where's Anne?' Ted asked

'She can't come.'

'Can't come? Why ever not?'

Michael paused. 'She's gone,' he said.

'Gone? What ... Gone where?'

'She's gone, Dad. Left. She's taken a job in Brisbane.'

'Brisbane? Brisbane, *Queensland*? She's nicked off? Just like that?'

'Just like that.'

'But Brisbane: bloody hell, that's halfway to Jakarta.'

'Yes, well—'

'When's she coming back?'

'I don't think she'll be back. She's left me, Dad. For good.'

'But ... But I really liked her. She had spirit.'

'She's not dead, Dad. She's just not here anymore. Do you want to bring the wheelchair?'

'Don't change the subject.'

'The subject is, do you want to go in a wheelchair?'

'I'd rather we drove.'

'Come on, Dad, we can't be late. Do you want to br—'

'But just like that? You had no idea she was planning it? Didn't you know she was unhappy?'

'Of course I did, Dad, but that's hardly the point, is it?'

'No? Isn't it? ... She didn't even come to say goodbye to me.'

'She said to tell you she'd write you a letter. Wheelchair?'

'No.'

'Walking stick, then.'

'Don't worry about me. I'll be fine. I'll lean against a sculpture. Or I can get one of Lea's sweet little friends to prop me up. That brunette with the funny nose and the red cheeks: I'll take her.'

'Walking stick or you're not coming.'

Ted peered at Michael. 'Don't take it out on me. I didn't tell her to leave.'

'It's quarter to six, Dad. Come on. What's it to be: wheelchair or walking stick?'

'I could get a taxi, you know. You can't stop me.'

'Oh, just come on, will you, it's only a stick. Ho Chi Bloody Minh carried a stick with him everywhere, didn't he?' Michael said, on the verge of tears. Ted recalled what Anne had confided one day about Michael. 'He's so sensitive,' she'd said. 'He gets upset about the oddest things. Don't tell him I told you: that'll just get him all hot under the collar.'

'Ho Chi Minh, eh? I can't argue with that,' Ted said.

Michael went to Ted's room and came back with his walking stick, an ugly gnarled length of oak with a rubber bottom. It was the last remnant of Ted's father, who'd hobbled for the last fifteen years of his life after his hip healed badly after a fall. When Michael held it out, Ted leaned close and grasped his shoulder.

'I'm sorry about Anne,' he said, almost too quietly for Michael to hear.

'Me too, Dad, me too. Come on, let's go.'

Half an hour later, father and son stood and stared at a photograph that was labelled 'L.I.f.E.' It was five feet by four feet, glossy blue with an indistinct object in the top left-hand corner. It was housed in an enormous gold frame that threatened to bring the whole wall down.

'I like it,' Ted said firmly. 'You could certainly use a couple of those around the house. And only three thousand dollars. Good value for the frame alone, I reckon.'

Michael smiled. 'I'll get us a drink.'

'Do you think that will help?'

'Keep your wits about you, Dad. It's a minefield in here.'

Lea floated into view, wearing an ankle-length dress that Ted thought had to be a nightgown. She took Ted's arm. 'You made it, then.'

'What a tail you've grown,' Ted said, indicating the men Lea dragged behind her and who, as she settled in beside Ted, fanned out, each choosing an image to ponder.

'What do you think, Grandpa? Be honest, now.'

'I think they're all too scruffy and too vacant. Especially him,' Ted pointed at one of her admirers, a short bloke with a bad haircut and three days of stubble who was dressed in jeans that didn't quite fit him and a red T-shirt that had lost its shape. 'And that one over there: Jesus, love, he's almost as old as I am.'

'What do you think about the photographs?'

'Well, I ... They're certainly original, I'll give you that.'

'You hate them.'

'I don't hate them, love, not at all. I think they're wonderful. All congratulations to you. Really. It's just that—'

'It's just that what?'

'If you'll let me finish – it's rude to badger your elders, didn't anybody ever teach you that? It's just that, I mean, for instance, if … Well, take this one: is it supposed to be called "life," or "ell-one-eff-*ee*," or … ?'

'It's up to you. Whatever you prefer. Whatever you see in it.'

'No, that doesn't help me, love. That's exactly the problem. I need to know what to call my art. Otherwise I can't tell you whether I like it or not because I don't know what it is I'm looking at.'

Lea laughed. 'You haven't got a drink. Are you ill?'

'Your dad's getting me one now. Now listen, why di—'

'I'm listening.'

'Stop interrupting while you're listening. Why didn't you tell me about your mum and dad?'

'He's told you, then. About time, too.'

'Why didn't *you* tell me?'

'It's his news, his private life, not mine.'

'But aren't you upset?'

'I suppose. A little, maybe. But honestly, Grandpa, it's been a long time coming. It's better this way. Better for everybody.'

'Better for your dad?'

'Maybe especially him.'

'I don't think he sees it like that.'

'He will. Eventually. Come on, I want to show you something.'

Lea took Ted's arm – as she did so half a dozen male heads jerked in their direction – and led him across the room.

'Close your eyes,' she said.

'Do I have to? One of these days they won't ever open again.'

'Close them.'

'You'll have to hypnotise me.'

'Close them or I'll start spreading rumours that you're senile.'

'Promises, promises,' Ted said, but he put his hands in front of his face. Lea led him through the crowd, collecting congratulations and pecks to both cheeks as she went.

'Okay, Grandpa, you can open your eyes now.'

Ted blinked. After the fuzzy lines turned sharp, after the green and black splotches faded, an enormous black and white photograph of an old man confronted him. All of a sudden he wished he'd brought the wheelchair.

'But ... is that me?'

'Of course it's you, Grandpa.'

In the photograph Ted stood in the ocean, his head and shoulders out of the water. Lea had taken it the one time she had cajoled him into going swimming with her at Henley Beach. He had endured it for ten minutes because she promised him that the cold salt water would be therapeutic. His white hair was stuck askew across his head, which seemed to have expanded to twice its normal size. His eyes were closed, his mouth open, his skin beaded. A triangular crease ran across the bridge of his nose, joining the corners of his eyes. It made him look, he thought, as if he was regressing into some lower lifeform.

'Well? Do you like it?'

'I'm not sure any man should have to see the shape of his skull. It's like peering at your own corpse pinned to a wall.'

'I think you look beautiful.'

'Why's it called "spiRit"? You should have called it "MoNsteR."'

'You don't mind, do you?' Lea asked.

Ted did mind. He minded very much. He wanted to rip the image off the wall and skewer it with his walking stick.

'Of course I don't mind, love. Anyway, you're an artist: you don't need my permission.'

Ted only lasted another ten minutes before he began to tilt and sway. When he began to dribble, Michael and Lea each grabbed an arm and shepherded him to the car.

They were passing through the intersection of Osmond Terrace and the Parade when a blood vessel ruptured in Ted's head. His closed eyes flickered. Michael thought Ted was asleep, and took the last corners to the Concertina Rest Home gently. Only when Michael parked did he realise that something had gone terribly wrong inside Ted's shell of a body.

Ted lay in a bed in the high-dependency ward for nearly a month. The doctors punctured him with tubes to feed him and to remove his wastes. He wore an oxygen mask. Nurses came from time to time to turn his body. Lea hated that most of all. While one nurse cooed in Ted's ear – 'It's a beautiful sunny day outside,

Mr Whittlemore. Not a cloud in the sky. Can you be a brave boy for me now? We're just going to give you a teensy-weensy jolt and maybe after, when you're feeling a little better, I'll have a little treat especially for you. Do you like chocolate, Mr Whittlemore? Everybody likes chocolate, don't they?' One nurse grabbed his shoulders and the other his feet and they yanked him like they were pulling a tooth.

Ted murmured now and again, indistinguishable sounds insinuating speech. His eyelids flickered and occasionally threatened to open. Once or twice one eyebrow raised when somebody spoke to him. It gave Lea hope, but he was toying with her. He never regained consciousness. He got pneumonia and his lungs slowly filled up until he drowned in his bed.

Ted Whittlemore died on a Tuesday. At the moment he stopped breathing, Michael was staring out the window. There were a few spots of rain colouring the red paving, and Pamela, that attractive administrator Michael had been thinking of asking to the Barossa Jazz and Wine Festival, was walking towards the car park. Michael watched her buttocks retreating and wondered whether it would be appropriate to knock on the door of her office, or if he should contrive to bump into her.

Lea was down the hall, buying burnt coffee from the vending machine adjacent to the fire stairs.

1998

Pol Pot spoke his last words to Nhem Kiry – Kiry forever believed they were his last words to any person – a week before he died. Sitting up in his camp bed, he half-listened as Kiry read aloud pieces from a week-old *Bangkok Post*. Occasionally, he made a comment – 'That Mr Clinton takes us all for fools,' or, 'Who scored the goals for Manchester United?' – but mostly he concentrated on keeping his head upright. After a while he slept so noiselessly that Kiry once or twice leant across to check that he was breathing.

Suddenly Pol Pot jerked awake.

'There is no simple answer,' he said. 'It depends entirely on the context.'

'What does, Big Brother?'

Pol Pot squinted at Kiry, confused. 'Who's there? Show yourself.'

'Can you see me, Big Brother?'

'Go away, whoever you are.'

'Calm yourself, Big Brother. Are you thirsty?'

Kiry put a bottle of water to Pol Pot's lips. He tried to swat it away but he didn't have the strength.

'Where are we?'

'Anlong Veng.'

'Still? We need to get away from here. There's not a moment to lose. The Chinese will welcome us, won't they?'

'I'm not sure, Big Brother. Perhaps not.'

'Thailand then.'

'They might allow you to visit the hospital, if you promise to be a quiet patient. But they will not let you stay.'

'Phnom Penh? Is there no chance, for you at least? You should climb up on Ranariddh's shoulders, like we always discussed.'

'Big Brother, I hoped to negotiate with Ranariddh. But Hun

Sen has crushed Ranariddh. Ranariddh is in exile in France. You know all this.'

'Then we will go to Yugoslavia?'

'Big Brother, Yugoslavia no longer exists. It has broken into pieces.'

'President Tito will embrace us, surely?'

'President Tito is dead. Don't you remember?'

'Dead? Are you sure?' Pol Pot's eyes clouded over. He sagged in his bed.

'Are you all right, Big Brother? Can I get anything for you?'

'Go away. I'm sick of you spying on me.'

An hour or so later, Pol Pot's daughter found him slumped on the floor of the hut. They lay him on the mattress. Ta Mok's doctor came to look, but he could think of nothing much to do other than force water and a little sticky rice down his throat. Every few hours soldiers shifted and shook his limbs so that he didn't bruise too much.

Some time after Pol Pot died, three of Ta Mok's bodyguards entered the hut. They greeted Kiry with polite, sympathetic murmurs. One bodyguard took hold of Pol Pot's feet. A second man brought his wrists together above his head. They lifted Pol Pot – 'He's so light,' one of them whispered – so that the third bodyguard could place a length of tarpaulin between the body and the mattress. They dragged several blocks of ice into the hut and wedged them under Pol Pot's arms and between his legs. They lit cigarettes, admired their handiwork and wandered off.

Kiry knew he should leave Pol Pot's body and offer his support to Mea, who was inconsolable. Or ask Ta Mok if he could spare a can of Coca-Cola to give to poor little Sisopha, who was outside drawing pictures in the dirt with a blank look on her face. Or just retreat to his hut and allow Kolab to comfort him, maybe massage his shoulders. But he stayed where he was, counting the drops of melted water dripping onto the dirt.

Nuon Chea entered the hut, limping badly. Kiry stood up to let him have the upturned wooden crate he'd been sitting on. Usually, Chea sought out Kiry to rant at him, to accuse him of some weakness or failing, to insult him for (it seemed to Kiry) no good reason at all. Today Chea was silent. Kiry wanted to leave but he sensed that Chea needed his company.

A group of Thai military officers arrived, chattering like children. They crammed into the hut, forcing Chea and Kiry against the wall. They filed past and peered at Pol Pot. The last officer in the queue took a camera from his bag and began taking snapshots of Pol Pot's corpse. He paused, stood in the middle of the hut and put a fresh roll of film into the camera. He crouched down and took a rapid series of photographs of Pol Pot's face. The camera's flash lit up the dim space and cast silhouettes across the concrete walls.

Kiry saw that Nuon Chea was about to erupt. He took his elbow and led him into the sun. They walked to the river, sat on a rock and watched the brown water flowing slowly past and around the bend, where they could hear women thrashing clothes.

'What now? What now but fishing?' Chea said.

They stayed sitting on the rock by the river, silent. Soon after midday, Kiry's granddaughter Kunthea came looking for him. But before she got close Kiry called out, 'Not now. Go back.' She ran away, crying.

'You spoke harshly to the child,' Chea said.

'Yes,' Kiry said.

Soon after, Chea's wife brought them food and water but Chea refused to take his medicine. When his wife insisted, Chea took the packets of pills and launched them into the river. Then he grabbed at his shoulder and let out a low moan.

In the middle of the afternoon, four soldiers carried Pol Pot to a clearing. They dumped him on a pyre made of wood and old rubber tyres and the sodden mattress he had died on. They set him alight.

Kiry and Chea stayed by the river until the last of the black smoke had cleared. By then, Chea's bad leg had seized up. Two of Ta Mok's soldiers came and carried him along the winding path that led back to the village. Kiry followed on behind.

*   *   *

On the morning of the press conference Nhem Kiry was nervous, then lethargic, then nauseous and then finally so deeply irritated that he could not sit still or think clearly. He sent his daughter, Yat, and his granddaughters, Kunthea and Minea, downstairs to the breakfast buffet. He supposed they would inflict permanent damage on his reputation for frugality by devouring more croissants and fruit than a peasant family could possibly consume in a month. But he desperately needed peace and quiet to prepare for the traumatic day that lay ahead.

The day before had been bad enough. It began before dawn, when Kiry had snuck out of the village – stealth was best, he'd decided, even though he doubted that anybody, least of all Ta Mok, now cared whether he came or went. A couple of soldiers waited for him along the track. Kiry had bribed them to make sure they turned up, but he suspected that they wanted out just as badly as he did. They drove a few kilometres to a rendezvous point, where a government helicopter swooped out of the sky and pulled them in. Kiry arrived in Phnom Penh in time to shower and take lunch with Hun Sen. The food was bland and, worse, he had to spend an hour genuflecting before him. Then Hun Sen told him he had to front the media to explain himself, and Kiry almost felt like fleeing back to Ta Mok in Anlong Veng.

He had brought little Kunthea and Minea to Phnom Penh because they were oblivious to tension. They treated nothing seriously, which was exactly the attitude Kiry wanted to imitate. The night before, he had urged them to drink all the Coke and Sprite in the hotel-room bar fridge. It was the best – the only – revenge he could think of, but the excess sugar had transformed his girls – Yat as well as the children – into a giggling mess of limbs spread-eagled across the king-sized bed. Kiry joined in by downing two cans of Heineken, the first of which he almost enjoyed. 'Cold and bitter,' he said. 'Just like me.' Then he opened a bottle of Johnny Walker Black, sniffed it and pronounced it fake. He tipped it down the bathroom sink, an act that deeply shocked Kunthea. Kiry took her hand. 'When we leave, let's steal the towels,' he said.

Kiry was relieved that Kolab had chosen to stay away from Phnom Penh. Not that she would have said anything much. But she would have denounced Kiry – herself too – with constant sighing, or by gazing at the ground in silence or by picking at her food. She had stayed in Pailin in their new wooden home. After everything he had put her through, Kiry knew she had hoped for a more palatial abode in a more cosmopolitan city. 'It's not Shanghai, it's not Paris,' she said. 'But anything is better than another year in Anlong Veng.'

Overnight, Kiry's sinuses had reacted badly to the air-conditioner. He blew his nose, one nostril at a time, but the tissue was bone dry. So he ran the shower hot and placed a few drops of eucalyptus oil on a flannel, a neat trick that a diplomat friend had once taught him. He stood under the shower, closed his eyes and allowed the fumes that rose with the steam to clear his head.

He shaved with a Braun two-headed electric razor. Although he preferred a blade – he liked the feel of steel on his cheeks, the smooth finish, the reliability – he had taken to cutting himself. 'Your skin gets thinner as you get old,' Kolab had told him. 'Thank you for yet another startling revelation,' he had replied. But he supposed she was right. And today, of all days, parading himself before all those people and cameras, he did not want scabs on his throat or blood spots on his collar.

Outside, Kiry's minders – government policemen with fake Ray-Bans and obsolete firearms – scrabbled about in the corridor like rats. He wished they would keep quiet, but he was grateful to have protection from the pushy journalists and the indignant locals.

He washed himself with a tiny bar of soap that came wrapped in waxy paper. Once wet, the soap smelt rather like over-heated peanut oil. When it had washed away, Kiry checked his skin for stains. He used his own shampoo: a few days earlier at a Bangkok salon – on the eighth floor of the 'Sixth Biggest Shopping Mall in Southeast Asia,' a claim he found ludicrous – a European-trained stylist had dyed his hair chestnut brown. Kiry liked the result, the colour as well as the wave she had blown through it, but he knew from experience that he needed to treat his hair with great care now or it would shrivel up.

He dried and powdered himself and dressed in a new camel-coloured safari suit which contrasted nicely, he decided, with his new hair colour. He put a single blue ballpoint pen, relieved from the hotel lobby, and a blank piece of paper folded in quarters into his breast pocket.

A government official nudged Kiry in the back. He took an erratic path, as if he was negotiating a minefield of microphones, spotlights and fat electric cords. The government official took his elbow but Kiry shook him off. He didn't want anybody writing that he needed help to stand up. But then the noise in the room hit him, the waves of people pushing towards him from every direction, and his legs turned heavy. The minder grabbed him again and this time Kiry let him lead him through the throng.

Kiry sat alone behind a table on a slightly elevated stage. He folded his hands on the white linen cloth and fastened a pleasant and patient look onto his face. The mob was already shouting its interrogation. Kiry was unable to locate a fully formed question in the tangle of accusations. It was as though everybody in the room was hurling burning words at him. Should he duck or douse the flames with his glass of water? Should he sit still and let himself catch alight?

He considered absconding. He could have snuck back to his room, legitimately too, for it seemed that no amount of sleep was enough for him at the moment. Or he could have retired to the hotel's piano bar, out on the balcony, with the *Phnom Penh Post* and a gin and tonic (he'd heard that the piano player, a backpacker from Finland, had a wonderful repertoire). Or he could have donned a wig and sunglasses and taken a stroll around the Central Market.

Instead Kiry leant into the microphone. 'Good morning, ladies and gentlemen. It would be most helpful if you could ask one question at a time.' He sat back, waited for the voices to dull and then pointed at one man.

'You: do you have a question?'

'Do you think that the Cambodian people will accept the blanket amnesty that has been bestowed upon you? Do you think they should?'

'As you know, Hun Sen, the very honourable prime minister of the royal government, has warmly welcomed me. I spent a most enjoyable time with the honourable prime minister yesterday and we agreed that the time for fighting is over. If you demand that I tell you who was wrong and who was right, if you carry on and on and on accusing particular people of this and that – and if you

expect me to do it too – then we Cambodians will never be reconciled. If we keep talking like this the war will never end.'

'Do you expect to see King Sihanouk while you are here?'

'If he invites me to visit him then of course I will go: he is my
king,' Kiry said. 'But I suspect he is a very busy king.'

'He's in Beijing,' somebody called. 'He's been there for weeks.'

'I'm deeply shocked to hear it,' Kiry said.

'You were a very senior member of the Khmer Rouge hierarchy.
Do you accept personal responsibility for the million or more
deaths that occurred in the Democratic Kampuchea regime?'

Kiry stared at the table as he replied. 'That story is old and stale.
When you persist in asking these questions, when you dig up the
past and turn it upside down and dissect it and examine it under a
microscope, well, I cannot see any purpose. The way this country
developed is so complicated ... too complicated for me to explain
in a few words today. Please don't keep stirring things up about the
war.'

'Will you at least tell the Cambodian people that you are sorry
for all their suffering?'

Damned BBC, Kiry thought. But, given the sudden silence,
there seemed no way to avoid the question. Kiry leaned close to the
microphone and whispered, 'I'm sorry. I'm very, very sorry.'

'Say it in Khmer.'

'Yeah. Say it in Khmer.'

Kiry sensed his face contorting. He tried to maintain a mild
expression, but the strain left him feeling as if the blood vessels
were popping in his eyes. With a supreme effort he controlled himself. '*K'nyom somtoah nah*,' he muttered.

'Do you have a message for Ta Mok? Is it time he surrendered
too?'

Kiry ignored the question, but he imagined Mok standing on
the veranda of his garish villa, one arm snaked around a fake
Roman pillar like it was a Thai prostitute, telling his followers that
Kiry had betrayed them all.

'Why should you go free when every single family in Cambodia
has suffered because of what you did? Have you no shame?'

'I know that some people talk about these things. I am not deaf.
I read. I recently listened to a radio broadcast in which some of my

countrymen were talking about the family members they lost. Even my own wife tells me such stories before she goes to work in the paddy fields each day. It is normal for people who have lost family over the years to feel grief and resentment. But I am sure that most of our fellow Cambodians have many more basic problems to resolve in the present and in the future. Let bygones be bygones: that is the only way for us to achieve peace and stability at last.'

'Why should the Cambodian people put up with your defection?' an American hollered from the back of the room. 'Why should the world?'

'The world? The *world*?' Kiry began, but then paused long enough to rein in his indignation. 'It is not for me to say, it is for others. But let me say this—'

'No. Answer the question. Why should the world accept your defection? Why shouldn't you face trial for crimes against humanity?'

'I cannot answer that. I cannot judge myself. History will be my judge.'

'Hasn't history already judged you?'

'It is far too soon to be talking about history. I'll be dead and gone – and you too, my friend – long before everything will make proper sense. What's good today will one day seem bad; and today's criminals are destined to be the heroes of the future. But I will say this … No: that's it. That's all. I've got nothing else to say.'

The morning sun was mild as Kiry and his family left Phnom Penh for a few days' holiday at the Seaside Hotel in Sihanoukville. The road was smooth. Kiry sank into the bucket seat of the late model Toyota minivan and was asleep before they passed Kompong Speu. Kunthea woke him ten kilometres out of Sihanoukville to show him a truck that had rolled off the road and was lying on its side. 'It looks like a buffalo,' Kiry said. Kunthea giggled.

After they arrived, Kiry sent his family to paddle in the Gulf of Thailand. 'Don't drown,' he called after them cheerfully. 'Take your time.' Alone at last, he sat cross-legged on the floor of the room and ate a plate of crabs which the hotel had brought in live from nearby Kep. He twisted claws. He cracked shells open with a small hammer. He worked methodically and made a pile of meat

before he began to eat. He sipped pineapple juice and looked for a
football match on the television but had to make do with a breath-
less, mildly amusing Thai soap opera set in a hospital ward.

He slept. Ants streamed up from the floor and invaded the crab
shells. Flies followed. A couple of geckos ran laps across the ceiling.
A waiter came to remove the plate but Kiry slept through his polite
knocks. Late in the afternoon, Kunthea leapt onto the bed: 'I went
into the water, all the way to my belly button.'

He stood under a cold shower with his arms raised and his eyes
open. He was still sluggish when he emerged, so he ordered coffee.
'Real coffee. Do you understand me?' The hotel manager brought
it himself, accompanied by a government official.

'Your car is here,' the government official said.

'What car?'

'Your car for touring Sihanoukville.'

'I don't want to go.'

'It's all organised. It's on your itinerary. Hun Sen insisted. Please
don't worry, the driver is very friendly.'

Kiry drank his coffee slowly, changed his shirt, tidied his hair
and stepped outside. A middle-aged man in a tuxedo grinned
broadly and ushered Kiry into the back seat of a Toyota sedan. He
stared out his window at the unremarkable streets as the driver
wound to the top of a hill so they could look down on the port.

The driver then sped from beach to beach and finally stopped by
a private patch of sand, halfway between two umbrella villages. Kiry
stripped to his shorts and, like Kunthea, went in as far as his belly
button. He stared at the flat sea and at the blurred horizon, where
the light rubbed out the water. It amazed him that Europeans came
here simply to go swimming.

The driver waded out, handed Kiry a banana and then turned
away and dived head first into the water. Kiry peeled the banana,
but it was brown and soft. He hurled it at a stick that floated by but
missed.

The driver lit a cigarette. Kiry looked back at him, appalled:
'Put that out. You can't smoke in the ocean.'

He stayed floating in the water for hours. Finally, his government minder appeared on the shore. He took off his shoes, rolled
up his pants and waded out to Kiry.

'I've decided to go out for dinner,' Kiry said.

'It's very difficult. Please reconsider. Too many people want to look at you. And there are still a few journalists hanging around.'

'I am going. Only me. You can come if you insist, so long as you get your own table. But I am going.'

Accompanied by the government official and three bodyguards, Kiry went to a restaurant on the hill above Victory Beach. Ieng Sary had recommended it for the sunset as well as the food, but by the time Kiry arrived the view beyond the balcony was black. Still he chose an outside table, away from the red-faced tourists who were watching *Rambo III*, the sound turned up high. His minders took a table near the television and ordered beer.

Kiry sniffed the air, enjoying the mix of salt air and the smoke from the mosquito coil burning in an empty Pepsi bottle at his feet. He ordered a gin and tonic and was delighted when it came with two triangles of lime, one drowning in the drink and the other on a small plate to squeeze over the ice.

His food came quickly. Kiry surmised that the restaurant owner hoped he wouldn't stay too long. He wondered, while he poked at the soft white flesh of the fish and waited for a glass of sauvignon blanc, what his family was eating. Cheeseburgers again, probably.

A couple of well-to-do Cambodians sitting a few tables away glanced at Kiry and then took a longer look. They drew their heads together and whispered. Their faces turned sour. They ate in a rush. Kiry smiled at them as they left and thought to himself, So you're the middle class.

He paid for his meal with a five-dollar greenback. The owner took the note and held it close to the candle on the table, checking for stains or creases or rips and making sure it wasn't counterfeit. The procedure amused Kiry. 'It's American money,' he told the owner. 'It's full of imperfections.'

As Kiry stood to leave he accidentally kicked the Pepsi bottle at his feet. The last curl of the mosquito coil, the stub still glowing, lodged in a crack. The bottle spun across the decking to a nearby table, where a Western couple in their thirties – tourists not expatriates, Kiry could tell by their beach clothes and their flushed looks – sat perusing the menu.

'Please excuse me,' Kiry said.

'No worries, mate,' the man said in an Australian twang, saluting him with a glistening bottle of Angkor Draught. 'It was an accident.'

Epilogue

After illness delivered Ted Whittlemore to the Concertina Rest Home, Lea converted the granny flat at the back of her parents' house into a darkroom and studio. She felt guilty about it; it was as though she were giving Ted's eulogy while he was still propped up in bed, still breathing (sort of), still swearing to himself, still ogling those nursing assistants. But Ted had told Lea he was never going back home: 'I'm stuck here, girl, and no pointless nobility on your part can change that. Take the bloody flat and do something useful with it.'

After Ted died, it was there that Lea began going through Ted's papers. But she found it almost impossible to do. Every time she sat down at the tiny pine table in the kitchenette, she felt as if she was spying on him. Finally, she forced herself to skim through Ted's Ho Chi Minh biography. She smiled as she remembered Ted ranting against the world's publishers: 'It's mass censorship, pure and simple. Nobody wants me to get my Ho book into print. It's a conspiracy funded at the highest levels.' But the frayed and stained pages Lea sampled seemed to her to be a mix of hero worship and banal detail: who cares, she wondered, how strong Ho Chi Minh liked his tea? Her first act as Edward Whittlemore's literary executor was to dump *Ho Chi Minh: A New and True Biography*, all 1009 pages of it, into a sink full of developing solution.

She put the rest of Ted's papers in the bottom of the built-in wardrobe in his old bedroom. She made a decent fist of forgetting they were there until the day a couple of boxes arrived in the mail from Ted's Vietnamese friend, Hieu. The boxes contained masses of drafts and notes: stray thoughts that Ted probably should have thrown out but which Lea now felt obliged to catalogue and archive. But there were also letters – it seemed to Lea that half the world wrote to Ted to tell him he was an asshole and the other half wanted to be his best friend – and bundles of photographs: jungles, cities, battle scenes and portraits of strangers, some dressed in rags and sitting in the dirt, some nursing horrific wounds, some weighed down by jewellery and superior looks. And there were snapshots of

Ted with an array of politicians and celebrities, the cumulative effect of which was to show the growing prominence over the years of Ted's balloon-shaped head.

Within a week of the boxes arriving from Vietnam, Lea retrieved the rest of Ted's papers from the wardrobe. There she found *The Confessions of Edward Whittlemore*. She had been certain that Ted had abandoned his memoirs, but here was a stack of pages, unnumbered, some typed, some handwritten, a muddle of events and people and opinions and grumpiness. The order was so illogical that Lea wondered if Ted had dropped the manuscript and retrieved the pages at random, or if, day by day, he'd simply recorded whatever stray memories popped into his head.

She found Ted's letter to Nhem Kiry inside an unmarked envelope lying between two pages of the memoirs. It was undated, but Lea suspected from the way the neat, small script intermittently gave way to a ragged scrawl that Ted had been in pain when he wrote it.

Dear Nhem Kiry,

I'm old and sick. I cannot begin to tell you how bored I am. I've got so much time to sit around and think, a curse I hope befalls you too. I don't mean that in a nasty way – although Christ knows you deserve every bit of nastiness that comes your way. I just mean that after you've lived the sort of life you've lived, you might appreciate having a good long hard think about things before you die.

I've been reflecting on my life, and it's annoying the shit out of me that I cannot stop thinking about you. Sometimes I find myself imagining I am you. I try to think like you think, rationalise like you rationalise. It drives me crazy: I wish I could banish you from my head forever.

I believed in you. Did you know that? I believed that you had some sort of key to unlocking the divide between the haves and the have-nots. Not just in Cambodia. I thought you might offer up some model for how to merge radicalism with compassion and decency. That's why I was always trying to get you to loosen up and have some fun: because I wanted us to be friends. Allies.

I had faith in you, and a person like me is not supposed to have faith. You let me down. You let a lot of other people down too: all those peasants who believed that you were their champion. Where was your unbending moral code when the people were dying by the millions? Did you have your eyes closed? Were you keeping yourself too busy to notice? Or were you up to your elbows in the murders yourself? And, in the end, what's the difference?

And don't tell me you were protecting your country's sovereignty. Were there any more mass graves after Vietnam invaded? You know there weren't.

And Bun Sody. You let Bun Sody down. He was a beautiful man. It's not too late – it'll never be too late – to tell me his fate. Maybe he just got sick. If you write and tell me in all honesty that he caught malaria and died, or that he had a heart attack or stepped on a landmine or got attacked by a feral pig, then I will believe you. It would comfort me to know that he died of natural causes or because of some ludicrous accident. I know these things happen. But if he got his throat slit or a bullet between the eyes, can't you just tell me? What does the truth matter now?

You let Sihanouk down. I know he was a clown but you never made proper use of him. And you never gave him credit for trying. And he did try.

I wish I could see inside your head. I imagine it must be as well ordered as a library in there, every idea, every fact, filed in alphabetical order and written in duplicate in Khmer and French. There's an index, no doubt, for ease of searching. There are summaries and footnotes.

But I don't want the facts. I want to know what you think about when you're tucked up in bed. Have you nutted out how the Khmer Rouge managed to kill all those people? Do you weigh up incompetence and malicious intent and xenophobia and megalomania and rotten animal instincts? Do you wonder which of those best describes you? Or are you just a garden variety psychopath? I wonder all of those things, and then I ask myself if communism is doomed to always be bloody. I answer 'no,' but that is never the end of the conversation: soon enough I find myself asking that same question again.

Do you ask yourself that question? Do you ask yourself anything?

Remember how I saved you and Sody back in '67? You thanked me once – remember? Well, nothing comes for free. It's time to pay up. Write me a letter. Tell me what's going on behind that urbane mask you wear. Give me an explanation, an insight. Give me something. Anything.

AUTHOR'S NOTE

Figurehead is not – and is not intended to be – historically accurate. Although inspired by recent Cambodian history, it is a work of imagination set in a familiar but imaginary world. The events and the political machinations were massively more complex and intricate than – and often just plain different from – the absurdist version of them I offer here.

In the characters of Ted Whittlemore and Nhem Kiry, some readers might recognise elements of two people: the Australian journalist/propagandist/agent of influence (depending on your viewpoint) Wilfred Burchett and the Khmer Rouge leader Khieu Samphan. But neither Ted nor Kiry should be equated with the historical figure who inspired him, whether in relation to his public life or, of course, his private life and inner world. They are new, fictional men; the bond between them is likewise fictional. Nevertheless, I have co-opted many episodes from Khieu Samphan's and Wilfred Burchett's histories and made liberal use of their writings and public utterances.

Similarly, other secondary characters – including those who retain their own names, such as Pol Pot, Prince Norodom Sihanouk, Henry Kissinger and others – are fictional creations even though they are often inspired and informed by actual people and by the historical record.

While I make no claim to historical fidelity, I nevertheless acknowledge my use of a collection of primary and secondary sources. I have made extensive use of such sources, sometimes directly and sometimes as the basis for my own interpretations and inventions. They include newspaper articles, opinion pieces, documentaries, motion pictures, photographs, memoirs, biographies, general histories, academic studies, novels, speeches and other documents.

ACKNOWLEDGMENTS

I wrote an earlier version of *Figurehead* as the major component of a PhD in Creative Writing at the University of Adelaide. There, I was fortunate to be supervised by the legendary Tom Shapcott and mentored by J.M. Coetzee. I'm grateful to both of them, and to all the academic and professional staff associated with the Creative Writing program and the Discipline of English. I also want to record my gratitude to my peers in the PhD program for their camaraderie and expertise: Anne Bartlett, Tony Bugeja, Jan Harrow, Sabina Hopfer, Christopher Lappas, Heather Taylor Johnson, Ray Tyndale and Malcolm Walker.

Thanks to my agents at Cameron Creswell, Sophie Hamley and (formerly) Siobhan Hannan, for their support and persistence. At Black Inc, Chris Feik and Denise O'Dea have offered empathetic, clear-headed and plain-speaking editorial advice. And a big thanks to the entire Black Inc team: thanks for having me! Thanks to Deborah Bogle at the *Advertiser*, Cath Kenneally at Radio Adelaide and the Wordfire team for giving me opportunities to try out earlier versions of *Figurehead*.

I can't begin to name all the friends, acquaintances, colleagues and strangers who have helped in various ways to bring *Figurehead* to fruition, but a few of these people are: Phally Hing; L.K.; Catherine Crease; Brian Pike; Jim Schoff and Dee Jones; the rest of the Thursday crew: Russell Bartlett, Mark Caldicott, Guy Carney, Katherine Doube and Niki Vois; Nick Jose; Mick and Sue Treloar; Annabel Kain and Glenn Smith; Carli Pfitzner; Nigel Palmer; Cath Palmer; Lenore Coltheart.

To Mum, Dad and Morag, Lisa and Harry, Matt, Kathy, Kaitlin and Maddie, Ros and John, Emma and Rami, Naomi and Kieran, and to my grandparents – and all the rest of the clan – my gratitude and love.

Special and heartfelt thanks to Thomas Berg and Zoë Gill.